GUNNING FOR
THE BUDDHA

To the Other Mike —

GUNNING FOR THE BUDDHA

MICHAEL JASPER

Thanks for the comaderie & feedback, from the other Mike down South...

[signature]

11-21-07

PRIME BOOKS

GUNNING FOR THE BUDDHA
Copyright © 2005 by **Michael Jasper.**
Cover art copyright © 2005 by **Jamie Bishop.**
Cover design copyright © 2005 by **JT Lindroos.**

PUBLICATION HISTORY: "Gunning for the Buddha" © by Michael Jasper, originally published at *S1ngularity*, March 2003; "Goddamn Redneck Surfer Zombies" © by Michael Jasper, originally published in *The Book of More Flesh*, October 2002; "Visions of Suburban Bliss" © by Michael Jasper, originally published in *Gothic.Net*, June 2002; "A Feast at the Manor" © by Michael Jasper, originally published in *NeverWorlds*, February 2002; "Unplugged" © by Michael Jasper, originally published in *SpaceWays Weekly*, January 2000; "Working the Game" © by Michael Jasper, originally published in *Future Orbits 4*, April 2002; "Explosions" © by Michael Jasper, originally published at *Strange Horizons*, July 2001; "Wantaviewer" © by Michael Jasper, revised from its original publication at *Strange Horizons*, September 2002; "Mud and Salt" © by Michael Jasper, revised from its original publication in *Writers of the Future, vol. 16*, September 2000; "Crossing the Camp" © by Michael Jasper, originally published at *Strange Horizons*, January 2001; "Black Angels" © by Michael Jasper, original to this collection; "The Disillusionist" © by Michael Jasper, originally published at *Would That It Were*, August 2003; "Coal Ash and Sparrows" © by Michael Jasper, originally published in *Asimov's Science Fiction Magazine*, January 2004; "An Outrider's Tale" © by Michael Jasper, original to this collection; and "Natural Order" © by Michael Jasper, originally published in *Asimov's Science Fiction Magazine*, July 2002.

Prime Books
www.prime-books.com

ISBN
HB: 1-930997-71-X
PB: 1-930997-72-8

CONTENTS

INTRODUCTION

In person, Mike Jasper has that blond, bluff Iowa farm boy look about him. I could imagine him on the high school football team with a crew of other corn-fed youths from the heartland. Yet when you hang around him for a while you realize that he is watching the world very carefully. He asks questions and seems vaguely amused at the answers. When he talks there is a suggestion of a chuckle in his voice.

I first met Mike when he enrolled in the graduate program at North Carolina State University, where I teach, intending to do a Master's thesis in creative writing. He took my graduate fiction writing workshop. At that time he did not seem to me to be headed toward a career in our genre, though in some stories he showed a facility for the strange. What I liked most about his writing was the way that, whenever he wrote fantasy or science fiction, he integrated the fantastic elements into the details of everyday American life. His stories hovered in the foggy region between contemporary realism and fantastic fiction. As Mike continued to write in this vein, I suggested that he look into the Clarion East writer's workshop at Michigan State University. He and his friend and fellow student Chris Babson were accepted by Clarion, and I had the pleasure of teaching them there in the context of a workshop dedicated to the strange in fiction.

Some of the stories in this book date back to those student days. Since he completed his degree and went out into the wide, cruel world, I have not always kept up with the fiction Mike has published, but I was aware of his increasing success, and reading these newer stories now I am pleased that he has continued to revisit that fertile borderland between the genres. The stories here range from near reality to horror to fantasy to science fiction. Some, like the tale of the surfing Dead, are playful literalizations of metaphors. In another comic horror story, we visit a fat farm that uses, shall we say, unconventional methods.

Others, however, engage with more serious matters. Take, for instance, the series of stories you will find here about the alien refugees, the Wannoshay, who have come to earth in the near future. In these stories Mike is not terribly interested in the conventional issues of aliens in the Star Trek mode. He doesn't dwell on their biology or their social structure. Though they suffer much mistreatment at the hands of humans, the Wannoshay in Jasper's stories aren't total innocents. In fact, we don't know exactly what or who they are. Instead, Mike uses the Wannoshay as a means of examining the middle American character —drug addicts, police, people in bars and in the street, a couple of Catholic priests, hunters in the snow—in the jargon of the current academy, the Wannoshay are a "site" for the expression of human nature.

Often Mike lets his characters tell us their stories directly, in the straightforward, reliable voice of a first-person narrator engaged in a struggle to understand precisely what is happening to him (or her) in a world where loss seems inevitable. Mike's characters are often marginal, on the outside looking in. At times they are even quite literally lost, trying to find a way to live or even simply to survive in a world that does not offer easy ways to prosper and yet remain whole. Sometimes these characters are completely ordinary, like the black man who moves to a lily-white gated community and deals with the consequences, psychological and otherwise. Sometimes, as in the first and last stories of this book, these people are more than mortal, doing strange work outside the normal circle of our lives. But they are always recognizably human.

And I guess that is the one thing I would commend the most to you about these stories: that in the end they are about people you might meet at the grocery store or the ballpark or in church. Mike Jasper brings the common touch to the most uncommon situations. Welcome to his world.

—John Kessel
Raleigh, NC

GUNNING FOR THE BUDDHA

We killed the Buddha for the first time outside of Berlin.

It was fitting that we caught sight of him walking barefoot next to the autobahn, where it would be a real bitch to stop in time to pick him up. But we were nothing if not up for a challenge. I brought our '75 Firebird screeching to a stop next to him on the narrow shoulder, giving him a few centimeters of breathing room between muscle car and blocky metal guard-rail, and opened the passenger door. Traffic screamed past us like bullets as the little man lifted his robes and stepped into the car. With a groan, Ari had jumped into the back and onto Marco's lap, crushing Annina, Marco, and Yeshev. The Buddha rode shotgun.

He was bald, of course, but a lot skinnier than I'd ever imagined. He'd been walking west, out of Berlin into the German countryside, probably headed for Madrid or Amsterdam or some damn place like that. I had to grin at the dirt trapped under his fingernails like brown scars. His face was made up of delicate bones, like a china doll I'd had as a little girl, before I broke it with my baseball bat.

When the Buddha smiled at me I felt the world teeter, but that could've been caused by the two oversized bottles of beer I'd already downed. Before tromping on the gas, I checked the rearview mirror for the first time all day, looking around the multi-colored faces cheek-to-cheek in the back seat so we wouldn't get into a wreck. I wanted to savor the moment, stretch it out like day-old taffy. It wasn't every day you came across someone who — for all intents and purposes — was a major player from the spiritual realm, thumbing a ride.

And you know, of course, what you're supposed to do when you meet the Buddha on the road.

In seconds the Firebird was hitting 190 kilometers an hour, the dashboard shimmering like an ocean at low tide. I watched him out of the corner of my eye while the others hissed laughter in the backseat, waiting for my patience to run out. They knew me too well, my fellow travelers. We were between gigs, regrouping. Our next rendezvous was with a bridge in downtown Frankfurt later that afternoon. Time was of the essence.

When we passed the first sign for Frankfurt am Main, still some fifty kilometers away, I'd finished off most of the bottle of German ale I'd been balancing between my legs, and my bra was flapping in the wind next to me, wedged between door and window like a flag of surrender. The breeze cooled me off, reminding me of the metal pressed against my side under my thin T-shirt. I was always amazed at the way our assignments took shape, usually at the last possible minute before or after a jump, in spite of — or was it because of? — all the chaos in the world.

Next to me, the Buddha had started talking. His soft voice carried clear as a bell over the wind howling through my cracked-open window.

"In some ways, my girl," he said, "I am helpless. I have what I have if only I will surrender to things as they are."

His lash-less eyes stared at me, *into* me in a way I'd rather not remember. I hated it when men called me "girl."

"We must return to the sea," he continued, "or the sea will return to us."

"You're damn skippy," I said.

The others in the backseat exhaled in disappointment. They'd wanted me to blow him away from the moment he got in the car. To hell with them — I wanted to hear what this Buddha had to say. Plus I was distracted; Frankfurt's Eiserner Steg was approaching, and I'd forgotten that this was a footbridge, and the pedestrians weren't cooperating. But the Buddha's time was coming.

We had to get it just right, hitting the midsection of the Iron Footbridge where the blue metal arches of the supports for the bridge dipped down. Then we'd be back into the ether, casting about for a new when and where, for more chaos to unravel. I needed to be rid of the skinny little shit by then.

Who knew what sort of cosmic balance he'd tip over if we jumped with him in the car?

"Trusting the young is the only hope of each aging generation." Pointing a delicate finger at me, the Buddha gave me a smile that made me think of cheap ceramic statues and sleeping lions. "However, pointing at the moon is *not* the moon itself."

"Like a fortune cookie you are," I muttered.

A man and woman dressed in black dove out of our way as we jumped the steps leading up to the bridge. I had my gun out by that time, the Firebird's wheels ba-dang-dang-danging onto the near side of the bridge over the Main. When we were a quarter of the way across I pressed on the brakes.

"Be a lamp unto yourself—" the Buddha began, but I didn't let him finish. I'd had enough of his whispering voice and his suspect wisdom. It was time.

I took two shots, but I think the second went high into the afternoon sky over the Main River. Ari pushed the false Buddha out the door at 140 k.p.h., and we launched ourselves off the temporal bridge backward — or forward — to some other damn when.

#

Anyone can travel back and forth in time.

A cynical creature would laugh at such a thought, but stop and think about it for a second. We do it all the time just by remembering the past and daydreaming about the future. But to actually take your *body* with you, you've got to go through some extra effort.

And if you want to travel temporally with the same group of folks, in the same vehicle you're currently whisking around in through the present, you've got to use a bridge. The more people you have, the more accurate the jump, but the shorter distance you could travel. It was the temporal quandary, the paradox of time. The Buddha and his Zen buddies would've loved wrapping their brains around that one.

To do a jump, any bridge or vehicle will work. The trick isn't the bridge or the vehicle — in our case, a sky-blue '75 Pontiac Firebird with a fat white stripe running up the hood and back to the trunk, but the *timing* you use on your way across the bridge. The secret is to jump at the exact midpoint of the

11

bridge. There's that frozen heartbeat of a moment — you know what I'm talking about here — when you're no longer coming onto the bridge but leaving it.

The strongest thought of any person in the vehicle at that temporally flexible juncture in the bridge wins the where and when game. So it's good to stay focused on your way across a bridge.

As the Buddha would've said (before I shot him, that is, and heard his slender body hit the girders of the bridge with a sharp crack), bridges put us in touch with ebb and flow of our own inner area of unrest.

To which I say: rest in peace.

#

We landed outside a three-story brick structure. The when was unclear, because there were no cars or people around. Unless it was the far future or the distant past, most buildings hid their timeframes well.

"It's a school," Ari said, pushing out of the back seat. My bare arms burst into gooseflesh at the sound of Ari's deep voice, followed immediately by the popping of the passenger door. Ari was a Muslim who'd lived his whole life in southern Missouri. He flipped his thick black hair in an arc around his head and somehow managed to secure it all under the turban he always carried in his back pocket. His turban had a John Deere patch sewn on it, along with the logo for the Kansas City Royals.

"Looks like America," he said, "from all the advertisements on the walls and used rubbers around the garbage cans. But *when* is it?"

I looked over at the shotgun seat, half-expecting our most recent Buddha to still be sitting there, legs crossed and grinning over at me. But the seat was empty, of course, his last fortune-cookie message forever left unfinished. I put the Buddha's words out of my head and got out, gun in hand, determined to live up to my tough-as-shiny-new-nails riot-grrl reputation.

The others unfolded themselves from the backseat and joined us outside, stretching and groaning. Marco was a former Soviet soldier with Jewish aspirations and no sense of the fall of communism, while Annina was a gawky Canadian atheist with bugshit eyes and a black sense of humor. Yeshev I didn't know much about. All of them I met on the road, and for the most part, we traveled well together.

And of course, we all tended to gravitate to times like this one, which are *supposed* to be periods of heightened chaos. Right now this place looked to be suffering only from a bad stretch of dullness and monotony.

"So," I said, looking at the slope of grass in front of the school and the sun reflecting off the evenly-spaced windows above it. "Who was thinking of this place?"

Nobody answered.

Great, I thought. Another at-the-last-minute job.

We drifted into the school, smelling the warm meat smell of the mass-produced lunch being prepared for the noon hour. Yet under that scent was a darker odor. A mix of gun oil and blown matches. Okay, I was thinking, there just may be some chaos activity here. We drifted inside, letting the waves of waiting energy pull us on invisible strings into the cafeteria, and then into the library.

The school reminded me of jail, the one I spent almost a decade in before I learned how to keep my mouth shut and fake my good behavior. Jail was shit, a constant battle of victim and aggressor, but I'd learned to always cover my back and trust the hunches that came over me. I was starting to recognize this place now; my hunches were rarely wrong, when I chose to listen to them.

A hot breeze blew across my forehead when I stepped into the musty school library. I was starting to think that today was a weekend or a holiday, the place was so empty. I'd wanted to check out the Reference section, where the computers were, so I stepped behind the desk, and then I felt a familiar tingle. I turned, and my heart skipped a beat when I saw the glint of black metal reflected in the rows of monitors in front of me. I was the first of our little group to see the kid in the army fatigues walk in, carrying an assault rifle in each hand, a WWJD pendant dangling on his chest next to his home-made dogtags.

My gun was out and pointed at the kid just as he was lowering the first Kalashnikov. I froze when I saw that Ari was in the kid's line of fire. The tall Muslim was motionless, staring at two other kids, a boy and a girl decked out in the same ugly green fatigues and carrying more weaponry than any zit-ridden sixteen-year-old had a right to.

The boy began shooting. He realized too late, of course, that his girlfriend and his buddy were standing directly behind Ari, guns lifted. Ari was caught in the middle of a mindless firefight that left us with four corpses and one less mind to muck up our travels through the ether. I still stood there, gun aiming at the space where the boy with the dogtags had been standing.

I may as well have been pointing it at the moon, for all the good it had done Ari. Ari was not the moon, either.

As we made sure the shooters were dead, Yeshev wrapped up Ari in his overcoat and carried him to the Firebird. Even as I felt myself want to puke on the card catalog next to me, I was already calculating how, on our next jump, we'd drop his remains somewhere and somewhen that wouldn't raise any questions. It wasn't the best we could've done for him, but we had a responsibility to leave behind no trace of our passing.

Annina and I gave each other a long look, my dry eyes taking in her tear-filled eyes. Was it worth it? Did we have to lose Ari in exchange for all the innocent kids and teachers who would've been shot by the three dead students now spread out across the Reference section of their high school library?

"At least we won't have to listen to his bitching about being carsick anymore," I muttered on my way out, but nobody was buying my act anymore. Not today.

At the door, I saw a bullet-ridden book splayed out over the outline of a perfectly-round, yellow face. "Have a Nice Day," the smiling sticker would have read, if the blood hadn't obscured the words. But I could still make out that smile, a perfect half-circle of self-contentment and wisdom. For all intents and purposes, the Buddha was still riding shotgun with us, his incomprehensible Zen koans echoing in my head like the bullets had ricocheted of the library's cinderblock wall.

I emptied my gun into the yellow happy face even as the others slinked out of the school like the shadow creatures we all were.

#

Back in the Firebird I was able to pull myself together. Yeshev had said something about not wasting ammo on smiley-face stickers, even though we were all reeling from losing Ari. Marco, even jumpier than normal, sat huddled into the backset, the gunfire probably bringing back old memories of Chechnya and ruined buildings. Annina pushed past me into the seat next to

Marco, swearing under her breath about not feeling carsick. We weren't having what you'd call good group dynamics.

With Ari gone, the Firebird handled much, much better.

I'd found the car the day I walked out of Folsom County Prison — no, not the one in the song by Johnny Cash, but don't you doubt that that damn song wasn't pumping through my damn head every second I was there. Because it was, believe me.

I was in a car graveyard when I came across her. The 'Bird. After getting out of jail, I found the gun under the Firebird's driver seat and saw it as a sign. So much for keeping up my "good behavior" — I stole the car from the toothless old man at the graveyard and learned her ins and outs as I chased chaos around the globe on my own. I'd learned about bridges and how they could move me through time with a little luck, concentration, and timing from my Folsom cellmate. Her name was Verity, and she had only one eye and lied every third sentence. She was also the one who told me about chaos.

"If you undo enough of it," she said with her permanent wink, "you can stop running and start finding order in your life again."

The sky-blue Firebird, with its big gas-sucking engine and dual glasspack mufflers, was a natural for moving through time and space and chasing chaos. The beauty of it was, if there was someplace I couldn't get to, the Firebird could bull its way through with the proper application of accelerator and momentum.

The difficulty came in when I started taking on passengers. The more people I had in the car, the easier it was to travel with some sense of accuracy, but at the same time, the more passengers I had in the car, the harder it got to jump longer temporal distances. With two in the car it was easy to go back to the grassy damn knoll, but with a gang of five — now four — it burned up a ton of psychic energy just getting out of the aughts.

Luckily I'd taught my fellow travelers well. They got quiet as the bridge over the Colorado River rose up in front of us. Emergency vehicles blasted past us like screaming mothers mourning their children, headed for the school. We ignored them, focusing instead on the invisible lines of chaos extending around the world like lines on a map, stretching out in billions of timestreams.

Ten kilometers southeast of the bloodstained school library and the ravaged Have a Nice Day sticker, we hit the middle of a slender two-lane bridge and jumped south and *way* east.

We landed in Afghanistan.

#

There was a very simple, almost elegant reason why I had to kill the Buddha. Not just *the* Buddha, of course, but *all* Buddhas. You'd be surprised at the number of imposters out there in the world, dispensing their suspect wisdom like a carnival attraction.

I had to kill all the Buddhas because it was their fault the world was riddled with chaos. I had to shoot any and all Buddhas, no matter what their incarnation, even if Ari had to get shot by teenagers, or if Yeshev had to die from multiple bullet wounds from the Afghanistan attack in '99. It was my duty to do it.

Don't get me wrong. I wasn't being bigoted in my choice of targets. If I saw Christ in a crosswalk in San Francisco, I'd gun the engine and splat him onto the windshield as quick as you could say "Peace be with you." Same deal for Abraham and Mohammad, for holy women and medicine men in charge of their flocks. All of them had to go. Too much of their misguided teachings had trickled down through the centuries, only to be misunder-stood by murderers and power freaks and oppressors. That was the only way I was going to get rid of the chaos.

The dispensers of false wisdom were the true agents of chaos out there in the world — I just rode along in their wake like a bicycle rider following a Mack truck.

But despite all of my best intentions, the Buddhas just kept finding their way back to me, in one form or another, no matter how many times I blew them away.

#

For close to three hours, the helicopters cut the night sky above us like man-made thunder, until Annina couldn't take it any more. Maybe she was thinking of Ari, and how he would've killed to see his homeland again, or maybe she was furious about the added destruction to a country already nose-deep in desolation. It was obvious she'd been the one thinking of this place. Damn Ari and his vivid descriptions of the poppy fields outside Kandahar.

The fields were on fire.

Shooting down from the choppers as they blasted overhead, the fire fell like slow lightning across the dry fields. We watched from the middle of the only road in or out of the valley, the Firebird parked sideways across the center of the dirt road.

When we heard the trucks of the poppy farmers and the laborers approaching up the road, we quit watching the Apaches crisscrossing the burning field and got back in the Firebird. The trucks piled up when they saw us in the middle of the road, turning off and running into one another even as we shot out of their way. I loved my eight-cylinder, six-hundred-horsepower, dual-exhaust Firebird.

The raid, instead of being foiled as it had been in the "other" past, was a success. We'd given the field-burners — oh hell, let me come right out and say it, the CIA operatives — the extra five minutes they needed. I could only hope that the Afghan time string would play itself out in a different, more orderly fashion over the next few years, and we wouldn't have to come back again any time soon.

We stopped outside a small village and got out to listen for any news about the burning fields and troop movement of the various alliances fighting or serving the Taliban. We kept to the shadows in the early morning light. On my way back to the Firebird, a blanket over my head like a birka to disguise my gender, I passed a donkey and a camel.

The camel was smiling at me.

"The river is wide and unmo-o-o-oving," the donkey next to the camel said in a high-pitched, whinnying voice. "I am but a rock in the river, worn smo-o-o-oth by its passing."

"Peace is everywhere," the camel responded. "You need only find it inside you."

"Peace is the bridge," the donkey agreed with a yellow grin. "And the bridge is inside of you."

I stared at their pleased grins and half-closed eyes. Damn that Buddha. Even the livestock had learned his ways. I reached for my gun, wanting to erase those smiles. But the crackle of automatic weapons made me let go of my gun and cover my head again in the blanket like a good Taliban maiden.

Screw it, I thought. I didn't have time to shoot the Buddha and his various incarnations every minute of every day.

I sprinted back to the Firebird, the gunfire building. I had a feeling Annina had lost her composure. She'd probably tried to do something to honor Ari's memory. I just hoped she didn't take anyone else from the Firebird with her.

I found them half a kilometer from the car, Marco bent over Annina and screaming Russian in her face. From his tone I didn't think the words were sweet nothings. Yeshev was crumpled on the ground next to them like a forgotten wad of paper.

I ran and got the Firebird, and Marco put the injured riders into the back seat. Yeshev was moaning and whimpering, but Annina was deathly silent. On our way away from the village, I passed the donkey and camel, still wearing their shit-eating grins. I fought the urge to turn the wheel and let the big bumper of the Firebird have them for breakfast. We were coming up on another bridge, the bridge that would lead us somewhen else, and I couldn't afford a delay, not with Annina and Yeshev banged up the way they were.

And anyway, I could only kill so many Buddhas before the bad karma finally caught up with me.

#

Yeshev didn't make it. The wounds were too many and too deep, and he died short seconds after we jumped away from the battlefields of poppy. I got the whole story from Marco as we drove. Annina had led Yeshev and Marco into a Taliban stronghold at the heart of the Afghan village and, bold as badgers, they'd tried to hold back the dam of chaos with their hand-guns and misplaced courage. Annina, as usually happened in cases like that, came out untouched.

Without Yeshev and Ari slowing us down, we were able to make it back to the eighties, but only the tail end. I tell you, that decade was a damn smorgasbord of chaos to unravel and rewrite in our own unique ways, and I made sure I had the dominant thought when we screamed across the muddy Afghan river on a bridge of rotting timbers. I was surprised to see that we actually made it to the time and place I'd been concentrating on when we hit the middle of the bridge.

We arrived in Berlin, in the fall of '89.

The wall was going down by the time we drove up. I took one look at the holes being punched in the wall and saw what I needed. Everyone in the crowd had pushed forward to get a piece of the wall, the crush of bodies like corpses standing up and leaning forward with their dead, stifling weight, but I was able to sneak in and get the chunk I needed.

I snatched the triangular piece of broken, graffiti-laced concrete with his face spray-painted on it. The corners had broken off in straight lines, cutting the face in half, but leaving that patented Buddha grin. Still he was smiling at me.

But this time I smiled back. I understood him now. He would always keep coming back, in one form or the other, and I would always be there waiting for him, as long as I had the Firebird and a friend or two. The secret was to stop looking. Then I could stop running and find the missing order in my life.

Even as someone grabbed my ass and tried to turn me around for a celebratory kiss, I slipped away with the Buddha in my coat pocket, leaving a horny German man behind me on the ground, clutching his nuts. I pushed through the crowd, the broken wall behind me.

But when I made it back to where I'd left the others and the car, I saw that the revelation I'd made at the wall had already become meaningless. Young men and women swinging sledgehammers had moved to the Firebird, doing to the car what they'd done to the wall. Marco must have realized that this was the end of communism, and he knelt ten feet back from the crowd, tears in his beard. Annina was one of the women swinging the hammers at the Firebird.

I wasn't going anywhere for a long, long time. And for the first time in my life, I was at peace with that knowledge. I walked away from the wall and, avoiding all bridges, I headed west, a tiny sliver of the Buddha held tight in my hand.

#

I lived in Berlin for a dozen years after that. After the wall came down, traveling the world in the ruined Firebird was no longer an option. I couldn't bring myself to look for some other car. Everything has to end, I knew.

And so, the others drifted away, promising to write and steer clear of all bridges, but most likely doing neither. I got used to walking most places, and it was getting harder for me to say no to the gearheads as well as a growing number of tourists near the Brandenberg Gate who were dying to buy the Firebird from me as a souvenir of the New World Order. I turned them all down, until yesterday.

I needed the money after all my chemo, and I was tired of waiting, one long fucking day at a time, for Buddha. *The* Buddha, not *a* Buddha. We had to talk.

I realized that gunning for the Buddha had gotten me nowhere, and somewhere in my travels I'd picked up the big C, probably from all the cigs and the power lines next to my apartment here in Berlin. But that wasn't going to stop me from trying to catch up with him one last time.

This morning I decided to go. But first, following my gut instincts, I plucked out what little hair I had left on my body, even eyebrows and pubes (I felt lop-sided with all that extra hair and none to cover my scalp, so it all had to go), and pulled on a robe. I was doped up on a lovely mix of my own creation — morphine, Maker's Mark, and marijuana — and I'd lost so much weight, my chest was non-existent beneath my robe. So much for my girlish figure.

Without anything on my feet, I started walking. Within minutes I came within sight of the Palace Bridge over the Spree. On the Bridge I could see the statues of men with swords growing closer, male guardians of a lost time. Memories of jumping through more recent timeframes flitted through my throbbing head. I hadn't crossed a bridge in over a decade.

I didn't even have to lift my thumb to get the big car to pull over. It was a mint-green '72 Monte Carlo with mag wheels and a crackling muffler. Nice. After climbing inside, I dug into the pocket of the robe and found one of the hundreds of fortunes on rectangles of paper from Guten Wok, home of the best tofu stir-fry in Germany. I savored the fortunes like most folks did the Bible, or *USA Today*.

"In some ways . . . " I began, reading from a fortune I held cribbed in my right hand, hidden from the unsmiling young woman behind the wheel. The pain in my head was gone.

In the driver's hard face I saw young boys and girls with guns, helicopters dripping with flames, and desert livestock spouting wisdom. I thought of bridges crumbling slowly, one second at a time, into dust. I had to find the Buddha.

I swallowed and started over. "In some ways," I said, my voice thick from lack of use. "I am helpless."

When she pulled the gun out, we were already on the bridge and decelerating. The four people crowded into the back of the car hissed laughter, like snakes or punctured tires. The driver steered with her left hand and pointed the gun with her right. I forgot all about my fortune-cookie messages and devised my own.

"Be a lamp unto yourself," I said, kicking out with both bare feet as my body slid low in the car's big front seat, "and seek your own liberation with diligence."

The shot went high, shattering the window above me. The blast nearly deafened me, but at last I knew the blissful release of a fortune told, a lesson learned, a deity found. At last. We hit the middle of the bridge, and we were gone.

GODDAMN REDNECK
SURFER ZOMBIES

People stopped coming to the North Carolina coast when the dead returned to the beach after four decades away. Got to the point where folks couldn't sit outside their own beachside trailers with a case of Bud without some rotting corpse staggering up and asking for directions to the cemetery or the bars or the bait shop, the whole time smelling like spoiled tuna. They killed us for most of the entire tourist season before we realized what they were up to and actually did something about 'em. Goddamn zombies.

Back then I spent most of my days down at the end of the pier, the longest one in the state, where the stink of fish innards cooking in the sun never got to me like the reek of dead-person guts in some walking corpse did. If you come out to Long Beach — which you *should* do, even now, with the zombies and all — to fish and swim in the bath-warm water during the day and eat seafood and drink cold ones with us at night, you'd find me there at the farthest tip of the pier, past the signs saying "No Spectators Beyond This Point" and "King Mackerel Fishing Only." If you give a shout for Big Al, I'd come over and say hey to you, long as the kings weren't biting.

I caught my limit most days by noon, smoking and drinking with the other old men with skin like leather and just enough teeth to hold their Camels in place. After the doc threatened to cut a hole in my neck, I stopped with the cancer sticks, but I still liked a cold Bud while I watched my lines in the salty hot Carolina air.

High point of my days that summer came late in the afternoon, when the pretty girls came up and visited with us after a day of sunbathing and gossiping. Oh Lord, to be young again. Their tanned stomachs were tight and their long hair was salty and wet from the Atlantic, and they acted like they wanted to learn about fishing. We all knew they weren't interested in any of that. They were up there on the pier with us for protection.

Because every afternoon, when the tide started to head out, the dead came lurching out of the brush on the other side of the dunes and headed for the waves. The girls don't want to be alone on the beach wearing just their bits of bikini as the zombies walked past, dragging their coffin lids behind 'em. Couple of the girls even recognized their grandparents, stripped down to their birthday suits, showing off their pale gray skin. That shook 'em up pretty good, let me tell you.

Far as I could tell, the girls didn't have nothing to worry about. These zombies were here for one thing only — they wanted to *surf.*

Some of us thought the zombies were attracted to the waves because of the pull of the tides. Mort and Lymon had their nicotine-and-six-pack theories about the moon's effect on the graveyards and the bodies buried in 'em. "Tidal forces from the moon," Mort said in his gravel voice. "Pulls 'em up outta the ground just like it makes the waves come in and out. They put that cemetery too close to the ocean, that's what. Yeppers. Tidal forces."

We all just laughed and tried not to look at the naked corpses falling off their coffin lids like the newbies we called grommets back in my surfing days. Ten of the dead were out on the water that day, flinging their rotting and bloodless bodies toward the next wave. I recognized Alfie and Zach, old buddies from high school (flipped their car into the Intracoastal Waterway one Saturday night in '59 and drowned in three feet of water) along with my own mother (lung cancer, '82) surfing next to four-decades dead Purnell Austin, forever twenty-one.

They took some tremendous tumbles, like the time Purnell was launched off his lid by a wave and slammed headfirst into the lid of the rotting girl next to him, sending pieces of nose and teeth flying. That one was so bad I caught myself moving out of my chair toward the water. But the surfing dead didn't need any kind of first aid, not any more. Purnell climbed back onto his coffin lid, twisted his head with both hands to the left once, hard, and got ready for the next wave with a laugh. Lucky he didn't lose his head on that one.

The zombies' laughter was like the cough of a lifelong smoker, and it made the hairs on my arms stand up. Must've been hard, laughing when you didn't need to breathe any more.

Quiet old Bob Mangum nodded his bald head toward the undead surfers. "It's the beginning of the end times, 'ats what it is. Nothing to do with no moon or no tidal forces." He hobbled back to his cooler of shrimp bait and his five fishing lines. "Keep an eye out for Jehovah 'n' the horsemen," he added.

Now, I'd always been one to just let things be. Long as the zombies left our people alone and no one went missing like last time, I was fine without getting into some sort of hassle with 'em. Cops didn't care about the zombies either, so long as no one was hurt, but someone must've told the reporters this time.

Luckily, the film crews didn't last long when they learned that the surfing dead didn't photograph well. All the zombies left were gray smears on film that looked like they'd been faked to even an old fart with bad eyes like mine. I could've told 'em they were wasting their time and their film, but who ever paid attention to a crusty old man like me? They were gone within a week with no story and a pile of worthless film.

Tourists were another story. Of course, they were scared shitless by the walking dead. Us locals can adjust to 'most anything, long as it doesn't get in the way of the fishing, but most tourists ran off the instant they caught sight of some old zombie woman limping up the beach, tits hanging to her belly button, dragging her surf lid behind her like the train to a wedding dress. Even worse were the dead young 'uns, the teens killed in drunken car wrecks that went 'round as if showing off their missing arms, legs, or the occasional head. Made it hard to concentrate on your John Grisham lawyer novel, or your gushy Fabio-on-the-cover romance paperback, I'm sure.

The tourists that did stick around, wasting their film with more damn photos, didn't last too long. The zombies were "quaint" at first — swear to God I heard one of the Yankee women say this, heard it all the way up on the pier — but when their stink filled the air and the chunks of dead flesh started washing up onto the beach, they skedaddled real quick.

Before packing up the kiddies and their plastic shovels and expensive umbrellas and chairs, I did catch some of the housewives sucking in their soft bellies when one of the fresher, not-dead-for-*too*-too-long male zombies whizzed past on his surf lid, as if these mamas had some sort of chance with a rotting old redneck boy whose last memory was red ambulance lights or a doctor beating on his chest a handful of years ago.

Now, I didn't mind getting rid of loud and rude tourists — most of 'em were Yankees anyhow, moved down here for their high-falutin'-tech jobs a few hours away up in Raleigh — but my buddy Lou at the Surf'n'Suds Pier Restaurant and Angie at the Wings store needed the cash that those tourists brought. They couldn't handle another bad season, not after three hurricanes in the past five years, including the near miss from barely a month ago that left half the beach underwater. It was hard enough getting folks to come to Long Beach the way it was, and then the goddamn undead showed up.

I'd lived here all my life, and I watched the landscape change as the ocean ate away the sand dunes and made the new hotels the developer fools built sink and dip like leaking ships, and in that time I saw the same sort of tourist come down to our beaches. They'd pack up the brats, soak up the sun 'til it burned 'em, spend their money in our shops, and try to catch fish off the shallow sides of our pier. Like clockwork, they'd leave one week later, not to return until the following year. At the end of summer us locals cleaned up their mess and got back to our own business. That was the way things went.

The only disruption in the pattern was back in '60. That was the summer I came back to Long Beach to find the cemeteries from here to Southport empty, and the dead walking the streets.

#

I'd been surfing for a decade by that point in time. I'd started with my older brother's board when I was 'most ten years old, most times falling off it like a grommet before a wave ever picked me up. But I stuck with it and spent most days surfing instead of in school with the other kids. I always figured one of these days I'd go back and get my diploma, but my sixtieth, then my seventieth birthday snuck up on me, and after that I just didn't see the point of it, really. I got all I wanted in life with fishing.

That summer of 1960, when there weren't waves big enough to go surfing, I learned all about pier fishing. I figured if I made friends with the fishermen on the pier, at the least I'd get fewer sinkers thrown at me on those days that I surfed a bit too close to the pier. Surfers and fishermen hardly ever see eye to eye, dealing like they do with the ocean from two very different angles. But bribed with enough smokes and brews, the fishermen warmed to me and taught me all I'd ever want to know. After that summer I never got hooked by a cast or thrown sinker.

And then the zombies came calling. It all started on a Monday morning right after Hurricane Donna blasted through in early September. I was half-buzzed by ten a.m., nursing my fifth beer, when the first body flopped onto the flooded beach west of the pier. Looked like a damn fish thrown onto the sand by a rough wave, except the ocean was dead calm for a change. The body was shedding its pasty white skin, along with the occasional body part, with each spasm. An eyeball rolled back into the surf like a stray golf ball hit by an idiot tourist golfer.

Me and the boys were down there in five seconds. In spite of all our bad talk about the tourists, none of us wanted to see one of 'em die. And no fisherman or surfer wants to see a corpse on their beach. That's what we all figured this was, judging by the white skin of the man flailing on the sand: a near-drowning.

The man wouldn't let us set him up to help him breathe, even though Bob was positive he couldn't get a pulse. For a mostly-dead fella, he had the kind of strength I'd never felt before. I grabbed his arm, nearly sicking up my beers at the cold and loose feel of his flesh, like the skin of uncooked chicken. He lifted me right off the ground with that one arm.

It took us an hour to figure out what he was. His face had swollen up, but I swore there was something familiar about that crooked nose and that anchor tattoo on his shoulder.

Luckily the Oleandar Drive-In in Wilmington had been playing a horror triple-feature earlier that summer, and my buddy Marty had seen all three flicks, including "I Walked With a Zombie."

"That's Jack Johnson!" Marty shouted. "Swear to God! He's one'a those zombers!"

The dead guy opened his one remaining eye and gave Marty what looked like a pissed-off glare. That's when I knew it was Jack, because of those Paul Newman ladykiller eyes. Or eye, I should say. His right one was floating up and down in the surf like a bobber. Jack was polite and didn't say anything about Marty's mangled terminology. Jack Johnson had drowned a week ago, caught out in the hurricane trying to save his boat.

"Ain't no such thing as a zom*bie*," Bob said in his quiet voice as we helped Jack to his feet. Bob had been old even back then. If I was a fool like Marty, who died in 'Nam when he fell over a trip wire after three hits of acid and blew his face off, I'd be wondering if ol' Bob wasn't a "zomber" too.

We didn't know what else to do, so we handed Jack his eye, which he popped back in its socket, and let him be. The fish were biting, that's all I can say in our defense. Marty left us to go surfing, and Jack walked off in the opposite direction of the pier.

We'd pretty much forgotten about him until we heard the screaming coming from the Dairy Queen up the road.

Purnell Austin, one of the biggest guys I knew back in school before I dropped out, had been stuffed into a garbage can outside the DQ. Both his legs had been broken, and they dangled out of the garbage can like dead flowers. But that wasn't the worst of it. When we pulled him out of the can, his head was split in two, and over half of his brain was gone. The top half of his head sat on a pile of bloody newspapers, looking like a hairy pottery bowl.

Before I sicked up my Budweiser breakfast, I saw two things that would stay with me until my dying day, and probably beyond even that.

The first was the teethmarks that had been left in the pinkish-gray brain matter of Purnell's battered skull.

The second was Jack Johnson's sky-blue eyeball, staring up at us from next to the garbage can.

#

This time most everything was different. The dead on the beach were just as bad as the crew from four decades ago for stinking and losing body parts — but at least this time no one living had gone missing. Back in '60 we'd lost almost a dozen folks before we could get the situation under control. We'd been able to keep the reporters and the other authorities away. Only Sheriff Johnson knew about the zombies back then, and he hadn't been keen on letting anyone outside of the Long Beach community know that his brother Jack was a "zomber" with a taste for brains. We kept it hushed up, for our own good.

For now, though, decades later, no dead tourists had turned up with their heads cracked open like walnuts, missing most of the gray shit that makes up people's brains. At least not yet.

Seems the zombies came this time just for the surfing, and nothing more.

#

I take full responsibility for that. I was the one who taught 'em how to surf. Goes to show you *can* teach an old dog new tricks, even if that old dog is dead. Or undead, however you wanna call it.

Nobody else was having any sort of luck keeping the zombies under control. You could shoot 'em and stab 'em with a filleting knife, but they didn't even flinch. If you were close enough to stab at 'em you were probably a goner anyway. We didn't figure out until it was almost too late that we should've been aiming at their heads the whole time.

After four of us young punks got killed by the zombies, and I'd taken the worst beating of my life from Marty's Great-Aunt Esther (dead of a stroke in '38), we had to regroup and find some other way to keep the zombies from chowing on our brains like undead stoners with the munchies. If the outside world heard about this, the town would shrivel up and die, and we'd be good as dead then ourselves.

It was me who came up with the idea of surfing. I loved it, I figured, so why wouldn't the dead? If there was a heaven, I figured it had clear skies and monster waves all day and night.

So we taught the zombies to surf. They took right to it even though their bodies were never as coordinated as they'd been while they were alive. At least we didn't have to worry about anyone drowning.

Old Bob had the idea of collecting the brains from the fish we caught off the pier to give the dead to eat, sort of a goodwill gesture, and they went along with it. For the rest of fall, nobody else went missing or showed up with a scooped-out skull. The zombies surfed up to the start of winter, until another tropical storm blew up in November. The zombies made one last surf as the storm passed over, and then they went to rest again back in their water-logged graves, pulling their coffin lid surfboards back on top of them like blankets.

\#

This was the summer for surfing, that was for sure. The waves had been unbelievable all summer, bringing with 'em the biggest fish I'd ever caught. Just yesterday I pulled in a fifteen-pound king mackerel from off the pier and nearly pissed myself. I was getting ready to fillet it up after Lou took my picture with it when I smelled the stink of zombie on the fish. I tossed it over the side of the pier, hoping no one saw me do it.

I should've known then that the dead had overstayed their visit once again. I tried to ignore 'em, I really did, but they were affecting my livelihood now. A man's got to fish, and a man's got to eat.

Some of the other guys were noticing it too. Most of the fish we caught went back over the side after a quick weighing and measuring. The too-sweet stink of rot was on our hands now, and we couldn't get it off no matter how much we wiped 'em on our shorts and shirts.

Like I said before, I'd always been one to let things be. If I got hungry enough I could cook the hell out of the fish I caught and choke down the zombie-tainted meat. If I had to. I'd just resigned myself to this when I heard a gaggle of our young girls on the beach. They were all screaming and pointing at the ocean.

Now let me explain something to you about a man and fishing. If his concentration was just right, with the sun keeping his head warm and the fish keeping the muscles in his arms tense, you could drop a nuclear bomb on the bait house behind him and he'd only check his lines and maybe blink once or twice.

So I never knew it had gotten this bad with the zombies. I set down my reel like I was in slow motion, like it was the last time I'd ever see it, and I turned to look at the beach, where the girls was still screaming.

The ocean was *thick* with the goddamn redneck surfer zombies.

They were perched on top of their coffin lids, leaning into the waves from the back half of the lid, just like I'd taught 'em decades ago. It was as if they had some sort of Stick-Em keeping 'em attached to their lids, because not a single one fell off.

And that was when I noticed that all the zombies were aiming in the same direction, their surf lids pointed toward a circle of blood fifty yards beyond where the waves broke.

Old Bob was already running down the pier toward the beach, with Mort and Lymon busting a gut trying to keep up. I dropped my line, grabbed the pneumatic spear-fishing gun from the crow's nest upstairs, and did the best swan dive off the side of the pier that a seventy-six-year old redneck could do, right into the salty waves. I thought I'd broken my neck until I resurfaced, eyes stinging and head reeling.

"Shoot 'em in the head," Marty had told me all those years ago. "It's the only way to take 'em out."

We'd been smoking and drinking all night on the beach, watching the corpses surf in the moonlight. Marty was leaving for Fort Leavenwood the next week for basic training, and then he'd be off to Vietnam a few years later, waiting for his encounters with acid and the tripwire.

"Blow their brains out, huh?" I finished off my bottle of beer and launched it at out at dead Purnell out there surfing. He was barely a month dead. It smacked him in the chest and knocked a chunk of gray flesh into the waves with a soft plop.

"Yeah. Go for the head," Marty had said. "Spread their brains out all over the place so they can't put 'em back together."

I'd always wondered later, after catching a midnight showing of "Night of the Living Dead," if that George Romero fella had been out to Long Beach that summer, checking out the situation, maybe even talking to Marty. In any case, Marty had been right about the head shots. The zombies were much more interested in learning to surf once we blew off a few rotting heads.

As I swam through the waves that summer day, my old heart pounding in my ribs, I thought about Marty and all the others from Long Beach, including those of us who were now zombies. I swam harder, wishing there had been enough of Marty left for 'em to ship back to us. He always loved catching a good wave.

Half a minute later I was there, outside the ring of thirty surf lids each holding one zombie apiece. They were surrounding the bloody froth, watching the struggling with dumb blank faces.

"Get back," I shouted, raising the gun and aiming it at the closest zombie. The coppery stink of blood was in the air, mixed with the zombie's odor of rot and the salty spray of the waves. I dog-paddled my way to the middle of the coffin lids and saw that the struggling had stopped in the bloody water ahead of me. I lowered the spear gun and waited. Just like that a zombie's head and shoulders lifted from the water, followed by the lifeless body of Janie Winters, covered in blood.

"Bastards!" I screamed as I pulled the trigger of the pneumatic gun.

I probably would have taken off the head of the zombie holding Janie if the zombie closest to the two of 'em — Purnell Austin, actually, of all damn people — hadn't thrown himself in front of the spear and caught it with the back of his head. The spear blew off most of his face before getting lodged in his skull. The zombies closest to him were showered with whitened bits of brain and dried strips of brown flesh.

"Daaaa-aaamn," Alfie the car wreck zombie said in his guttural voice. "Why'd ya do thaaaa-aaat?"

Just like the summer of '60, it made me want to retch, having to kill someone who used to be my neighbor. But just like last time, they'd left me no choice. Or so I thought.

I dropped the gun when Janie moaned. A jagged gash ran the length of her thin arm, and that's when I realized how close I had come to making a huge mistake.

Blinking saltwater and sweat out of my eyes, I saw what had *really* been going on. The corpse of an eight-foot-long shark floated behind the zombie holding Janie, its side peppered with bloody, fist-sized holes. Four of the zombies had been torn to shreds fighting off the shark that had gone after Janie, but they'd survive.

Well, maybe "survive" isn't the right word. But you know what I mean.

#

We made an agreement, the zombies and us living folks. They could come surfing every couple of years during the low season, long as they left when we asked 'em to and stuck to eating fish — not human — brains. Otherwise, us humans would start digging up graves and blowing off some zombie heads.

To our shock, they agreed, even though I could tell it was killing 'em — ha ha ha — to leave the waves behind for the year. The surfing was *that* good 'round here.

And hey, if they were willing to keep the waters shark-free for their surfing pleasure, that was fine with us.

31

Janie was doing better, and was most likely going to get most of the movement back in her arm after the shark bite healed. She stayed on the shore all the time these days, concentrating on her tan instead of swimming or surfing.

Meanwhile, I kept a close eye on the cemeteries from here to Southport, as well as the Weather Channel. You never knew what the next hurricane might stir up, and I couldn't say I was partial to cooking my fish until the taste of zombie was fried out of it.

But at the same time, I knew I was getting on in years, and I was sort of looking forward to surfing again someday soon. Got a coffin lid all picked out, too.

VISIONS OF SUBURBAN BLISS

Richard Tolliver was proud of the fact that his was the first black family to move into the Olde Carriage Ridgewood subdivision in Cary, North Carolina. His job as an electrical engineer at Implement Telecom in the Research Triangle Park, nestled between the three cities of Raleigh, Durham, and Chapel Hill, had allowed him to spring past his childhood neighbors from the housing projects of Southwest Raleigh. Many of his old neighbors were still living there, either working one to two hourly, minimum-wage jobs, or working the streets, hustling crack or coke or the old standby, transparent baggies of pot. They'd all been going nowhere fast, Richard knew.

But I made it out, he thought, enjoying the power he felt sitting up high in his Ford Expedition, crawling through eastbound I-40 traffic after work, only seven short miles from home. It was a drive that averaged thirty-five minutes, one way. After escaping the slums of Raleigh, Richard was proud to be able to call himself a resident of Cary.

He rolled up his windows and cranked the AC. The humidity of a Southern summer was fast approaching, and he wasn't ready for it. He'd put on fifteen pounds since moving into the management job at the telecom company, spending more and more time in front of his computer, reading status reports and timesheets instead of working on switches and routers.

But the money was worth it, he'd told himself so many times he thought he'd print it out and tape it to his office monitor. Larissa loves the new house.

And with Junior on the way, we'll need all the extra dough we can get our hands on.

Richard Tolliver leaned back in his massive sports utility vehicle, letting his foot off the break every fifteen seconds, inching closer to his new home in the gated community of Olde Carriage Ridgewood in Cary, North Carolina.

#

Thirty-nine minutes later, after creeping through stop-and-go traffic ("Onlooker delays for a three-car accident at the Harrison Avenue off ramp has traffic backed up to the Page Road exit," the radio announcer shouted every five minutes), Richard waited to make the left turn into his new subdivision.

Gonna need a left-turn arrow here soon, he thought, watching the unending line of cars coming at him. He'd never seen so many Beemers, Mercedes, and Lexuses since moving to Cary. He rolled forward until he was halfway through the intersection, hoping the cars would relent long enough to let him dash across the road.

As the light slipped from yellow to red, Richard punched it. He blasted in front of an oncoming Cabriolet that had to slam on the brakes to avoid hitting him head-on. A white hand with the middle finger raised shot out of the honking Cabrio. Five cars behind the Cabrio joined in the raucous chorus. Richard turned hard into the main entrance of his neighborhood, the Expedition rocking like a trailer in a tornado.

Three Mexican men from the landscaping company contracted by the subdivision — operating a lawn mower, leaf blower, and weedeater, respectively — looked up from their equipment for a long moment to stare at Richard. Their gray shirts were stained with sweat, and their dark faces were lost in shadow under the lowered brims of their matching caps.

Richard nodded at the three men and stopped at the eight-foot-high black gate that sealed off his neighborhood from the rest of the small city. Fumbling for his key card in his back pocket, he dropped his overstuffed wallet onto the floor. Credit cards, licenses, and photos spilled out, hitting his dress shoes and sliding under the seat.

The Mexican men had returned to their work, motors buzzing like oversized insects.

"Crap."

When Richard bent to pick up the key card, his right foot slipped off the brake, and he had to slam his foot on the brake to keep his Expedition from running into the gate in front of him. The SUV jerked to a stop, and he smacked his forehead on the steering wheel.

"Crap!"

For a split second, Richard saw stars. Blinking hard and shaking his head, he put the car in Park and bent carefully to pick up his key card from the spill of cards around his feet. As he was bent over, he felt the blood rush to his forehead. His vision went black for a moment, and then went white. Finally things came back to normal.

"Oh boy," he muttered, holding his head. He reached the key card out the door and aimed it at the reader. With his suddenly-blurry vision, it took three tries to get the magnetic strip of the card through the narrow slit of the reader. The gates slid open toward him. He backed up his big SUV to allow them to open all the way.

What a day, he thought, shifting into Drive, his head throbbing. In the rearview mirror, Richard Tolliver saw a faint lump begin to rise on the dark skin of his forehead. *It's enough to make a person lose his head.*

#

Richard kept his window down as he drove toward his two-story house at the end of his cul-de-sac. Down Bent Tree Lane, toward Forest View Heights Avenue. On his right, five black men were working on a brick wall separating the Emerson's back yard from the Andrews' lot. The wall was half done, and skinny, blonde-haired Nancy Emerson sat on her back deck, watching the men and sipping a glass of iced tea. Richard felt his face grow hot at the sight of the men working hard in the hot sun. He gave Nancy a quick wave and sped up the tiniest bit.

Half a block up on the other side of the street, Tim Johnson was watering his dark green lawn again, just as he was every afternoon. Johnson was a day trader, and he'd made a killing in '99 flipping Amazon, Cisco, and Microsoft stocks all day long, just before the economy's downturn, to the point where he'd moved his office and his computers to his house and never left home. Richard watched Johnson, in a baggy pair of jeans shorts and a sleeveless white T-shirt, yammering into the cell phone in his fat hand.

His fat, *black* hand.

Richard hit the brakes of his SUV, staring at Johnson.

"What the hell?" he said, forgetting his window was open.

Tim Johnson turned to look at him, his dark, curly hair sticking up in spots. *Nappy,* Richard would have described it, if his attention hadn't been caught by the color of his neighbor's skin. The pigment of Johnson's face seemed to darken even more from its already-deep-brown color as he looked without recognition at Richard.

"Got a problem?" Johnson said. His eyes were bright white in contrast to his dark skin, widening for a second before narrowing with suspicion. "Can I *help* you?" he said, his voice deepening, with a slight twang.

"You're not . . . " Richard tried to say.

"Fuck off," Johnson said, turning the garden hose on Richard and his SUV.

Richard recoiled from the icy blast of water that hit him through his open window. The sudden movement made his head spin again. He closed his eyes and felt the world go sideways.

Was this their idea of a joke? he wanted to scream. Are they trying to make some kind of point here?

A second later he opened his eyes. Wiping his face, he turned back to Johnson, who had dropped his hose and was running up to his car. Richard fought the urge to punch the accelerator. By the time Johnson reached the side of his SUV, Richard could see that it was Tim Johnson after all, big, unkempt, *white* Tim Johnson.

"Ah, gosh," Johnson was saying, panting for breath. "I'm so sorry about that, Mr. Oliver! I mean Tolliver. Hose got away from me for a second there. I'll pay for a car wash for you, is that okay? I'm so sorry."

As Johnson spoke, his cell phone beeped twice and went dead. Richard looked closely at the big man next to him, squinting slightly.

What was I thinking? This guy's as white as Wonder Bread.

"No problem," he said at last. "Don't worry about it. It's just water, man." He gave Johnson a big smile and waved, spattering water onto the steering wheel. "I've gotta run. The wife is making spaghetti and meatballs. Can't be late."

"Sorry," Johnson said again as Richard pulled away. He held the hose in one hand and his dead cell phone in his other, looking very much like a little kid waiting for his punishment.

"Jeez," Richard said, glancing at the man receding in his rearview mirror. "Crazy fella."

#

He wiped the last of the water off his face at the Stop sign at the end of Bent Tree Lane and caught his breath. Risking another look in the mirror, he winced at the knot on his forehead, which had almost doubled in size.

Crap, he thought. That's going to leave a mark.

He was about to turn right onto Forest View Heights Avenue when he hit the brakes again. If he would have pulled forward any further, he would have run into a dark blue low-rider pickup that had come out of nowhere. The pickup now sat sideways in the street in front of him.

Before Richard could back up, three long-haired boys leapt out of the door on the opposite side of the Nissan pickup. All three wore dark, loose-fitting clothes, and in each of their small hands was a gun.

Richard punched first the button to raise his window, then hit the button to lock the doors. In his rearview he saw another pickup slam to a stop behind him, close enough to touch bumpers.

Carjacked! his mind screamed. I'm being carjacked!

Larissa had told him all about the reports of the gangs running through Southwest Raleigh, stealing cars from foolish drivers on the wrong side of the city. For some reason, she had told him, most of the carjacking was being done by gangs from the Chinese section of the projects. They only stole American cars, and they had a preference for Ford's line of sport utility vehicles.

Before he could activate his hands-free cell phone to dial 911, six guns were pointed at him from outside his window. Dark-eyed faces looked at him from under their hoods. This was one of *those* gangs — all the faces were Oriental.

"Get out the car," one of the boys shouted through the glass. His accent was thick, making his English sound choppy and harsh. He tapped on the glass with his gun. "Give us keys!"

"This isn't happening to me," Richard muttered, taking his hand away from his phone. He'd only managed to hit the "9" before being caught.

"Get out the car!"

Richard nodded and opened his door. Each movement took most of his strength, and his head throbbed with every shallow breath he took. He stepped down from the heights of his SUV. How did these kids get in here, past security? Especially with those awful low-to-the-ground pickups with the tiny wheels?

"Keys! Now!"

Richard looked at the six boys standing next to him. All of them were a foot shorter than him, if not more. But the guns in their hands looked huge, almost as big as each boy's head. He looked down at his empty hands. He'd left the keys in the ignition.

"No fun stuff," the boy said. "We watch you close!"

"Let me get them," he said, moving back toward his SUV. As the boys lifted their guns higher, pointing them at his face, he leaned up and in to get the keys. He heard words that could only have been Chinese curses coming from the boys below him.

I'm going to throw these keys as far as I can and run for it, he thought. Soon as I lean back out of my Expedition.

But once he'd made up his mind to act, Richard couldn't move. With his hands wrapped around the keys still in the ignition, he stood half in and half out of his SUV. He could feel the slick leather of his Implement Telecom key fob, next to the key to his house, the key to their storage units, the key to his tool shed, the key to Larissa's parents' house, and the slick plastic of his MVP card for Harris Teeter. He leaned on the leather seat, one hand on his keys, the other hand on the hot door frame. He couldn't move. He closed his eyes.

"Hey!" a voice shouted. "Mister!"

Richard waited for the bullets to enter his soft body.

I'm gonna throw these keys, he thought without energy. But I know before I run, they'll shoot me in the guts and watch me bleed.

"Mister!"

When bullets failed to pierce his body, Richard opened his eyes. He looked down at four small boys and two girls, staring up at him with a mixture of fear and impatience. They all had brown eyes and a dark tan tint to their skin.

"I think he's havin' a heart 'tack," one of the dark-haired girls said. Like the others, she looked Oriental.

Maybe Chinese, maybe Japanese, Richard thought.

"My uncle had two heart 'tacks, then he had a highway bypass put in him."

Richard let go of his keys and pulled himself out of the SUV. After another head rush, he looked around him. A red kid's bike with a black, banana-shaped seat lay in front of his Expedition. There were no pickups, anywhere.

"What are you kids . . . " he said, trying to catch his breath. I am *not* havin' a heart 'tack, he told himself. "What are you kids doing in the street? It's not safe out here."

"Duh — my mom says this is the safest neighborhood in Cary," one of the boys said. Richard recognized him as the Lawrence boy from three houses down. "The chain on Janey's bike came off, and we couldn't get it back on."

"Can you help me fix it?" the blonde little girl who had to be Janey said. Tears had worn two clean trails down her dusty white face.

All these kids are white, Richard thought with something close to shock. Why did I think they were Oriental at first?

"Well," he said with a smile. "I'm a little late for dinner, but I think I can help you fix your bike. You see, you have to get the chain on the sprockets at the back first, then you take the wheel and . . . "

As Richard, still talking, walked away from his Expedition and led the children and their bike to the safety of the grass next to the road, he felt the pain in his head begin to lessen.

Everything's okay, he told himself. The heat was making my imagination get away with me. He chuckled softly in the middle of his bike-chain lesson. I should know better than to think such things could ever happen here.

#

At the intersection of Forest View Heights Avenue and the entrance to Lakefront Trail, Richard's cul-de-sac, someone had set up a sweat lodge.

Richard realized that the sight of the low, domed teepee made of canvas and bent branches next to the road didn't even surprise him. Not after the strange things he'd imagined already today. He took a tentative lick from the sucker in his right hand, a gift from one of the kids for helping with their bike. "I only licked it a coupla times," the blue-eyed boy had said.

He parked his Expedition next to the curb and, sucker in hand, walked up to the smoking structure sitting next to a humming electricity box. Low chanting came from inside the front flap.

"This should be fun," he said, bending down and lifting the flap. He crawled inside.

Through a haze of smoke and steam, perched on the far side of a fire made of green sticks piled onto a metal garbage can lid, sat a wrinkled, brown-skinned man. The man had wiry gray hair tied back with a piece of leather. Three white feathers stuck up from behind him, jammed into the piece of leather and his hair. The man stopped chanting. He nodded and, without a word, motioned for Richard to sit across from him.

Richard started to sweat even before he sat down next to the fire. The teepee seemed much bigger on the inside than it had on the outside. He felt like he was shrinking.

The man across from him wafted smoke from the fire into his sweat-stained face and breathed deeply. Trying to cool off, Richard pulled his dress shirt over his head. Before inhaling the smoke, he passed the Indian the barely-licked sucker as barter. The man across from him smiled as he took the gift, then closed his eyes.

Richard did the same, still breathing deeply. Sweat had already covered his chest and soft belly, trickling from his armpits onto his pants.

When he exhaled, he saw a vision.

A white man on horseback chased a brown-faced woman, heavy with child, his gloved hand reaching down for her. The image blurred and coalesced into an ancient wooden boat, listing badly as it pulled into a port city, thin black hands reaching out into the air from the barred windows of the ship. The image changed into a scene of nimble, black-haired men scurrying with their hands over their ears onto an unfinished railroad track, just in advance of a dynamite explosion that opened a gap through a mountain pass. The explosion melted into a cluttered construction site just outside a gated community, where Spanish-speaking laborers in plain white T-shirts carried heavy panes of glass with suction cups held in strong hands up five flights of stairs. The reflection off the pane of glass morphed into a ghetto in India, where a gang of boys tormented a thinner, older boy carrying math books and his passport through the dirt streets. A worn, rectangular sticker bearing the image of the American flag was plastered to one of the boy's folders gripped in a dark hand.

I know you, Richard whispered inside his own head. I know all of you.

Then the images faded away, and the thick smoke was gone. Richard was still sitting cross-legged, but he could feel bright sunlight on his eyelids.

He opened his eyes and saw two brown faces staring at him from less than a foot away. His shirt was off, and he was sitting on top of a rickety, sticky card table. The sucker was stuck to his forearm.

"Are . . . " he whispered, his throat painfully dry. "Are you boys Indians?"

"We are from India," the older boy said with a lilting, staccato accent. "But my father says we are Americans."

"Uh-huh," Richard said. The sun was so bright he could barely see. "So where's your sweat lodge?"

The boys gaped at him without responding.

When he tried to move, the card table under him groaned. His legs were asleep. Richard moved to the table's edge, slapping life back into his legs, and in the process he spilled a pitcher of lemonade onto the table, soaking into his dress pants. He lost his balance and pulled the card table over on top of him, the plastic pitcher landing on his hand.

"Shit!" he shouted, bringing his headache back with a vengeance. "Shit shit SHIT!"

The two boys ran off, yelling something about a "crazy black man wrecking our lemonade stand." Richard could plainly tell that the boys were light-haired and white. Just like all the other kids in the neighborhood.

He eased himself off the card table, put his shirt back on, and pulled off the sucker that had been attached to his forearm. He walked back to his SUV, his face burning and his pants dripping with lemonade.

I really need to get out of this sun, he thought to himself.

#

When he at last made it to the front door of his house on Lakefront Trail, the door was locked from the inside. Richard didn't even bother to swear. Fumbling in his pocket, he set down his briefcase and pulled his keys from his ruined dress pants. Inside the house, someone walked up the hallway as he unlocked the lock in the door and twisted the deadbolt. Larissa was coming to greet him, probably ready to explain why she had the house locked up tight in the safest neighborhood in the greater Raleigh area.

He opened the door, inhaling the warm, spicy smell of spaghetti and meatballs, and was met by the double barrels of a shotgun.

"Who the hell are you?" a woman shouted. Inches in front of Richard's face, the two barrels of the gun never wavered. "And how did you get my husband's keys?"

"Larissa?" Richard felt the sweat falling from his face as he blinked hard. His eyes were burning from the bright sunlight. His headache had returned.

"Get back!" the woman screamed. "I'm pregnant and emotionally unstable!"

That was Larissa's voice, Richard thought. He barely even registered the shotgun pointed at him. Just another weird illusion from my headache, he figured.

"It's okay, miss," he said, squinting into the darkness of the house. He could barely see the woman holding the gun. It looked like Larissa. He smiled. "I'm just a lost black man, that's all. Trying to find his way home."

The shotgun wavered. "What are you talking about? How did you get past the gates?"

Richard felt himself relax.

What a day, he thought. Larissa and I are gonna laugh about this tomorrow.

"I snuck in after a fat white man in his Mercedes," he said, stepping closer. "I've got your white husband tied up in the back of your Expedition. When I'm done jumping your bones I'll let him out and you can live happily ever after."

Richard could see the woman just inside the door. It *was* his wife, and it *wasn't*, just like everything else he'd seen and done since entering the gated community of Olde Carriage Ridgewood that afternoon. But it was okay; he understood the rules now. He reached up with his hand — his black hand — and pushed the door open further.

"I *knew* it," the very pregnant white woman said, pulling the triggers of the gun.

Richard felt white-hot pain for a split second, his head rocking back as twin blasts of exploding metal pierced his skull, spreading the contents of his head onto the front lawn like strawberry preserves. Then Richard Tolliver knew no more.

#

"Crap!"

Larissa Tolliver rubbed her shoulder where the butt of the shotgun had recoiled into her. Richard always told her to be careful of that, but she hadn't been thinking straight. The man on her porch had shifted her into protective-mother mode, and all rational thought had taken a hike.

When the pain in her shoulder began to lessen from its original white-hot level, Larissa lowered the gun and set it on a chair. She caught herself before peeking out the front door.

I just shot a man on my front steps, she thought.

Rapist. Robber. Thief. Murderer.

We're safe now, she thought, rubbing her belly with her left hand. She pulled her cell phone from its waist holster with her right and punched in 911. The skin of her hands, along with the skin covering the rest of her, was a deep brown color.

Her headache from the past few days returning, Larissa hit Send on her cell phone and stepped heavily back to the kitchen to take the spaghetti out to drain.

A FEAST AT THE MANOR

Outside the Manorhouse Hotel, Rob Heying and his big, beautiful wife tried to catch their breath in the desert air. He felt like his lungs were melting into so much taffy, while Melinda simply moaned with each exhalation. The airport taxi motored off, pushing hot air onto them with a foul whiff of exhaust, a cruel imitation of a breeze. The driver of the taxi hadn't stopped yammering on and on about the Barringer Meteorite Crater — "It's only ten miles from here!" he'd shouted back at them over the blasting radio — and how they *had* to visit it before they left. Rob just hoped his heart wouldn't give out and leave his body floundering on the hot sidewalk of the hotel next to his wheezing wife. There wouldn't be time for sightseeing on this trip.

He looked up at the bright white Manorhouse stretching out in front of him. The ten-story hotel stood in harsh contrast to the flat expanse of desert that surrounded it. Row upon row of double-paned windows looked down at him and his wife, each rectangle of glass boasting its own window box filled with cactus and purplish-blue desert flowers. Double doors awaited them at the top of a dozen curved steps.

"You'd think there'd at least be someone here to greet us," Melinda said, a whine growing in her voice. Rob made himself turn to her with a smile, but she stepped away from him. "There better be AC. We pay all this money, and they can't even treat us like we matter."

Rob bent for his bags, filled to bursting with two new pairs of cross-trainers, snacks, workout clothes, and books. He watched his wife make her way up the front stairs of the Manor. His dark-haired love since the day they met at South Dakota State, he still found Melinda and her curves arousing, despite the padding that had been added after ten years and three children. When they'd married, she'd been a size six. Now she cried every time they left Lane Bryant or the plus sections of regular clothing stores. As the years passed, Rob had thought he was helping — in a misery-loves-company kind of way — by gobbling up his meals and clamoring for seconds. He'd let his own weight slip from two-thirty to five pounds shy of the big three double zero.

The thing was, unlike his wife, Rob didn't mind being big. *Big*, not *fat*. He hated that word. As long as there were pants with elastic waists and adjustable seatbelts and floppy shirts that didn't need to be tucked in, Rob Heying was okay with being big.

Melinda stood wiping sweat from her forehead at the top of the ten stone stairs in front of their home away from home for the next two weeks, waiting for him. He could still feel the stupid grin he'd created for her hanging on his face like paint left out in the sun too long. Inhaling a deep breath of hot Arizona air, he made his way up to the front double doors of the hotel just as a black limousine pulled up behind him.

"Don't gawk," he muttered breathlessly to Melinda when he reached her side. He'd seen the California license plates of the limo, and Rob knew of only one person who would *drive* all this way. The man had such a fear of airplanes that he demanded a limo take him everywhere.

"It's got to be him," Melinda said, her puffy hands unconsciously pulling at her shirt and adjusting her hair. "He always comes here before he starts a new movie. He's such a sweetie when he's on Rosie."

"Weren't you the one dying for the air conditioning two seconds ago?" Rob said. He grabbed at the ornate wooden door, surprised at its heft. "Let's go on inside, Mindy."

Cool air streamed onto Rob as reward for pulling open the big door. Inside the hotel, he saw a bustling of concierges, bellhops, and maids, flowing around an occasional slow-moving, oversized guest. A tinkling of piano music carried over the voices and footsteps on the worn marble floor. Before turning back to his starstruck wife, Rob thought he could smell a hint of something sour, like rotting carpet or mildew. He hoped there weren't any bugs. He got enough of them at work (the software kind) and in his basement at home (the creepy crawling kind).

It's an old hotel, he thought, remembering the pamphlet he'd read almost a year ago now, before he'd saved up the thirty grand for their two-week "vacation" here. Of course it's going to smell old. Most of the Manor, the pamphlet said, had been built in southern California just after the turn of the century, then it had been dismantled and moved — in over a hundred large pieces — to southeastern Arizona. The endeavor had taken close to two years. Why they had even *wanted* to do such a thing, the pamphlet hadn't explained.

Rob reached behind him for his wife's thick upper arm.

"He's coming this way," she said, her voice growing whiny again. "I'm so embarrassed to be here for this, with someone important like him."

Here it comes, Rob thought.

Melinda's voice was equal parts self-pity and disgust. "I'm so *fat*."

"Melinda," he began. He'd stopped telling her she wasn't fat long ago, after she'd had such a hard time bouncing back after Bobbie was born. She'd argue with him that she *was*, indeed, very fat. Sure, she wasn't the slender girl he'd married, but he still loved her. Though it rarely helped his cause to remind her of that at times like these.

Rob grinned with sudden inspiration. "You should feel good that a movie star like him has trouble with his weight, too. Maybe we'll get to know him better in the next two weeks."

Melinda didn't look convinced. "Let's just check in, okay? Before he *sees* me. Okay?"

#

The concierge was all smiles and untraceable accent. "You're in room 504. It's a suite. Bedroom in one room, living area and kitchen in another room." The thin man on the other side of the desk gave him a quick, almost harsh laugh. "Though I doubt the kitchen will get much use during your stay, hmm?"

Rob felt something twinge in the back of his brain, like a tiny red light that began to softly blink. Those light blue eyes across the desk from him weren't right.

Melinda answered the man by snatching the keys from his hand and bending for her bag. Ignoring the bellhop approaching, she swung her head from side to side until she found the elevator, bags clamped to her side. She walked deliberately toward the closed elevator doors.

Great, Rob thought, waving off the bellhop. Mindy was pissed.

"She must be jetlagged," he said, smiling for the concierge. "It's a long trip from Fargo."

The man looked at him blankly, and then jotted some notes in the ledger in front of him.

All righty-then, Rob thought as he grabbed their remaining bags and trudged after his wife. Not only was Mindy going to be a holy terror, but he was surrounded by a bunch of folks who'd had their senses of humor surgically removed. What could be funnier than a bunch of big people converging in the desert for fourteen days of intensive dieting, exercise, and therapy? It made *Rob* want to laugh.

Melinda hadn't held the elevator for him. I know one thing, Rob told himself, waiting at the elevator door. It was going to be a long two weeks.

#

When Rob made it to their hotel room, Melinda was standing naked in front of the mirror.

This was a relatively new thing, Rob knew. Ever since she'd put on another thirty pounds, Melinda had started obsessing over her looks. Strangely, she had become suddenly un-self-conscious about her body with him. She would show him her stretch marks from her pregnancies as if trying to repel him. Rob just rubbed them and said they'd get them removed with a laser if it bothered her so much. He'd work extra hours at the call center if he had to.

For some reason, that hadn't been the reaction she'd been looking for.

"Excellent," Rob said, leering at her as she prodded her soft stomach and rubbed her veined thighs. He dropped his bags and began pulling off his clothes. "Let's get it *on*, baby."

Melinda turned to him, her full breasts sagging down, the brown nipples stretched too wide. Her pubic hair was dark and inviting. Rob felt himself getting hard. Then he saw the tears on his wife's round face.

"Mindy," he said, walking toward her.

"Stay away," she said. "I'm fat and disgusting. I don't deserve to be touched. Not until I lose—" she gestured at herself in the mirror, her face filled with pain "—all *this*."

Rob pulled up his untucked shirt. "Look at this," he said. His white belly jutted out like bread dough rising. "Do *I* disgust you too?"

Melinda turned away without answering, crossing her arms in front of her breasts. She pulled a robe with a monogrammed MH from the hook next to the bathroom. Luckily, all the robes in the hotel had been sized for the new residents; otherwise, the tight fit of the robe would've sent Melinda into hysterics.

Rob felt like a fool, his dick hard and his belly hanging out. He felt a rumbling in his exposed stomach, and he wondered how long it would be until supper.

#

Supper was an adventure. Rob and Melinda entered the cool expanse of the Gardenfront Restaurant on the first floor, careful to avoid pricking themselves on the potted cacti filling every nook and cranny. Rob felt like a balloon in a room full of needles, and he saw the same apprehension in his wife's soft facial features. They were escorted through the main dining area, past tables of people dressed in dark suits and dresses hunched forward close to the candles in the middle of each round table. None of the patrons in this room was big.

Rob, all too aware of his faded imac T-shirt, sweatpants, and sandals, smiled at each patron as he lumbered past. Dress code? he thought. We don't need no stinkin' dress code.

Their hostess, Agatha Bronwyn according to her nametag, welcomed them into their dining room. The room felt ten degrees warmer than the main area of the restaurant. As he shook hands with the tall, lean, fifty-ish woman smiling down at him, Rob knew he was in trouble. He doubted Agatha had ever been big in her life. She was going to be merciless.

"Nice to meet you," he said, trying his best to suck in his gut.

Agatha pushed a loose strand of her long, gray-brown hair out of her face. "Relax, Rob. We're all here for the same reason. We all understand."

Sitting around an oval table were the other guests, chairs pushed back a healthy distance from the table to accommodate their large bodies. The table was painfully empty; no little baskets of bread with saucers of butter or even glasses of water. The big people glanced up at him, then quickly looked away, as if sizing them both up: "He's bigger than me"/"She's not as fat as I am"/"Get a load of the big couple," and so on.

"Let's get started," Agatha said, motioning Rob and Melinda to the remaining two chairs — big chairs — at the narrow end of the table. Melinda took a seat, smiling at the others around the table, until she saw Mark Chandler (a.k.a. Lone Wolf, a.k.a. Sergeant Blinker, a.k.a. Dead-Eye McQuaid) sitting at the far end of the table. She stiffened visibly. Rob sat and rubbed her upper arm until she relaxed. His stomach growled.

"Welcome to the first meal of the rest of your life," Agatha said, standing behind Rob. Her voice was filled with the kind of melodrama Rob heard at awards ceremonies like the Oscars. "After your first full day here," she was saying, "you'll start to notice a difference. And more importantly, your mindset will have already changed. You will find that your *perception*, along with a carefully planned diet, has more to do with your physical well being than genetics, lifestyle, and physical state. Outlook is everything."

Rob nodded at that. The bearded man next to him gave him a doubtful look and shrugged. The man had a round head and body, like the top two sections of a human snowman.

"Before the meal is served," Agatha continued, circling the table and making eye contact with each big person at the table, "I'd like to give a brief history of the Manorhouse and how the Nutrition Institute came into being here in Arizona."

I've got a great pamphlet that'll sum this up for you, Rob wanted to say. The other folks around the table were fidgeting, rocking in their chairs or tapping their fingers on the table. Skip the damn history lesson, their body language said. Can't you see we're starving?

"The original Manorhouse was built just outside the California desert, close to what is now Hollywood and Vine. Until 1920 the Manorhouse was just another fancy hotel for the rich new celebrities to visit. But a fire changed all that. Half of the first floor was ruined, and the owner sold the hotel to the highest bidder. Charles Thoroughgood, our founder, saw the potential of the hotel, but after he bought it he immediately dismantled it.

People thought he was crazy, but he'd seen the beauty of northern Arizona, the energy and potential it held. So he simple moved the Manorhouse here."

"In a hundred pieces," Rob piped in. Melinda elbowed him as the other people around the table gave him dirty looks. Don't interrupt, those looks said, if you want to *eat*. "Sorry," he said. A look of irritation flashed across Agatha's face before her smile returned.

"The rest, as they say, is history. Charles Thoroughgood began his work and research right here within these walls. On your tour tomorrow — after your morning workout, of course — we'll show you his lab on the second floor, along with the elaborate gymnasium he built in 1925, surely the most advanced facility of its time. We've of course updated much of it," she said, walking to the door and rapping on it three times. "But some of the original . . . equipment remains to this day."

Agatha's smile was bright white as she opened the door with a flourish. After all this buildup, Rob thought, supper better be *damn* good.

Three waiters in white coats and black pants whispered into the room, carrying round trays filled with metal canisters.

"Dinner," Agatha said, "is served."

With a metallic clank, silver canisters with pop-tops were placed in front of Rob and each of the fourteen other guests. The others grabbed their cans without hesitation, and the sound of seals breaking whooshed around the cramped dining room.

Rob and Melinda shared a quick look with each other, then opened their dinner. As he drank, Rob saw that Mr. Movie Star Chandler had already polished off his meal and was waiting for the rest of them to finish. Rob swallowed his meal. In his opinion, chocolate-flavored chalk water would have tasted better.

#

Just like snowflakes or fingerprints, every big person Rob ever met had a truly unique body shape. Some were all belly with almost non-existent butts (mostly men, Rob conceded, though *he* was definitely not built that way), others were more stout and thick all over than chubby (like Rob's father and grandfather), and others had this sort of droopiness about them, as if their fat collected in certain areas, like their waistline or butts or under their chins (this was Rob, in all three areas). But no two big people looked alike.

Rob was busy analyzing the spandex-encased bodies in front of him as they sweated through their first workout in the Manor's basement gym. It was twenty minutes past six, and he was pretty sure he'd start screaming in agony if he didn't keep his mind off the leg lifts and roundhouse kicks he was being forced to do.

The night before, after two hours of lectures by Agatha and other members of the Nutrition Institute, Rob had felt light-headed and dying for a pizza with the works. The chalk cocktails, as he called them, had kept him full for all of fifteen minutes. Double crust would've been heaven.

Instead they were ordered to their rooms to complete their homework. Jogging painfully in place, Rob wondered what kind of trouble he was going to be in for not reading the first five chapters of Charles "The Man" Thoroughgood's book, *Nutriology*, Book One. Agatha couldn't say enough wondrous things about the late scientist/adventurer/renaissance man. Rob had watched the end of the Chiefs game instead, and Melinda was still studying when he fell asleep.

"Cooldown," the blond aerobics instructor barked. His name was either Steve or Vince, but Rob thought of him as Sven with his light blue eyes and perfect skin. The man was barely out of breath, while Rob's shoes squeaked in the puddle of sweat he'd created on the floor in front of him.

Andy, the man built like a snowman, leaned close to him. Sweat beaded off every inch of the bearded man's skin, soaking into his T-shirt and sweatpants. "Check out the equipment, eh?"

Rob followed the man's nodding head to the north wall, where the arcane exercise equipment of Mr. Thoroughgood ("The Man," Rob added silently) was arranged. Taking up the entire length of the wall, over two dozen barely-recognizable exercise stations sat waiting for their next victim. Pulleys and blocks of cement were attached to uncushioned metal seats and benches, everything looking less like Nautilus and more like Mengele.

"Wonder when we get to use *those*," Andy said, then added "eh?"

"Hopefully never," Rob said. He was slowly getting his wind back.

"All right, folks," Sven called out. "Let's hit the saunas and keep that good sweat going."

Rob turned to whisper a comment about their workout to his wife, but she was no longer at his side. He caught a glimpse of her round, spandex-encased rear as she walked out, chatting and grinning up at Mr. Mark Chandler, Hollywood's one and only heavyweight action hero.

#

When they returned to their room that night at nine, the first time they'd been there all day, every single mirror was gone.

Rob looked at Melinda, who had flopped onto the bed, sweaty clothes and all. Rob winced at the tightness in his legs and looked at the wall where his wife had stood naked only a day ago. In front of a full-length mirror.

"Mindy," he began, but she was already asleep. Rob pulled off his sweat-soaked shirt and limped into the bathroom. An oval-shaped mirror had hung over the sink; he'd looked into it last night while he was brushing his teeth. A photo of Mr. Thoroughgood at twenty-five, wearing black jeans and a black leather jacket, hung in its place. The Man as a biker. Rob glanced back into the bedroom, at the blank space on the wall next to the dresser.

"It was there yesterday though," he whispered. The sound of his voice was off, as if he'd been speaking in a much larger room than the tiny bathroom. Hadn't it been there? Rob, feeling empty inside and mentally disconnected, was starting to wonder.

He stripped off the rest of his clothes. His sweat pants came off easily, but Rob was too tired and distracted to notice. If there had still been a bathroom mirror, it would have reflected the vision of a big, exhausted man, squeezing into the stand-up shower and blasting hot water onto his tired body until he fell asleep standing up. When the water went cold he woke, turned off the shower, and dried off with two big towels.

"Maybe I can cancel our wake up call," he said, flopping onto the king-sized bed next to his snoring wife. His muscles twitched and hummed. "We *are* on vacation, right?"

#

In hindsight, after plenty of time to contemplate what he'd done, Rob would admit that planning the pizza party the night of their third day at the Manorhouse had been a bad idea.

But the constant exercising, the endless classes, and the thrice-daily chalk cocktails were making his usual happy demeanor turn grumpy and desperate, and he needed something to lift his spirits.

He'd talked with his new friend, Andy, about his plan all day Wednesday.

"Pizza," Andy said, doing the world's slowest set of ten sit-ups in the gymnasium that Thoroughgood built. He reached the top of his arc, meaty arms up around his head, sweat stains running down either side of his gray University of Toronto Athletic Department T-shirt. "Pizza is the great human bonding experience. Think anyone will deliver out to this hellhole?"

Rob started to speak, then bit his tongue as Sven walked past. He forced himself to do another sit-up before addressing Andy again. That morning, he'd noticed the looseness of his T-shirt and the fact that he'd had to tie his sweatpants tighter than before to keep them up.

"There's no phone books anywhere," Rob whispered. "How we can we call Domino's?"

"Dial Information," Andy said. "Don't give up so easy, eh?"

Rob smiled and did an extra ten sit-ups. Loose sweatpants and all, he felt better already.

The pizza arrived at ten p.m., the nervous driver looking to her left and right as she approached the big double doors of the Manor. Rob and Andy were waiting for her with their luggage. Rob paid the girl and made sure she got the $10 tip while Andy slid the twelve hot boxes of salvation into Rob's garment bag and Andy's suitcase.

Almost all the men and women from their group, minus one very absent movie star, were waiting for them in Rob and Melinda's room. Melinda had been there when Rob left, but when they returned, she was gone. Rob felt an instant of remorse, then Andy and the others had started opening boxes of pizza, and he was lost to all worry.

"Extra cheese," a pear-shaped man moaned. "There *is* a God."

"We shoulda got beer," Andy said around a mouthful of mushrooms and sausage and cheese. "Only thing this party's missing."

Rob laughed and licked grease off of his plump fingers. The room fell silent for almost five minutes as everyone ate, eyes half-closed and jaws working overtime.

Rob was about to polish off another slice when there were three sharp knocks at the door. Agatha and Sven walked in. Three other Institute people stood behind them, dressed in black and not smiling.

"Who is responsible?" was all Agatha had to say.

Rob tried to chew the big bite of pepperoni in his mouth, but he couldn't. He saw Andy start to step forward, then he put a hand on his big new friend.

This was all my idea, he thought. No way is he taking the fall. He swallowed his pizza and stepped toward the Nutriologists.

"It was me," he said, trying to smile as six slices of pizza curdled in his stomach.

Agatha shook her head sadly at the other big people standing around them. She nodded to the people from the Institute waiting behind her.

Rob pictured them slapping cuffs on his wrists and hauling him out of the room to a dungeon while the people in black confiscated the remaining pizza and ordered the others down to the gymnasium to work off their ill-gotten gains.

Except for the handcuffs, his vision had been accurate.

#

"I don't understand you people," Agatha was saying as they led Rob down the stairs. "You pay all this money to come here, you use your vacation time from your work to make this trip, and then you throw it all away on a night of debauchery. All your hard work for the past days has been wasted."

"But debauchery is *fun*," Rob said, giving her his winningest smile that faded when he thought of Melinda. Where the hell had she been tonight?

Before he could come up with an answer, he and his entourage stopped in front of a metal door at the end of a darkened hall. They were in the basement.

"I want you to think about what you've done," Agatha said as one of her assistants unlocked the multiple locks in the door. "We'll be back at five a.m. to get you for tomorrow's sessions. I suggest you do some exercise to work off your pizza. Tomorrow we start anew."

The door creaked open, and cool air wafted toward him. "This isn't legal," he croaked.

"Ah, but Mr. Heying," Agatha said. "You agreed to this when you signed your waivers."

Rob winced. He never read the small print.

He stood in the middle of the dark room after the door closed, listening to the locks click. The sound of the Nutriologists' footsteps died away, leaving him completely and utterly alone.

"Debauchery *is* fun," he whispered. The happy looks on the faces of his fellow inmates had made it worthwhile. At least my stomach's full, he added silently. His only regret was that he hadn't been able to try a slice of the Meat-and-Cheese Lovers pizza.

To his right in the semi-darkness sat a stationary bike and a weird contraption made up of ropes, rubber straps, and pulley-mounted weights. Rob wasn't about to go anywhere near what had to be yet another whacked-out Thoroughgood creation. Of course there was no cot. He sat on the seat of the bike instead of lying on the cold, hard floor and began pedaling.

Half an hour later, his rear end sore and his forehead damp with sweat, Rob began getting claustrophobic and paranoid. Drips of water from the wet walls echoed inside his brain, and strange scurrying noises were amplified in his imagination. He envisioned insects crawling across the floor and up the wheels of the bike. Coming to get me.

Clicking on the light of his watch, he rose from the bike at two minutes after twelve. He stepped closer to one of the walls and pulled up short. In the sickly green light from his watch, he could see a jagged scar in the concrete that ran from floor to ceiling. When he was less than three feet away, Rob saw something inside the crack. He leaned closer for a better look.

In a horizontal jag of the crack, a creature no bigger than Rob's littlest toe waddled through the rough terrain of the broken concrete. It was round and brown, about the size of a peanut M&M. Over a dozen tiny black feet propelled the creature along. Rob's mouth dropped open. Ten more round creatures followed the first. On the back of each tiny critter was a series of tiny, concentric rings that formed the shape of a bull's-eye.

Bugs? he tried to say, but all that came out was a squeaking sound.

Something rustled on the opposite side of the room. When Rob turned, he could barely make out another crack on the opposite wall. This one wasn't as wide as the other, but it ran from floor to ceiling, and from the skittering sounds coming from it, it wasn't empty either.

Rob stared at the round bug-like beings inside the crack closest to him for a half-minute longer. Then it hit him that he was locked in her with them, all night. Rob scurried back to the door, forcing himself not to hyperventilate. He wanted to slide to the floor, but it was too damp and cold. He got back on the bike with a groan.

When the knock came at five a.m., Rob could not have been gladder. After lifting himself painfully from the bike seat, he sucked down the shake Agatha gave him without complaint. Soon he was promising to do his best to lose weight and change his bad attitude.

"I thought the night would change your *perspective*," Agatha said with a cool smile.

Rob only nodded and wiped the chalky mustache from his upper lip. He'd spent the whole night pedaling with his fingers in his ears, envisioning trucks hauling a hundred pieces of hotel across the desert, past the Meteorite Crater his taxi driver had raved about, and then arriving here to put the pieces together like a gigantic jigsaw puzzle. The whole time the bull's-eye critters swarmed onto the workers and over the new structure.

Just get my wife and me back to Fargo, he wanted to say. Before the bugs took over.

#

When Rob returned to his room at half past five, his wife wasn't there. His stomach felt full of acid at the sight of the empty room, making him wonder what exactly was in those chalk shakes. The bed was untouched, and the closet door stood open from when he'd pulled his garment bag out of it last night, on his way to pick up his illicit pizza.

The only aspect of the room that was different was what sat on the dresser, between one of the four volumes of *Nutriology* and Rob's Microsoft manual. Melinda's wedding band.

Rob stopped in the middle of pulling off his pants when an image struck him. He pictured his big, beautiful wife, standing naked in front of Mark Chandler. Melinda would be standing in front of him instead of the mirror — since the mirrors had been removed days ago — and she'd be smiling and soaking in his compliments.

I guess when a bigshot movie star gives her compliments, Melinda listens to *him*. I guess it means more coming from him than some fat joe who happens to be her husband.

Someone knocked on the door, three sharp raps that knocked Rob out of his reverie.

"I'll be right down," he said peeling off his musty shirt and looking for his workout clothes. He was running late for the day's activities already.

When he kicked his pants off, shooting pain entered the left side of his abdomen and ran through him to his right side. He dropped to the bed, breathing hard and thinking about the end of his marriage. His gaze kept returning to the gold ring sitting on the dresser.

His stomach rumbled once, then again. He pushed off from the bed and ran to the bathroom. He got his shorts down just in time.

"What the hell is in those shakes?" he muttered before burying his face in his hands.

#

They'll be coming for me soon, Rob thought, pulling on fresh clothes after a quick shower. He had to retie his sweatpants twice after they nearly slid down off of him each time. He felt like he'd lost twenty pounds in the bathroom that morning alone.

While he was showering, he'd decided to skip his workout today and use the time to find out for sure just what Melinda and Mr. Movie Star were up to. He left his room and stepped into the hall. The musty odor he'd first smelled in the lobby on his first day there was back. Rob tiptoed down the steps past the fourth floor landing. As he approached the first floor, he saw two cleaning ladies in their black and white French maid outfits, sneaking cigarettes next to an open window. He crept back to the second floor and started down the hall, toward the other stairs.

Adultery, his mind whispered. What the hell was Mindy thinking? Did she hate herself and me so much that she had to go and do something stupid like that?

His stomach convulsed once as if in warning, and Rob forced himself to think of something less worrisome. Like the cracks in the foundation of the hotel, where over a hundred odd pieces of hotel had been attached almost a century ago. Yes, that was *much* less worrisome.

He was almost at the end of the hall when he heard a buzzing sound coming from an unmarked door. He thought he heard the sound of someone moaning after each buzz.

"Door's probably locked anyway," he said under his breath, reaching for the knob. To his surprise, it was unlocked. Rob cracked open the door, just enough to see inside.

Four big people sat against the wall, electrodes attached to their temples and left wrists, eyes closed in a strange mix of pain and euphoria. A long table covered in wires and boxy machines sat in front of them, and a red bowl filled with what looked like peanut-covered brown M&Ms rested next to their unfettered right hands. Agatha and another woman stood with their backs to Rob. Agatha held a black object in her hand that looked like Rob's remote from home.

What the hell, Rob wondered, but before he could finish the thought, Agatha pressed a blue button on the remote control in her hand, and a loud buzzing filled the room. A whiff of ozone filled the air, and all three of the big people at the table reached into their bowls. They shoved one of the M&Ms into their mouths, chewing and moaning with pleasure.

Rob stared, mouth dropping open, and as he did, he realized that the man on the end was Andy. He hadn't recognized him because Andy no longer looked like a snowman. He looked more like a scarecrow. Andy was losing weight. Big time.

"I know you will not regret speeding up your treatments," Agatha said to the smiling men and women in front of her. "Think of this as two month's worth of exercising and drinking shakes, all in one morning. Your outlook — your future — is changing with each passing second."

I just saw him last night, Rob thought. Andy had been as big as he'd always been. Maybe a *little* thinner. But nothing like this.

When the buzzing filled the room again, Rob watched Andy's now-slender fingers dive into the bowl. Those weren't M&Ms. Just before Andy shoved the round object to his mouth, biting down on it with a moist crunch, Rob had seen tiny circles on it, in the shape of a bull's-eye.

Holding in the shout that was threatening to explode out of him, Rob pulled the door shut. They'd been eating the tiny creatures he'd seen last night, scurrying around inside the cracks.

"Oh my God," he whispered, his voice thick with fear and disgust. Stepping away from the room as if in a daze, he somehow made it down to the first floor workout room without being caught. His skin felt like it was crawling with bugs. They were *eating* them.

A thought struck him when he was just outside the workout room: if it helped people lose weight, they were probably putting bugs in the shakes, too.

Rob lost it. He grabbed the nearest wastebasket, pulled off the lid, and lost his breakfast shake into the canister. He hated bugs.

With a groan, he put the lid back on and tottered away.

All thoughts of bugs left his mind a minute later, however, when he peeked into the aerobics room, where Sven was putting his people through their paces. Rob saw Melinda, glowing with sweat, just three people down from Chandler. With a start, Rob realized that almost everyone in the room looked thinner. Including his wife.

"Five more minutes before morning break," Sven called out. "Let's double-time it."

Rob had caught the look passed between Melinda and Chandler the instant Sven had spoken about their upcoming break. With a sick, dizzying sensation of knowledge, Rob had a pretty good idea how the two were going to be spending *their* fifteen-minute break.

#

Instead of following his wife and her new lover back to Chandler's room after the morning workout, Rob jogged back up to his room. Something about the look of helpless pleasure on Andy's face, along with the confident grin on Chandler's big mug, had inspired Rob with an idea of vengeance. Armed with two butter knives and a garbage bag from their unused kitchen, Rob hurried back down the stairs into the basement.

Agatha had talked about changing my perspective, Rob thought. Using a butter knife to jimmy the three locks on the door to the basement room where he'd spent last night, he wondered why Agatha hadn't told him his world would turn upside down in the process.

The lock finally relented, and Rob entered his former cell. He jammed the knife into the doorframe to keep the door open and went to the biggest crack.

The crawling creatures were gone.

"No," Rob whispered, hurrying to the other crack. It was empty as well. "No no no."

He stepped back into the light and stared at the rotting concrete in the wall. He poked it with the second butter knife in frustration. Chunks of rotting foundation fell to the floor. Rob thought about all he'd seen this morning, and his legs gave out on him. He slid to the cold, hard floor, his hand covered in wet grit from the ruined wall.

"Why the hell did we ever come here?" he whispered, stabbing the floor with his knife. We'd been happy, he thought. We had good jobs, great kids, a happy marriage. We were big, but happy. Right?

Rob was preparing to jab the knife into the basement floor again when something crawled across his neck. A dozen tiny legs tickled his skin. Stifling a scream, he jumped to his feet, his pants sliding down again. From where he had touched the wall earlier, round black creatures bubbled up like an oil gusher. Rob watched, fascinated, as bull's-eye creatures filled the crack.

Finally, he pulled the garbage bag from the pocket of his too-big sweatpants and filled it with the ugly little critters. He was going to pay a little visit to Mr. Movie Star Mark Chandler and see how badly the superstar wanted to lose weight. All at once.

#

Less than ten minutes later, sitting in a storage room on the top floor, Rob saw his wife and the movie return to Chandler's room on their fifteen-minute morning break. They slipped into Chandler's room, giggling like schoolkids cutting class.

Rob stifled a shout of pure rage from inside the storage room. Holding his bag of critters, which he'd grabbed on his way out of the basement, he ran for Chandler's door, catching it before it closed and locked. From the laughing and carrying on he could hear inside the room, he had a feeling they wouldn't notice that the door wasn't closed all the way.

Mindy, he thought. How could you do this to me?

"Mmm," Chandler said, his voice thick. "You look so good. I could just eat you up."

The bed squeaked twice. Rob pictured two large bodies crawling onto it. A sound like plastic rustling filled Rob's ears. What kind of twisted, kinky shit were they up to?

"Oh my," a lusty female voice moaned, "you are *so* good."

Rob couldn't take it any longer. He burst through the door, a butter knife in his left hand, a bag of critters in the other. "Stop it right—" he began, then stopped. "There?"

Mark Chandler and Melinda Heying were sprawled across the king-size hotel bed, just as Rob had imagined. But they were both fully clothed and nowhere close to each other. Separating them were five bulging paper bags, overflowing with Twinkies, Doritos, candy bars, Jelly Bellies, and just about every other kind of junk food imaginable. Chandler had a donut in each hand and powdered sugar around his lips. Melinda held a handful of chips in one hand and a Snickers bar in her other, her beautiful blue eyes wide.

"Oh Rob," Mindy gasped. "Please don't tell anyone."

"What are you doing here?" Chandler said with his mouth full, finishing off a donut.

Rob let the door close behind him. He shook his bag of critters. "I'm her husband, numbnuts. The one she's been cheating on. With you. Now you're gonna have to pay for it."

"Cheating?" The man who was Dead-Eye McQuaid looked from Rob to Melinda and back to Rob again. "What are you talking about?"

"I think the word is *adultery*," Rob said. He shook the bag open, looking down at the roiling mass of brown creatures. He was going to enjoy shoving them down Chandler's throat. "Isn't that what you'd call it, Melinda?"

"Rob—" Melinda began.

"Listen, friend," Chandler began.

"I'm not your friend."

"Let me finish. I know this looks bad, but it's not what you think. The only cheating that's going on here is our little snacking sessions." He stifled a belch. "I don't like to snack alone, so Mindy here agreed to accompany me. It's more fun that way. And we feel less guilty."

Rob glared at him. "Am I supposed to *believe* that?"

Mindy slid off the bed, leaving her can of Pringles behind.

"Rob, listen to me," she began, and the emotions in her words made Rob drop his butter knife. But he held onto his bag of critters. For now. "You were gone last night, and Mark stopped by while you were getting the pizza. We talked about the food he had here, and I snacked with him. I was too ashamed to come back to the room. I knew how much it meant for you to lose weight."

"Hmm," Rob said. Chandler had gone back to his donuts. "What about your ring?"

"It didn't fit anymore," Melinda said with a grin, licking chocolate off her fingers. "I've lost too much weight. It kept sliding off, so I left it . . . " She stopped talking and looked over at him, her face frozen with dismay. "Oh, Rob. You must've really thought—"

"Plus I'm gay," Chandler said, rattling a package of Chips Ahoy. "My boyfriend would kill me if I ever cheated on him." He gave a nervous smile. "Ah, could we keep that our little secret, though? I've got some fans who love thinking of me as a lady's man."

Rob looked away from Chandler to take in his wife, glowing with sweat. She had crumbs on her T-shirt and chocolate on her fingertips. The tightness he'd been feeling in his chest broke loose. She'd never been more beautiful.

Rob smiled at her and held up the garbage bag in his hand like a kid at Halloween. "Mr. Chandler," he said, grabbing a jelly donut. "What can you tell me about these critters?"

#

Rob and Melinda Heying left the Manorhouse exactly two weeks after they'd arrived there, a combined four pounds heavier, and happier than ever.

They had suffered through the workouts in their last week and a half there, but they both skipped the voluntary "eating treatments" held on the second floor so they could "better focus on" their physical exertions. Which consisted mostly of trips to Mark Chandler's room for snacks.

In his room that day, Chandler had explained to them how the creatures from the cracks worked, how they entered a fat — *his* word, not Rob's — person's bloodstream and sucked up the fat. Their effect was heightened by exercise and electricity, so the Institute kept the guests as active as possible and claimed their teachings were why their patients lost twenty to thirty pounds in fourteen days. For a hefty fee, guests could pay to get zapped while they ate critters.

"I know exactly what you're talking about," Rob had interrupted with a shudder.

"The critters are why they moved this place, you know," Chandler said. "Old man Thoroughgood was camping close to that crater just south of us back in the forties, doing his peyote or whatever it was he did, and he came across some rocks. This was during his scientific period, so he did some research on them and found the rocks were covered with single-cell microbes that weren't, ah, shall we say, from around here. It took years of research, but he was able to figure out the effects the microbes had on people. Especially fat people. So he moved the Manorhouse here so he could harvest the microbes and grow them into those critters.

"The only drawback," Chandler added with a grimace, "is that the effect of the critters is temporary. Very temporary. That's what keeps me coming back, month after month. Do you think I *like* riding across the desert to get here?"

For the rest of their time at the Manor, Rob and Melinda had pretended to drink their shakes, pouring them into sinks or plants or whatever was closest. They wanted to remain critter-free. Mr. Chandler — "Please call me Mark," he kept saying to Rob — made sure they had plenty to eat. Their little secret, Mark had called it.

Just before takeoff on their flight back home, Rob squeezed himself into the seat of the plane next to his wife. He kissed Melinda's round cheek and rubbed his even rounder stomach.

"Feel good?" he asked, extending the seat belt out as far as it could.

Melinda nodded. "Never felt better in my life," she said.

When the flight attendant brought their lunches, they both opted for the salad.

UNPLUGGED

I'm on the front porch of Rubin's place, staring across the lawn at the silent cars slashing past, feeling old and empty inside, when the new guy walks out. He's got the cowboy twitch, the uncontrolled jerk of the head to the right or left, that all of us have when we first arrive here. I suddenly want to scratch the back of my head, down at the base, but I fight the impulse. The new guy sits next to me, sighs, then pulls his head up suddenly. It goes down and up again three times before I look away. Nobody likes watching someone else short circuit.

"Hey," he says after a few awkward seconds. His hand is held out to me, close but not touching. "My name's Jonathan. My two weeks just started."

He gives a quick laugh, and I shake his hand. His palms are dry and cracked, but his grip is strong.

"Mickey," I say, watching him.

The first two days are the worst here at Rubin's non-tech health facility. Staying unplugged is not an option for a lot of cowboys, but the alternatives — stims coursing through the nervous system or triggering the built-in lightning viruses just about every system has nowadays, not to mention the unnatural act of plugging metal into the back of your head — the alternatives aren't so tasty, either.

Jonathan relaxes slightly next to me. At least he's stopped twitching.

"I knew that flack would catch up to me," he mutters. His voice is high, unsteady, and his scalp is bright white under buzzed black hair. "That's what got me here. I had the cheap stuff put in me when I was sixteen, just starting out. How was I supposed to know it melted after prolonged use?"

"Yeah," I say, the veteran cowboy trying to clean up his act. For the second time. The treatments after my first interment at Rubin's held for about six months, then I started sneaking trips to Lia's com line for a fix when she was asleep. Pretty soon I was popping her stims and jacking in every time she was gone. Lia found me in the bathtub, the stripped com wires attached to the miloprene plugs in the back of my skull jolting me with enough juice to cause paralysis.

"Should've left you in there to dance yourself to death," she'd said. To break the connection she'd had to prop my head up with an antique wooden chair.

"What's your story, Jonathan?" I say. I keep my gaze away from him, following the traffic instead.

Rubin's is surrounded by transparent soundproof baffles at the edge of the front lawn, so the silence is complete. Rubin likes the rustic feel, even though there isn't much peace and serenity left to spare these days. Behind the baffle, the ten lanes of satellite-guided traffic are only a few feet away.

After a few seconds, Jonathan flicks his gaze over to me. "My story?"

"Talk, man. We've got to talk to get through this, to pass the time." A wave of nausea passes through me, and I fight off fresh, unfamiliar panic. "You know?"

Jonathan gets up and leans on the porch railing. "Yeah. Guess you're right." He adjusts his white jumpsuit with a quick, smooth arc of his hands. Despite the erosion that must've hit his synapses when the flack at his brainstem melted, I can tell he still has some of the old moves left in him. "I started jacking in back when the weather controllers started malfunctioning, and everything went cold for a couple years."

"I remember that. You've been in that long?"

Jonathan shrugs, smiling. "Oh yeah. Had the best rig in the New England systems, which isn't saying a lot. But it was something. My buddies from the old Webscapes helped me get the specs right. It was rock and slide, grab and go for about five years. Then I met Marta."

"She Russian?" I ask.

The west Europeans and Russians had a stranglehold on the sturdier old-tech that had outlived the flashy plastic-and-laser tech from the past decade. Once the flack was installed inside your head, you no longer needed to worry with virching lenses and rings on your fingers; all you needed was your head, and lots of adrenaline. Flack had landed most of us here at Rubin's with battle scars melted into our heads. Prolonged use was what we were all about.

"German," Jonathan grins. It takes me a second to figure out what he's talking about. "But she was a real girl, no prosthetics on her or in her. She made me go back to my old face." His skinny hand flicks toward his chin, where I can make out a tiny white line that sweeps back to his ear. "Anyway, she came over to get away from the old ghosts in the eastern corridor. Her family was wiped out by an old nuke in Berlin that detonated by accident. Some baby cowboy, thirteen years old, thinking he was downloading some American Defense Department holos, activated it with his rig."

Jonathan's voice stops abruptly, and we turn back to the front yard, silent. Something itches at the base of my skull. Electric two-man coaches and Japanese ginsu bikes rush past on the other side of the transparent baffle, a world of speed and motion and tightly-controlled energy. On our side, a black squirrel pats the ground with tiny fingers, trying to jack in on some acorns. Rubin's quiet world of healing and silence exists alongside reality like a dinosaur in rush hour traffic.

Jonathan's head has started twitching again. "Must be about time for the circle-go-round," I say, clapping him on the back. He tenses his shoulders, and his head stops moving. "Let's go back inside and talk to Rubin."

#

There are ten of us at Rubin's this week. We sit in a circle on gel-filled bags in the muted lights, staring at each other without meeting eyes. The cowboys and grrls at the end of their treatments — Penny, Chase, Vanya, and Marsden — sit and watch with their hands on their knees, trying to convey a sense of cool in their non-descript jumpers. The rest of us twitch or scratch ourselves in varying degrees of intensity. We're a sorry-looking bunch, out of date and out of circulation.

"Eddie," Rubin says, nodding toward a kid in his mid-twenties next to Jonathan. "Why don't you start us out today." Rubin's voice is soft, almost inhuman in its monotone. But his eyes are pure intensity under his shaggy eyebrows. Rubin used to be a cowboy, too.

"Oh, okay," Eddie says. He's a short, fat kid, sideburns down to his chin, and he won't stop turning his head around the room, as if he could get all of our attentions by a simple glance. "I told you guys about the time some anti-intelligence agent laced my stims with metal shavings, right? Least I think he was some government agent. And how the next day — I swear to you it's all connected — the plastic in my head melted?"

Jonathan shifts next to me, both his legs tapping on the floor in discordant rhythms. I cough and catch his eye: *take it easy*. He lifts his chin a fraction of an inch.

"Yeah, so, the next day I woke up," Eddie says, scanning the room with his head rocking like a metronome. "And some tall skinny plugger was in the rig room with me, watching me. This guy sticks something into my matrix simulator, without even jacking in, and then clears my rig's memory." His voice rises and becomes a warble. "The whole time I'm trying to get the hell up, but I can't lift my head, like my head weighs a ton. He knocks over my snort, knocks it into my rig, and leaves. It took me all day to get up and read what he burned into it."

Eddie falls silent, staring at the floor in front of him. His sideburns look like a grotesque smile.

"Eddie," Rubin murmurs. Rubin's voice is so cool it makes me shiver, and when I start shivering I don't know if I can stop.

"'Sleep the sleep of the extinct and obsolete'," Eddie says, his voice cracking on the last word. His face is white and empty. He doesn't move.

"Eddie," Rubin says, louder. "Eddie, keep talking. You've got to talk about it."

But Eddie's not home. He's jacked in, a surfing cowboy high on a noseful of stims and metal shavings. And he's seizing.

The gel bag splooshes under Eddie, giving a flatulent honk as his legs kick out in front of him. His stubby body stiffens, synapses hungry for more stims. He cracks his head on the thinly-carpeted floor behind him. I hear Jonathan's gasp beside me like an interrupted sigh, and I feel a sharp kick of sympathetic pain for Eddie from the plugs at the base of my skull.

Rubin is at Eddie's side in two seconds. He has something in his hand, a small black Tazer-like gun, which he touches to the back of Eddie's head.

Whitish-blue current shoots out of the end. Eddie punches out with both hands, barely missing Rubin, then he lies still. Only his feet move, his heels drumming on the floor weakly. When I look back at Rubin, his hand is empty again.

I gaze around the room. Nobody else wants to look at Eddie or Rubin. Jonathan's eyes are wide open like a double-lensed dronecam, recording everything as his mouth drops open and his head jerks spastically to the left. Some playback that'll be, my mind laughs crazily: a blurred shot of Eddie's feet kicking at the floor as the perspective teeter-totters around the room, capturing the blank faces of worn-out cyber-cowboys, suddenly aware that at any instant, this could happen to them.

#

Something tugs at me later that night, pulling me out of a dream with Lia next to me in our shared sleep-tube, her glowing red lips and matching fingernails shimmering across my waking vision. Her voice was softer in the dream than it had been a week ago in reality, and she was so close I could taste her fluorescent lipstick. I wake up when another pulse tugs at my head.

I cut under the black dot of the dronecam tacked above my door and pad into the hallway barefoot. After a decade and a half of being plugged in, and now after going six days without, I feel like I could sense the white noise distortion from a rig, any rig, from miles away. It starts in my teeth, where the fillings used to be before Rubin removed them on my first visit. The carpet pulls at the soles of my feet on my way down the stairs.

One of Rubin's assistants must have gotten bored of watching the display from the cams. The front desk is empty, and beyond it is the freeway. Headlights slash by, teasing my eyes. I couldn't leave if I had the strength to try; the whole place is magnetically sealed. Next to the desk, a pencil-thin line of light peeks out of a crack next to a piece of soundproof wallboard. The hum that I'm feeling and hearing, almost tasting, is coming from this room.

I roll my weight forward, barely breathing, until I'm at the crack in the wall. I lean forward and look inside, knowing Rubin would not be happy if he found me here. A whiff of ozone tickles my nose from inside the closet.

The son of a bitch working the front desk has brought in his own matrix simulator, big as a wallet and emitting a shimmering gray light that barely lights the room. He is wearing a pair of clunky specs and a glove. His stuff is so old, it barely passes for a rig. His simulator is hooked up to the com line, and from the back of his head sprout two thin cables. One cable leads to the specs, the other leads to the simulator. His head moves to a silent beat as he skims through another world, a world I've promised myself I can never revisit.

But all I need is a handful of stims and that could be me, weightless in a landscape of information.

My head jerks to the right. The stims make everything more vivid, more than just energy and data. Right now I'd be willing to jack in without them, even with the damage it would do to my raw, burned-out nerve endings. Just a minute inside, then back to bed.

Before I realize what I'm doing, I'm inside into the cramped room, two meters from the tiny hand-held rig, my mouth dropping open and full of metallic spit. I can feel my hand reaching for the cables in the man's head.

I stop. Eddie. Think of Eddie, today, in the circle, his heels tapping on the floor as he gets reformatted by Rubin.

Think of Lia, waiting for me outside, pissed off as ever. She told me this was the last time she'd bring me in and pick me up from Rubin's: "Don't think you're so important that I can put my life on hold every six months to save your flacked-out ass." Her eyes had been two wheels of fire in the darkness of my short-circuited vision. Soapy water covered her shoulders. "Don't think I'll wait for you much longer."

My hand drops to my side, and I step back. The jacked-in cowboy riding his ancient rig doesn't even see me. The muscles in my neck clench. Another week and I can see Lia. In the gray, buzzing darkness, it's a quick walk back to my room.

#

I've been here for eight days now, and everything's starting to hurt. My hands and feet, almost numb from my slowed circulation. Inside my chest, my heart hammering with the memory of near-overdose levels of stims. But mostly the pain comes from my head: my temples and the base of my skull. I want to rip the miloprene plugs out of my body with my dead fingers.

Jonathan isn't much better. I can bypass the physical treatments, since it's my second visit, but this morning was treatment number two for him. Detoxification. All the stims clinging to his hypothalamus and pituitary, as well as the inner lining of his stomach and intestines, have been flushed out. Leaves you feeling pretty raw, especially after the depolarization he underwent two days ago as part of his first treatment. I know he's not going to want to talk.

"The first job Lia and I cracked together was down in Tijuana," I say. Some of the pain recedes as I talk, but there's still the humming epidermal twinge of the D.T.'s. Jonathan's head doesn't rise, but I can feel his eyes on me. "We had to go there to get the right frequencies, since the Mexicans didn't give a flack about the air pollution it caused. Border patrol let us through cheap, even provided us an armed escort through the city. Cuervo for everyone. Ever been south of the border?"

Jonathan blinks twice. A muscle in his left cheek tenses and relaxes. I take that for "yes."

"We lost the soldiers in a meth bar and kept going deeper into an old barrio Lia knew about somehow. She was clean that night, and her eyes — shit. She had the most intense, unaugmented eyes I'd ever seen. Pacific Ocean greenish-blue." I watch a bullet-shaped bus shooting past silently behind the barrier, a long blur of gray and black. "At least she said they weren't augmented. Never could tell with Lia."

It begins to sprinkle, and everything goes gray. I rub my chin, thinking of Lia on the outside. Each Saturday we got ten minutes' com time, the only access to any kind of tech we were allowed. Not a lot you can do with an old touch-tone and a handheld screen, but it's better than nothing. I didn't call her last Saturday, but maybe I'll call her tomorrow, tell her how clean I am. Again.

"Anyway," I say, stretching my cramped back and legs, "we met some connections in a tin shack, and I got busy jacking in. It was a cold jack, no stims, because we just couldn't afford it in those days. God damn, that visual from the matrix simulator was crystal clear, almost blinded me with the light show."

I relax into my chair again and watch Jonathan's unmoving head. He starts to slide down in the adirondack.

"Those were the good old days, before the brownouts and the mutating electronic viruses. We didn't even need the stims then." I grab Jonathan, stopping his downward slide. "Didn't even want them. Know what I mean?"

Jonathan jumps as if hit with feedback.

"Yeah," he mumbles, straightening up. He rubs his face. "What were you talking 'bout?"

"Mexico. Tijuana." I grin in spite of the deadness in my body. Lia would laugh at me for being so fatherly toward this kid. She doesn't understand, with her addiction to the easy-to-find pharmaceuticals and the escape holos on public access. "I can stop whenever I want," she'd say, touching the back of my head with a cold, cold hand. "Can *you*, Mickey?"

Then she'd flop onto her bed and forget about me for an hour, watching holographic people enter our efficiency and live their lives for her amusement. She said I was behind the times, a fossil. But she was always waiting for me when I jacked out and her pharmaceuticals were gone, holding herself tightly with an expression of anger and fierce need on her face.

"I was jacked in, moving faster and faster through the systems, nothing sticking to me but Lia's hand on my shoulder a million miles away. We got in, picked up some specs from one level of Arcnet, turned around and sold them back at an upper level for an insane profit. Rock and slide, grab and go, just like you said. Jesus. Being a cowboy's all I knew how to do then."

"Yeah," Jonathan says. He's pulling out of it. The vomiting will start later. "What *are* we supposed to do once we're cured?" He says the last word like he's spitting out something that tastes rotten.

"Good question," I say. A tenth of a mile above us, rain falls on Rubin's baffles, protecting us from the wet and cold. Down below, we sit like inert lumps of clay, devoid of warmth and power.

"I don't think Marta's coming back," Jonathan says in a small voice. His words skitter up my back and stick in my head. "She likes the pharms too much to remember to come back in twelve days and get me. I don't think I'll ever see her again."

I turn back to him, lowering my gaze from the sky. He's balled up, a thin young man regressing into inert mass and electric impulses. The white of his scalp shines under his buzz cut. He barely twitches. It's a long time before I look away and bring him inside.

#

I'm awake the second the buzzing starts. Sweat covers my chest and forehead, my body trying to clean itself out through my pores. I pull off my T-shirt and wipe myself off. Maybe I should've agreed to the optional treatments. I still haven't shaken the emptiness filling my body, like a hunger that spreads from my stomach to all my organs and limbs. I'm going to end it tonight.

I float down the steps to the front desk on feet that don't even feel the floor. I pause only for a nanosecond when I see the desk man stuffed under his oak desk, shuddering slightly like a new member of Rubin's exclusive club. Two tiny trails of blood slip down the back of his skull, underneath his cheap, implanted plug.

The piece of wallboard is wedged back in place, and I'm able to open it on the third try with my twitching hands. The electric buzzing is almost deafening to my ears now. I slide the paneling down the wall and look inside. Jonathan sits hunched forward, his body gyrating slowly to a silent beat, two monofilaments snaking out of his skull like intravenous tubes. I'm not at all surprised to see him here.

There's a subtle magic to the way he's moving, like a snake charmer facing the mother of all cobras. He has no idea I'm even here, I realize, walking around him. His eyes are open, blinking quickly and darting across the room. He is seeing cybernetic objects in his mind's eye more real than anything here at Rubin's, more real than anything else in his life right now. More real than Marta.

Jonathan starts to sweat and moan after a few minutes; the lack of stims in his system and the melted flack in his head are taking their toll. He's fading fast, eyes blinking like crazy. Stupid kid. He's going to make a mistake, trip a virus. I want to pull the plugs and get him out of there, but an ugly part of me lets him play on, trying his luck as a cyber cowboy a little longer. I should hate myself more than I do as I watch his thin face tighten and redden with each passing second. He's gasping and trying to speak when the simulator pops. Pent-up static electricity shoots into the air with a white spark as big as my fist. Jonathan jerks forward, and I instinctively rip out the cables from the back of his head before he falls into my arms.

The next two minutes in the semi-darkness spin past, as fifteen years of jacking in tells my quivering hands what to do. I don't have much time to reboot and redigitize, but I luck out and find the echo of the last address on the matrix simulator, so Jonathan and I are in business. I put the rig on standby, then I'm ready to go back on-line. I grab the jacks. The live cables shake in my right hand like a two-headed snake.

My hand stops an inch from the plugs in the back of my head. Jonathon's breathing is irregular and ragged. Lia. I need to talk to her. Beautiful, angry Lia.

I may not come out of this.

I glance at Jonathan's body next to me, his breathing shallow. There's no time. The virus will have eaten through his nervous system within half an hour, if that's what he got himself into. I have to go in, find some kind of antivirus.

My hand jerks in a final, involuntary arc toward my skull. In and out, and Lia never needs to know. I close my eyes in anticipation of the rush and the flash and the pain.

But I can't push the plugs into the back of my head. It's not the shaking in my hands that denies me my final jack, but the time I've lost with Lia. All I have is her, here in the present, and me, trying not to admit that history has passed me by. That the future has made me obsolete.

I ease the plugs into Jonathan's head, flick on the rig, and hope he can find his way back to the antivirus himself. If he wants to be a cowboy so badly, that's his future. I turn away, willing myself not to hear his floundering movements behind me as I think of bright red lips and Pacific Ocean eyes. I walk back to my room without twitching, ready to finish my treatment.

WORKING THE GAME

I knew it was going to be a bad day when I saw the scrag almost get cut in half twenty minutes after work began.

I was working on a crew off Hodges Street, a mile from the wall that separated us from the rest of Raleigh. I'd been on the job for eighteen days now. For my first two weeks, the oldest workers — the ones with years of breakdown and restructuring in their hands and backs and legs — constantly watched me for any hint of weakness in the chilly fall air. For all of them, half an instant's distraction could mean a painful, crushing death. So I showed up early and worked late with the rest of them, and they were starting to trust me. I was finally working the game.

Before, I'd been just a scrag, doing the scut work no one else would do. At ten points an hour, this was my first legit job. At a hundred thousand points, I could put in an application to go over the wall, and at two hundred thousand I could pay for it. Kwabe and Natalie had the highest point totals at our worksite, so they had been chosen by the govvie to lead the job. They had the most to lose.

Maybe Lia and I'd be gone, too, someday. If we both kept working, and if Lia could hold out that long in the cold. This morning, my wrist had read fifteen degrees F, and the front door of Lia's box had been blocked by half a foot of new, blue-tinted snow. It wasn't supposed to be this cold, not in October, and especially not here in Raleigh. I'd been chilled to the bone since late August, and Lia hadn't stopped coughing since June.

So, to keep my points flowing and my mind off the cold, I worked. Each day was a new list, relayed to the group leaders through their wrist implants. The routine was the same whether you were at a restructuring or a breakdown: you make or take down your quota of walls, you get your points. You don't get enough walls put up or taken down, the points get taken away. Three of the scrags in my group had decided not to show up this morning. We'd have trouble making our quota with just the five of us.

On the top floor of the reconstructed building off Hodges Street, I melted a six-inch-thick border onto the floor with my fuser, getting it ready for a piece of duraplast. Coated with a thin lining of nanodes, each new wall on the fifth floor would get fused to the top-most piece of duraplast on the fourth floor. As long as we got the new piece of duraplast in place before the plastic cooled, the outer wall would be immobile in just over a minute. By that time the tech inside the new wall would have talked to the tech in the existing wall, and then you had a smart wall that controlled the heat and cold, blocked the sounds of the outside and neighbors, and even showed old vids, all according to the preset govvie settings. At least that's how Natalie had explained the tech to me.

Nat had given me her leveler at the start of the day. Only team leaders used these yard-long tools, digital versions of the old levels that Nat said used to work with *water*, somehow. Half the junk she told me about old jobsites had to have been made up. But she'd lent me her leveler, and she'd kill me if the first wall I did on my own was crooked.

Takeem and two other scrags had a piece of duraplast waiting for me. Takeem was a good kid, and smart. When I popped off the fuser, the scrags hefted the duraplast over me and fit it into place, careful not to let their bare skin touch the melted floor before the wall was fused. If they did make contact, they'd be infected. Nat knew a scrag — there was *always* a scrag — who got sucked into a wall that way. He was now part of a smart wall in a ten-story outside Durham.

Once the wall was in place, I slid the fuser up the right-hand side, bonding it with the existing wall. I held the leveler next to the wall, squinting at the readout. The wall was level.

When I looked up from the wall, a stupid grin on my face, it happened.

Twenty yards away, two scrags were struggling with the wiring for one of the northern walls. The girl jerked at the wires being fed up from the scrags below, her hair falling into her face. The guy reached over to help her, and the wire in his hand touched her wire. The wires were hot, and they were both thrown by the electric contact. The girl skidded back into the building. The boy was knocked into Kwabe, who was working his cutter on a bad piece of recycle. The boy's legs crossed the blue-white beam of the cutter, and the screaming began.

Kwabe shut off the cutter in time to keep from slicing off the boy's legs, but the kid was still cut badly. There was no blood where the cutter had hit the boy, though a chunk of red flesh lay on the ground next to Kwabe. The cutter must have cauterized the wound on contact. I wanted to help the boy, but he wasn't in my group, and my own group was already behind.

I felt a hand on my shoulder. "Twenty-four to go," Nat said, out of breath. Three scrags carried the boy to the steps as Kwabe talked into his wrist, calling up an emergency unit. She tried to make her voice sound tougher. "Bet you a beer we don't get out of here before it's dark."

"You're on," I said, feeling the weight of the leveler in my hands.

Work had stopped for all of five minutes. The other workers and I returned to our work at the outer edge of the floor, picking up our fusers again. I rubbed my left wrist, feeling the hard sliver of the implant under my skin. So much for watching the jumpers tonight after work, I thought. I'll be here until the curfew, if not later.

As I worked, I kept thinking about what life must have been like without the wall. According to the stories, Raleigh had already had the Beltline walls in place years ago, twenty-foot-high brick sound barriers blocking the noise of traffic for the North Raleigh residents. Raleigh was a divided city even back then. The new wall built on the existing walls, adding layers of duraplast until the wall gave off an electromagnetic pulse from all of its stored energy.

I looked outside as the sun rose, bringing some heat to the morning. The wall — the big one, the only wall that mattered — jutted up into my vision to the north, a pinkish-blue bruise in the growing daylight. Lia blamed the cold on the wall, built back before either of us had even been born. Supposedly the poor people living on this side of the wall had fought against it during the month it took the government to put the wall up. According to the stories, the govvie had used cloneslaves, the faceless drones that didn't need to eat or rest. Or earn points.

I drew in a long, icy breath of air. We'd never finish in time. Not with this crew full of scrags. And as long as the wall was there, we were *all* scrags.

#

With the help of shoulder lights, Nat, Kwabe, Roberts, and I finished the last wall on the fifth floor by ourselves. Stars glittered above us, stopping abruptly to the north, blocked by the wall. When I turned my wrist up, it read five minutes to ten. Twenty degrees F, Ninety seven point eight degrees F. Sixty-two bpm. One hundred twenty-two mmHg over seventy-three mmHg. Always too much information, scrolling past, every time I looked. But that's the way the govvie liked it — vitals, communications, points, and satellite tracking of my exact location at any time of day. They thought they were doing all of us some kind of favor, fitting us with the implant the day we turned one. Some birthday present.

"Guess you owe me a beer," Nat said. Her narrow face was red from the cold.

Kwabe sat wiping down the fusers left in disarray by the scrags. The dark skin of his face still looked ashy after the accident that morning. "Beer? Who's got beer?"

I looked at the fifth floor. Such a stupid way to track your work, counting off your progress in ten by twenty rectangles of smart walls. Takeem and his buddies had left around seven, when it had started getting dark, not caring if they lost points or not. There was a wall-jumping tonight, and they weren't going to miss it for a measly twenty or thirty points.

I could query my wrist for my point total, now that Kwabe had connected to the satellite with his linking unit and authorized the day's work, but I vowed never to do that unless I absolutely had to. At the max of a hundred fifty points a day, the numbers added up way too slowly for my taste. It was better to just put your head down and work through each day, whether you were a scrag or a real worker. That was the scrag's mantra: one point at a time.

#

I made it home before eleven o'clock, but the sound of Lia coughing and sniffling in the pallet next to me drove me back out into the streets, to the wall. I was too wound up from the accident today, and her coughing was killing me. One day we'd get her to the health center. We just needed another five thousand points first.

The jumpers were just starting their last race when I got to the wall. Fitted with wings made of scrap duraplast and wire, the jumpers used the energy of the wall to deflect themselves up and away, crossing the dead old highway towards the boxes where we all lived. Once they were in the air, they'd lift their wings and glide, hoping to catch a friendly wind current and be the first to the finish line half a mile away. Ten feet beyond the finish line was a three-story brick wall. At least one over-eager jumper a night, flying high on stolen energy and a good breeze, hit the wall after crossing the finish line. It kept the jumpers honest, to be sure, and it also kept me from ever wanting to try jumping.

The jumpers were positioning themselves into their harnesses, aimed at the wall, when I got there. I saw some of the scrags who'd abandoned the site early, and they guiltily led me to Takeem, strapped into his bungee rig and wings. He was trembling against the resistance of the blue cord pulled tight at his back, the cord secured at either end to posts jammed into the ground. He looked like a big fly caught in an oversized slingshot.

"Watch this, Chapman," Takeem said, a wild grin plastered to his face. "I'm gonna take this race. Already won two tonight."

"Do it," I said, stepping back. In my mind I could hear Lia wheezing, and I shook my head like a dog to clear it.

A whistle blew. Takeem lifted both feet, launching himself at the wall. He lifted into the air, skinny body in a ball. An instant before he hit, he raised his dainty wings and straightened his body, arching his back. The pulse of the wall hit his wings, pushing him up and away. Takeem was flying.

"Damn," I whispered, grinning.

As Takeem unfurled his thin arms inside his wings, gaining altitude as he pulled ahead of the other jumpers, I glanced back the wall. My grin died on my cold face. One of the jumpers hadn't gotten his wings up in time. His friends were picking him up off of the old highway, his wings crumpled and a fresh red smear following him down the wall. "Damn," I said again.

After Takeem won his last jump of the night, I realized how late it was. Tomorrow was another day of work. I'd gotten used to only a couple hours of sleep each night, but now that I wasn't a scrag, I wasn't going to be able to do that much more. Things were changing.

I was about to turn back towards our box when I ran into Jaime. Four hundred pounds and growing, Jaime lived under the ruins of the old Capitol building. Jaime was one of the few people I knew who not only didn't have an implant in his wrist, but who refused to work the game like the rest of us. He also rarely left his basement home, which was filled with illegal tech he'd salvaged from the garbage pits or bought from the black markets. Tonight must've been a special occasion.

"Hullo Marcus," Jaime said. He rolled up to me in his go-cart, his hand on a little red joystick. Despite the chill in the air, his light brown skin was covered in a light sheen of sweat. "How's the construction business?"

I shrugged. "Booming. I've got more work than I know what to do with."

Jaime looked at me. "And you think that's a good thing, don't you?"

"It's *points*, amigo. What's new?"

Jaime grinned, his small white teeth flashing. He pulled a square paper container from his jacket pocket and tossed it to me. "Try one of those. Take the damn paper off it first, Chapman," he said. I slid one of the thin pieces of paper-wrapped material out of the container. "It's gum. You chew it."

I raised an eyebrow, but popped the rubbery white rectangle into my mouth. Jaime always had the best stuff. I could feel my eyes go wide with surprise as I chewed, and Jaime almost fell off his go-cart chair laughing. It was sweet, like sugar, but it never dissolved.

"Found some interesting things today," Jaime said, nodding at the wall rising next to us like a wave that never crashed. "I've been checking on the govvie's plans here in Raleigh. They keep all this stuff on an unsecured site, figure we aren't quick enough to slip into it. You'll never guess what's coming next, or why they've been working so hard on perfecting the cloneslaves." The wheels of his go-cart groaned as Jaime pulled back on the joystick, sliding him closer.

"Thought the cloneslaves were myths," I said, trying not to swallow the gum he'd given me. "You know, just some stories people made up about how fast the wall got put up."

"I wish they *were* just stories," Jaime said, and looked at a tiny readout on his go-cart. "Damn. Party's over, Chapman. Stop by the basement sometime, and we'll talk."

Something was throbbing in the air. Jaime was already rolling away, heading for cover as the throbbing became a low rumbling. The govvie choppers were late today. Usually they came before the wall-jumpers were done with their races. I hurried after Jaime.

"What about the cloneslaves?" I shouted to him over the pounding of the govvie choppers. Instead of answering, he rolled into an old warehouse three blocks away from the wall. I followed him, knowing I was probably going to regret it.

"So tell me," Jaime said after the thunder of the choppers had died away. "What do you think is going to happen to you when you earn your magic number of points?"

"What are you talking about? I thought you had some important news to tell me."

"I do. But humor me first. Tell me why you want to work your whole life like a cloneslave."

I chewed the gum for a second, thinking of the best way to explain it. Work was something I'd lived with for so long, something that was so much a part of my life I couldn't even *see* it anymore. "You're supposed to earn points so you can go over to the other side. And when you're there you get fitted for your cocoon and all that shit. Live the easy life, everything you need right there in your cocoon."

Jaime started to laugh, a hissing sound that filled my stomach with acid. "Cocoons, huh? Is that what you think is in there? Think you've got a cocoon waiting for you with your name on it when you earn your points?"

I stared at him in the dark of the old warehouse. That was exactly what I'd thought. That was what I'd been told, all my life. That was what got me through each long day of work.

"May have been that way once," Jaime said, digging his right index finger into his left wrist as if searching for an implant. "Not anymore. 'Least here in Raleigh, they're all full up."

I moved away, walking in a wide circle around Jaime and his go-cart, trying to keep away the chill creeping into me. "So do we get to go to other cities when we earn our points?" I said. "Because that doesn't matter to me. I don't care where I go, as long as I get inside with Lia."

Jaime didn't respond for a long moment. When I walked back toward him, he was looking up at me, his eyes like the eyes of an old, old man. "How long has that girlfriend of yours been sick, Chapman?"

"Couple months," I said automatically, then stopped pacing. "Why? What's it to you?"

"The other little tidbit I found out today. The govvie's been cutting off funding to the health centers on the outside. They want to channel all their money and energy into perfecting the cloneslaves." Jaime shrugged his rounded shoulders. "Why waste time and money on keeping a bunch of point-grubbers healthy?"

Jaime was waiting for an answer, but I was too tired to argue. All I gave him was silence.

#

I stumbled back to Lia's box, my heartbeat too strong in my chest. Even as I made my way into the tiny front room of the box, pulling in new snow behind me, I knew I wouldn't get much sleep that night. In the main room, Lia was sprawled across the mattress, coughing and rolling from side to side in the cold air of our shared box. I felt the familiar ache in my back from fifteen hours on the job.

Lia coughed and reached for me. "Where were you?" she whispered, her voice ragged from coughing. "You weren't working late, were you?"

"No," I said, kissing her hot forehead. "Not working. For once."

She was already falling back to sleep. I could hear the phlegm rattling in her lungs with each breath. She sounds bad, I thought. She's been sick for way too long. Maybe Jaime had been right. Even if we went to the health center, would they be able to help?

I rolled onto my back, my body aching for rest, but my brain wouldn't let me relax. Maybe I just worried too much. Once we got over the wall, life would be different. Maybe, on the other side, if she still had this damn cough, there would be doctors to help. The people in their cocoons surely got sick once in a while, even though — at least from what Jaime had told me — most of the cocooners never left home.

I ran my tongue across my teeth, tasting the sweetness of the gum Jaime had given me. All he told me had to be just another story, a stupid rumor. He pulled too much information from inside the wall and the govvie. It wasn't good for a person. I closed my eyes and inhaled the chilly air of our box. It was better to just work and earn your points. And hope for the best.

#

As if to prove my point, when the reconstruction project off Hodges Street was completed and the building had been activated, Kwabe made his point totals.

"It's possible," was all he said to me as we packed up our equipment two hours earlier than usual. "It can happen, Chapman."

Getting your point totals was something that didn't happen every day — I'd never known anyone in my years of working the game who'd actually made it. We worked until five, when Kwabe hit his numbers, showing everyone the numbers in his wrist as they flipped over all zeroes. Then he treated us to the beers he'd been saving. He only had ten, so I was able to get two short pulls before passing it on. I'd never tasted anything better after a day's work, and I couldn't stop thanking Kwabe and wishing the big man good luck on the other side.

The next day the govvie had his replacement. Watts had the whitest teeth I had ever seen. And he flashed them at us every chance he got. Watts came in at just below Nat's point level, keeping the number of senior workers high for the sake of safety and order. If he continued working his current twelve-hour days, Watts told us minutes after meeting everyone, he would go over the wall in exactly 452 days, sixteen hours, and forty-five minutes. Give or take an hour or two, he added with a grin, adjusting his cutter with his slender fingers.

Despite the man's odd accent and obsession with numbers, I liked Watts at first. While we hauled our equipment two blocks down to the next site, a breakdown job at the edge of the dried-up Crabtree Creek, Watts talked with me and Natalie and the others in their group.

"It is suppose to rain much more this winter," he was saying. He was full of strange facts, I was quickly learning. "Not snow. The hole in the ozone, they say. It is opening again. Good news for us, huh? Not so cold, you see. More sunshine."

Watts and Nat led the way to the top of the ramshackle building, the scrags following us with the cutters. I carried my own hand cutter, used for the smaller pieces of wall and foundation. We were supposed to have the six-story building down by the end of the day.

After dropping most of the northern wall down the side of the building, I felt my wrist buzz. I clicked off my fuser and pretended to be checking the gun's trigger mechanism. We weren't allowed calls on a site, but my first thought had been Lia. *Something's happened to her.*

The words scrolled past on my readout almost too fast for me to read, the wrist screen covered with dust and slivers of plastic. It was Jaime, telling me to meet him that night at that week's jumping. Something about the wall, as usual.

When I looked up from my wrist, the new guy was watching me, a small smile on his face. I gazed back at Watts and nodded, the air cold on the sweat that had broken out on my neck. Then we both returned to our work.

#

We leveled the building by ten, just four of us again, this time Watts instead of Kwabe, along with Nat and Roberts. I'd tried to keep the new guy in my sight most of the day, and it wasn't until just before quitting time that I realized Watts was doing the same to me.

I left the site and walked back home, enjoying the cool air as I thought about the building coming down in big chunks of plaster, insulation, and wood. It was good work, and it was good to feel the ache in my body after a hard day. I was about to go inside our box and get some sleep when I heard Lia's cough again.

"Damn it," I whispered, my hand on the door.

She needed her sleep, and I was still wide awake. Too many of the other people Lia worked with at the factory had been coming down sick, just like her. And the govvie didn't do anything about it. Just as long as we stayed on our side of the wall and didn't cause any kind of problems. Jaime's words from the night of the last wall-jumping came back to haunt me.

I turned, pushing away the fatigue in my legs, and walked towards the wall. Even from here I could hear the jumpers shouting, caroming off the duraplast and into the night on their rickety wings.

Takeem, as the reigning champ, had the night off as other jumpers tried to perfect their form so they could challenge him at next week's jumping. Judging from the three sets of wrecked wings tossed like garbage against the wall, there'd already been quite a few jumpers in need of some work on their form tonight. Some of the broken duraplast wings had already started melting into the wall from where they had been abandoned.

"Hey Chap," Takeem said, glancing over at me from his crowd of admirers. "Things have been weird today, man."

"How so?"

"You must've been asleep on your feet not to see it, man. Watts was bossing me and Nat around all day at the site, and Roberts was acting all scared of him." Takeem pulled away from his crowd. "And I heard something about Kwabe."

"Kwabe?" I gave Takeem a look as something tickled the back of my neck. "He's long gone, Takeem. He's probably forgotten all about us."

"Nah. Someone said they saw him. Out at the pit east of town. Saw his body." Takeem's shoulders were overtaken by a sudden shudder, as if he hadn't thought about what he was saying until just that minute. When it came to the wall, everyone had a damn story. "What happened to him, do you think? Someone must've had it in for him, on the other side, huh?"

"Come on," I said, scanning the crowd for Jaime, trying to shake off the tickling at the base of my neck. "Don't believe everything you hear."

"You gotta admit that it's goddamn weird. Guy earns his points then—"

"Yeah, yeah. It's weird." I said. I didn't have time for this. "Now get on back to your fan club, Takeem. I gotta find someone."

I pushed through the crowd and felt the spit in my mouth turn sour the closer I got to the wall. Most of the people at the jumping were younger than me, scrags, trying to find any kind of thrill before they had to return to work the next morning. I passed some other workers I knew from my first job, then walked onto the old Beltline, still looking for Jaime.

I was ready to give up and go back home when I found myself in front of the wall, the sound of the jumping crowd drowned out by the low vibration it gave off. I looked up at the twenty-plus feet of duraplast. The exterior of the wall was like bruised skin, and I fought the urge to walk up and touch it. If I got too close, would it suck me in like the scrag Nat liked to talk about? I tried to swallow, already feeling nauseous from being so close to it. I hated feeling sick. Touching my wrist implant, I turned away from the wall and the cocoons it protected.

I had to get home, back to Lia. The air was like sandpaper on my skin, biting me through my worn-out jacket. Whatever Jaime had to say, it could wait. I walked away from the wall as young boys and girls flew over my head, bouncing off the wall. Trying to fly.

The walk home took fifteen minutes. Back in the box, I sat next to Lia, waiting for her to wake up. I watched her for close to three hours, until she stirred. I had to do something, and this was as good a place to start as any. I didn't care how much it would cost.

"We're going to the doctor," I said when she woke up at last.

#

The tests at the health center cost me a year's worth of work. Still reeling from the loss, along with a lack of sleep, I stumbled off to the jobsite at five past six. A gray ball of anger was building behind my eyes, pushing away the cold around me. I was tired of working the game.

The initial tests at the center early that morning had been inconclusive. The young doctor, a lightly-accented Indian woman with short black hair, told us that they'd seen more cases like Lia's than she cared to admit. It wasn't tuberculosis, it wasn't pneumonia, it wasn't a virus, but more like select elements of all three. And it didn't seem to ever go away. She promised to keep Lia there longer, a look of nervous frustration on her face as she held out the point reader to me. I'd forced myself to stay calm as I slid my wrist into the metal coupling of the reader, looking away as the points came off. I'd lost this round of the game.

Back at the site, with slabs of old walls piled on the ground where the building once stood, I poured hot coffee down my throat and blinked my sore eyes. Only four of us were at the site, doing cleanup detail. In my rush to get to work this morning, still half-asleep, I'd left my cutter in the front room of Lia's box.

"Hey Marcus," a voice said. I jumped at the sound. I'd been thinking about the redness in Lia's eyes, and the blueness of her lips in the harsh light of the health center.

Nat stood on my left, looking at me quizzically. "You okay?"

"Yeah," I said, tossing my empty cup onto the pile of walls. I listened to the sizzle of plastic dissolving. Nat must have already poured the nanode agents onto the old slabs of wood and drywall. The pile of rubbish would be gone in less than two hours, and then we'd seal the ground for the construction crew moving in today after lunch.

The walls sizzled louder as the agents caught, speeding up the disintegration process. Watts came walking around the corner of the wrecked building.

"Just a rough morning," I said, looking at the pile of rubbish. My cup was gone already.

"Yeah?" Nat said as Watts approached. "What—"

"So," Watts said, leaning close. "What have I miss?"

"Nothing," I said, and stifled a yawn.

Nat gave Watts a long look, then shook her head. "Listen. I've got to check on a new site with Roberts. Can you two hold down the fort here for me?"

"Sure," I said, stepping away from Watts.

Nat walked off, leaving me with the new guy. We stood staring at the pieces of the building as they dissolved in front of us. I was tired, almost asleep, when my wrist buzzed.

I moved away from Watts and held my wrist close to my face. It was the center, about Lia. They were out of space and couldn't help her. They needed me to come get her. I stared at my wrist as the words rolled past again and again. They couldn't help her.

At the edge of the pile of walls, Watts was cutting chunks of wall down to size with his cutter. He glanced over at me. I felt my mouth go sour, as if I was standing in front of the wall again.

"What are you *looking* at?" I said at last. The hiss of the nanode agents filled my ears.

"Wonder who calls you," he said, his voice low. His eyes were shadowed and hidden, but his smile was still there. "You're not suppose to take calls on site."

It was all I could do not to grab to the grinning man next to me. Instead, I looked at my own wrist, at the metal imbedded in my body.

"Watts," I said, my voice tight. I knew I was right about Watts. Here he was, Kwabe's replacement, while Lia coughed her lungs out at the center. Where they couldn't help her. Here was one of *them*, right in front of our noses. "Could I borrow your cutter for one second?"

Without hesitating, Watts held out the cutter.

"Always more like me, you know," Watts said. He let go of the cutter, his smile gone. "Points or no points. The wall has made your people extinct."

"Shut up," I said, activating the cutter. Before I could stop my own hand, I swung the cutter in a low arc and sliced Watts in two.

There was no blood. But that wasn't because of the fuser's ability to instantly cauterize a wound. There was no blood because Watts had no blood inside of him. My wrist began buzzing like a hive of hornets. Already the govvie knew what I'd done.

Squeezing my left hand into a trembling fist, I bent down next to Watts and risked a look at his — *its* — melted innards. Wires, circuits, chips, and pinkish-brown duraplast were sealed together on the severed top and bottom of its body. Jaime had been right after all.

"Just avoiding extinction," I whispered, lifting the cutter again.

With a sudden intake of air, I cut off my left hand just below the wrist. The buzzing and shaking stopped before my hand hit the ground.

There was no blood, only pain as I fell to my knees. I bit off a scream and pushed my hand and the implant it held away from the two halves of the cloneslave. My hand fell into the sizzling pit of nanodes with a tiny thump. I'd learn to live without it.

In spite of the pain, or maybe even because of it, I felt like a new man. The future spread out in front of me: after I picked up Lia from the center, we would go someplace without walls, someplace warm where they still knew how to heal people. We would live in a small house without smart walls, close to the ocean. We could start living for the first time. And that would be worth all the points I could ever earn in a lifetime of labor.

EXPLOSIONS

Of course everyone blames the aliens. But they were working right up until ten minutes before the blast, that's what really bothers me, and that's what makes me think it was all just bad timing. Bad timing for Toshera and me, too, if I stop and think about it. We'd be long gone from here if it hadn't been for the Wannoshay. Now I'm out of work, we've moved everything out of our apartment once again, and the police are asking me what I know.

What I know is this: the Wannoshay had been here only five months when the brewery blew up. They'd crashed to Earth — "fell out of the winter sky" was how the anchors on the Netstream described it — in the middle of a January snowstorm. The few bits of footage I'd had time to download and watch had shown mostly shots of the fenced-off landing site a mile outside Milwaukee, and they hadn't told me anything. Give me good solid facts, not something hidden under a bubble next to someone's soybean field. In any case, work kept me too busy all spring to worry about the aliens.

So it was a surprise to me when Angie, our supervisor, told us in early May that the Wannoshay were coming to the brewery to work, loading and unloading the casks in refrigeration. It was all part of the integration process, Angie had said.

"The mayor wants to show everyone how open and welcoming the people of Milwaukee can be. I think he just wants to earn brownie points with the Wantas so he can check out what's left of their spaceship outside the city."

I knew Roberta would throw a fit when she heard that the aliens would be starting the following Monday. Roberta was ten years older than me, but she looked closer to fifty than forty. Someone told me her Bible-thumping husband, out of his mind on Blur, had stormed a church back in January when the aliens first landed and killed someone there before killing himself. Roberta hadn't been the same since.

As for me, I planned to be down south when I was her age, relaxing in a prefab house close to the beach with my daughter Toshera. I'd 'loaded a program about Myrtle Beach off a neighbor's Netstream, and five seconds into the program I had decided I wanted to smell salt in the air instead of burnt barley and factory smoke. I imagined Toshera's future boyfriends banging on our flimsy door and calling all the time, with the sound of the ocean in the background.

"Shontera," someone said next to me. "*Shontera.*"

I jerked my head up and blinked. Brown bottles were backed up behind my sorter like bugs outside a screen door. Angie stood next to me, holding an inspection keypad and a stamp gun.

"I need you to inspect the last shipment for me again," she said. "Some of the bottles haven't been sealed right, and they're getting skunked. You up to it?"

"Sure," I said, my face hot. I'd been thinking of spaceships falling from the sky like stars, hitting the sandy beach outside our Myrtle Beach dream home with sounds like gunshots.

Angie nodded and walked off, disappearing behind a pallet of twelve-pack boxes.

"Wantas are coming to get you, dreamer," Roberta's voice called out. "Better start paying attention, or they'll steal your *job,* too."

The racket of bottles sliding down the conveyor on their way upstairs to shipping drowned out what I was about to say back to her. It wouldn't have been a friendly response.

I walked along the line, clicking a stamp on an occasional bottle with a crooked cap or a broken seal, pulling them off the line. Sweat dripped into my eyes from the heat of the machines. After a few minutes my mind began to wander again, but instead of thinking about the beach, I found myself thinking about the Wannoshay.

Ever since they came here — "made planetfall," the Netstream anchor's voice blared inside my head — they'd caused nothing but trouble. First was the violence, like Roberta's husband in the church, and then the protests and integration riots when they moved into the old neighborhoods downtown. More troops were patrolling the streets now, including most of the men who used to work next to us in the brewery. Toshera and I, along with all our neighbors, had to leave our apartment complex in February when the landlord raised the rent too high for any of us to afford. Then, after we'd all moved out or got evicted, he cut a deal with a businessman who started renting it out at lower rates to the aliens, hoping to get some free publicity.

A bottle, broken off at the neck, rattled down the line toward me, and I nearly cut myself on it.

"Pay attention, dreamer," I whispered to myself, as the bottles kept coming, never stopping. I clicked the stamp again and again, tallying up the rejects. Each day here on the line was another day closer to leaving Milwaukee behind, forever. Aliens or no aliens.

#

"What's the difference between a Wanta and a Wannoshay, Mom?" Toshera asked the next morning at breakfast. Baked potatoes, left over from last night, and toast. She had on her orange sun earrings, and her brown eyes were almost hidden behind the lenses of her thick glasses. She flattened a mound of sour cream on her potato, then sprinkled sugar on it. Almost all of the other kids in her fifth-grade class had perfect vision, but I couldn't afford the keratotomy like the other parents could. Not if we wanted to get to Myrtle Beach before both of us were old ladies.

"Mom?" Toshera asked again.

"They mean the same thing, honey," I said, swallowing hot coffee, trying to wake up. The apartment felt extra stuffy this morning after the ninety-five-degree temperatures of the past two weeks. Of course the air conditioning had gone out again.

"One is just uglier. I think they like to be called Wannoshay. Why?"

"The kids at school're talking about them. You know, um, ugly stuff."

Toshera pushed up her glasses and watched me. She was growing up so fast, and I felt like I never got to see her.

"I don't get why their kids can't come to school with us."

"They're different, honey. I don't think they can speak our language yet. Though someone at work said *they* can understand *us,* somehow . . . " I swallowed hard and fluttered my T-shirt for a breeze. "Don't worry about them. I imagine they need their space, too, just like us." They already took *ours*, I wanted to say. "Ready to go?"

"Sure," Toshera said, gulping down the last of our milk. I needed to get groceries, but it was only Wednesday, with my next paycheck not until the end of Saturday's shift. We'd get by, somehow. It's not like we had much choice. I handed Toshera her keypad and backpack, and we headed out into the early summer sun. In five more days, the aliens would come to work.

#

Angie, my supervisor, had known for months about my plans to move away, but she never held it against me. She passed me a beer from the mini-fridge in her office, steam rising from the ice-cold bottle. My stomach wanted to turn over at the sight of another bottle of beer after ten hours of staring at bottles on the line, but I twisted off the top anyway and sucked down a big gulp that I could feel all the way down to my toes. Nothing like six o'clock on a Saturday after a long week of work. Hopefully all this overtime will get Toshera and me to the beach that much sooner.

"Monday's the big day, you know," Angie said, adjusting her bra strap with an expert flip of the wrist. "Some of the jokers in shipping are calling it the invasion of the beer snatchers."

I grinned and shook my head. "How come they get stuck down in refrigeration?"

Angie leaned back in her chair, polishing off half her beer. "You really *were* daydreaming the past few days, weren't you? Roberta's been talking non-stop about how the Wannoshay have this ultra-thick skin so they can handle the cold. And they're strong, too. Said she heard all about them from her brother-in-law. He's a cop downtown, on their side."

"So how come they're just starting to work now? What have they been doing the past few months?" I took another long swallow from my beer and thought about their apartments. It all made me want to gag.

"Stuff like this takes time," she said. "Remember how everyone was convinced back in January that the aliens were invading, that when their ratty old ships crash-landed they were just the first wave of some army of killer space aliens? At least we didn't have riots here like they did in Minneapolis."

I nodded, thinking about the packed churches after earlier this year. Lots of folks had thought it was the Second Coming or Armageddon, or both. I thought of Roberta's husband and shuddered. "I guess you're right. Maybe if there *had* been an invasion, I wouldn't have gotten evicted from my old apartment."

Angie opened another beer and gave a quick laugh. She leaned back again and flipped the bottle top onto the table. "This is like nothing else we've ever experienced, Shontera. The company's trying to send a message to the rest of the country by bringing the Wannoshay here to work so quickly after they arrived. But hey, what do you care? You're going to be long gone soon, right?"

She's right, I thought. But for now, I had to get home. I stood up too quickly and swayed a little — too much cold beer on an empty stomach. Angie walked me to the door and patted me on the back, and my T-shirt stuck to me where her hand had touched me.

She must have seen something on my face, because she said, "Don't worry," and then laughed. "What are they going to do, kill us all and take over the place?"

I wanted to laugh, but my mouth was too dry. I opened the door and walked past the second-shift workers on our line, busy sorting bottles and inspecting labels. Even if the economy was crap, people still wanted to drink beer, probably even more so in times like these. It wasn't until I got outside of the brewery, smelling and tasting stale beer with each step, that I realized I'd taken the long way out, avoiding the refrigeration cellars in some kind of unthinking fear.

#

I opened my eyes a minute before the alarm. It can't be Monday already, I thought.

Toshera stood next to me, her hand clutched to her head. God, not the headaches again. The school nurse claimed it was from the out-of-date prescription of her glasses. When we went down south, we'd be able to buy new glasses. Maybe even get the laser treatments.

"Morning, honey," I said. "You okay?"

"My head hurts." Toshera gave me a look that told me she hadn't wanted to admit it.

"It's okay, honey," I said. "Let's get you some extra-strength painkillers and get you off to school, okay? Only two more weeks before summer break, you know."

"Yeah," Toshera said, rubbing her temples. She put her glasses back on with a grimace. I'd have to take her to the doctor this weekend. It would be too late to get her into the clinic tonight when I got off at six. I wanted to think of the beach and Toshera in her bright red swimsuit next to me in the sand, but all I could think of was what Roberta had said in one of the gossip sessions I'd tried so hard to ignore. "They have snakes for hair, and they eat dirt."

"Mom," Toshera said, breaking me out of my daydreams. "Can we go to the Wanta section of town this weekend?" In the kitchen, I put two pieces of bread into the toaster. "Our teachers say they need volunteers to teach the Wantas English. Could we go, do you think?"

"Wannoshay, honey," I said, too harshly. They'd be at the brewery at eight o'clock this morning, ready to start work. "Don't call them that ugly name."

"Okay, okay. So can we go over there sometime?"

I smelled something burning. I snatched the toast out of the toaster. "Go where, honey?"

"Mom! Quit being such a dreamer."

I turned on Toshera, dropping pieces of burnt toast on the floor. "No. No, we're not going over to see the aliens. Not this weekend, not ever." I could feel myself starting to yell, but I couldn't stop myself. "Can't you see that we have enough problems right here? Leave the Wantas alone, Toshera."

Toshera shrugged her shoulder out of my grip. I hadn't realized my hand had been there until that moment.

"Call them Wannoshay, Mom. Wanta's an ugly word. You said so yourself."

#

That first morning, Roberta was early for a change. Her voice echoed through the quiet of the brewery at ten minutes before eight, and I couldn't help but listen to her.

"They all live in the same house and sleep in the same bed. They don't have families like we do. Just a whole bunch of aliens with snakes for hair, all huddled together like rats. They're probably tunneling their way under the city right now, as we sit around with our thumbs up our butts. I even heard

93

they can have sex with any other Wanta they want, and they think we're childish for having husbands and wives."

"Well, my husband's pretty childish," Ann-Marie said, and everyone laughed but Roberta. I turned away when I saw the flash of pain on her wrinkled face.

The first-shift buzzer went off and the line started. Toshera's painkillers should have kicked in by now, I hoped.

"Heads up, Shontera," Juanita whispered next to me, on her way to her station. She pointed up at the stairway and the steel double doors leading down to our section of the factory. Mark Stevens stood there, sweating through his white dress shirt and holding the door open.

This must be them.

A tall, thin person with what looked like thick dreadlocks walked through the door, swaying his back in a strange, jerky motion with each step. His legs were too short, and his ragged-looking pants were cuffed four or five times. Another person stepped through, then another, all of them built the same way. Before I knew it, a dozen of the thin, gray-skinned aliens stood on the landing next to Mark. Up and down the line, everyone else had stopped to look.

"*Dios mio*," Juanita whispered, stepping up next to me. Her eyes were wide.

When I glanced back at the doorway, Mark had gotten the parade of Wannoshay moving again. I looked closer at the aliens as they made their way down the steps. None of them wore shoes, and each narrow, grayish-blue foot had only four toes. Their hands and feet seemed to have been switched — their hands had toes, and their feet had fingers. At first I thought their oversized rib cages and long backs meant that they were all men, but then I noticed two aliens in the middle of the group with what must have been breasts.

They won't even *look* at us, I thought.

As I watched, the third Wannoshay in the slow parade began to sway. He looked like a tower blowing in the wind. The muscles in my stomach clenched when his wide shoulders swung violently from side to side, and he began moaning. He dropped to all fours, and I saw scars crisscrossing the backs of both of his big hands.

The aliens on either side of him put their hands on him, one on his back and the other in his quivering hair. A low humming drowned out his moaning. As quickly as it had begun, before Mark had even noticed the disturbance, the Wannoshay was back on his feet and walking toward the cellars as if nothing had happened.

"*Dios mio,*" Juanita whispered again, but this time the wonder in her voice had been replaced with fear and a trace of disgust.

The other aliens hurried past me, but one of the two females walked slower, her dark eyes taking in everything around her. She wore faded, cuffed-up jeans and a too-short Packers T-shirt that looked twenty years old.

Is she going to try and talk to me? I wondered. Do they even talk? Maybe they used some sort of sign language, or telepathy. I knew I should've paid more attention to the stories Toshera had downloaded from the Netstreams.

The rattle of glass on glass brought me back to reality. Bottles had backed up for ten yards on the line. I reached for a bottle, checked the label and the seal — and it slid out of my sweaty hands. It bounced off the rubber bumpers on the belt and would have smashed to the floor if a gray foot hadn't stopped its fall.

It was the female Wannoshay, the one with the curious eyes.

She balanced easily on her left foot and stretched her right leg up to me, at chest level, holding the stray bottle. Her four long toes were wrapped around the neck of the brown bottle like thick fingers. Her hands hung down almost uselessly at her side, fingers hooked like claws that glistened like metal. Her eyes were totally black. All three of them. The line in the middle of her forehead had parted, becoming a sideways eye that stared at me.

"Thanks," I whispered, my voice high. I could smell a musty odor coming from her, a salty smell stronger than the bitter hops-and-barley odor of the factory.

Her wide mouth moved in a strange way, rippling almost. "'Angks," she said. I felt her voice in my head more than in my ears. It *was* some sort of telepathy. I shivered, and grabbed at the bottle clumsily. I couldn't seem to get my breath back. Something ugly inside of me made sure I touched only the bottle, not her foot.

With the bottle tight in my grasp, I looked back at the line and saw Roberta watching me, her face puckered with concentration. When I turned back to the Wannoshay woman, the alien was gone, leaving behind only a strangely comforting tang of salt that made me yearn for an ocean I'd never seen, at least not yet.

#

The E bus was late that night, and the sun hung just below the tall buildings on State Street when I got back to our apartment. I passed through the flimsy security arch and skipped the rickety elevator. Panting in the hot air of our hallway at the end of six flights of stairs, I unlocked the three deadbolts to my door, and opened it. I stood there for a moment, the key still in my hand. The place was quiet and hot, and there weren't any lights or fans on. Toshera never went to bed this early. I walked inside. The place smelled stale, just like the attic in Mom and Dad's old house.

"Toshera," I said, opening the bedroom door and letting it bang against the wall. It was even hotter in here, and the air felt like cotton in my lungs. A lump stuck out of the mattress, covered in the thick woolen blankets we had stored in the closet.

"Mommy," Toshera's voice peeped out at the head of the bed. "My head hurts, bad. The nurse sent me home." Her voice was thick from crying. My hands curled up into fists against my legs, thinking about her by herself all day in the stuffy apartment.

"Toshera, honey, let's get you out from under there," I said. Under the two blankets, the sheet covering her thin body was soaked with sweat. She wore her heavy University of Wisconsin sweatshirt and two pairs of sweatpants, and she was still shivering.

"Mommy, I'm sorry I'm sick," Toshera whispered. Closing her eyes, she rested her hot forehead on my shoulder. We were going to have to go to the clinic and pay the after-hours fee. Another week or two of saving down the drain.

"Enough about that," I whispered. I pulled out my money card and called a cab. We struggled down the stairs, Toshera leaning on me. She was crying when we reached the lobby. I started talking without really thinking about what I was saying.

"They came to work today, Toshera. The Wannoshay. I got to meet one. They're really, really tall, and they don't have hair like you and me." I described the aliens as best I could, and the words fell out of me faster and faster, like the way the bottles on the line flew past when everything was operating right. I told Toshera about their gray skin, their three black eyes, and the way they walked half-hunched over as if they'd rather go on all fours like a horse. I even told her about the way the female alien had saved the bottle of beer for me, catching it with her narrow foot and finger-like toes.

The cab came at last, and Toshera and I crawled in. It had air conditioning, and it felt cold, wonderfully cold. Like the way jumping into the ocean must feel on a hot day.

"What was her name?" Toshera asked, sitting up straight.

"Her name?" I looked at Toshera and thought about the alien woman's three eyes staring at me. She had no name, as far as I knew. No name. "Nonami," I said, almost laughing out loud.

"What kind of name is that?" Toshera asked.

"An alien name," I said, squeezing her.

The cab stopped in front of the clinic, and the driver swiped my card through his reader with a clicking sound. More money down the drain. But we'd make it out of here yet, I promised myself, sooner or later.

#

The day everything went to hell, two weeks later, Roberta claimed she'd lost her money card, and she kept saying one of the aliens had taken it.

We'd finally cut back to eight-hour days, but the temperatures outside stayed in the nineties. I saw Nonami every workday during those two weeks, on her way to breaks and at the end of shifts. We never spoke. She was always with the other aliens, and ten more had been hired at the start of this week. Angie told me they could work all day and all night if we wanted them to.

"What are you going to do about this?" Roberta shouted at Angie that day at the end of May. "I need my money, and I know that damn Wanta has my card." Roberta turned toward me. I felt my face burn. "I bet *she* knows all about this. She's been talking to them."

"Shut up, Roberta," Angie said in her quiet way. "Shontera's not a thief."

Things might have blown over then if the aliens hadn't been on their way back down to the cellars after their ten-thirty break. They shuffled past on their short legs, swaying as they walked. They always looked like they were about to fall over.

"Don't you dare look at me, you thief!" Roberta screamed at one of them, her voice cracking. I'd never heard her sound so angry, or scared. The group of Wannoshay hurried past the lines, but the male she had yelled at stopped in front of her, standing up straight. He looked like he was over seven feet tall.

The alien raised his hand toward her, palm out. I think he was only reaching out to Roberta to explain. Or maybe he wanted to silence her, to permanently stop her lips from moving. Even now I don't know for sure.

What I know is this: he touched Roberta, and something *changed* in her. As if she were a balloon full of anger, and the alien had sucked the bad air out of her with his touch. When he let go of her, Roberta looked at him for a long moment with her face deflated, then she started moaning. It was loud and high-pitched, full of fear, and it lasted close to ten seconds. She didn't sound *human*. The memory of it still keeps me up at night.

The sound brought the other women on the line running, along with some of the people up in shipping. Roberta was that loud. The Wannoshay male stepped back, even more unsteady than usual, then he suddenly bent down. He touched his hands to the floor like a runner waiting for a starting gun. Both hands had a set of scars, like a strange tic-tac-toe pattern. Each alien had a different design carved into his or her hands, I'd noticed. Like fingerprints.

Staring at the Wannoshay, along with the rest of the humans who stood back from him at a safe distance, I realized that this creature wasn't human. I'd never understand him the way I would another person. The thought scared me, but it also made me feel something else. Sadness, maybe.

After hunching there, quivering, for five seconds, he ran down to the cellar on all fours like a huge dog, and Roberta fell forward onto the line, knocking bottles of beer to the floor and shattering them in tiny explosions, one after the other.

#

Ten minutes later, the noises began in the refrigeration cellars. I recognized the hissing sounds from when the coolers went off-line a few months ago, but this time there was a banging down there that kept getting louder and louder. Like someone was punching at the walls, trying to get out. Angie hadn't come back yet from taking care of Roberta, and Juanita and the rest of the women on our line were getting scared.

After another ten minutes, the rattling became a booming. Then the cellar doors crashed open and one lone alien male, Roberta's Wannoshay, ran out on all fours, his skin glowing white with frost. His mouth was a perfect circle of agony. Every place his hands and feet touched the floor, he left a crystallized footprint that immediately condensed into a puddle.

Seconds later, the remaining Wannoshay came running up out of the cellars, their hands and feet pounding on the concrete floor. I saw Nonami for a second in the middle of the pack. They sprinted past us, running on all fours, and disappeared up the stairs. Everyone else on the line followed them in a blind panic.

Except me. I heard the blasting sounds in one part of my mind, but in the other part I kept hearing Roberta's moaning. I walked away from the lines, where bottles of beer had started slamming into each other. I had to see what had happened in the cellars.

I walked down the cold, wet steps as if I was in some kind of dream. A smell filled the air, mixing with the familiar smell of barley and smoke. It was the salty smell of the aliens. It was also the smell of blood. I tiptoed down into the first refrigeration cellar, a square room filled with hissing and churning valves. Half of the valves were broken, spewing out coolant, and fist-sized holes covered the metal walls.

On the floor, three bleeding Wannoshay men lay motionless. The whimpering sound was out of my mouth before I could stop it. I'd never seen a dead person before. Or a dead alien, for that matter.

I felt more than heard the first explosion only two rooms away, my eardrums aching and my sinuses clogging. Maybe this was what the ocean was like when the waves got too rough for swimming. I was staring at a handful of wires dangling like snakes from one of the holes, spitting sparks, when something touched my back.

"Leave," a voice whispered in my head, loud and clear despite the noise of the malfunctioning equipment around me. I turned my head to see Nonami. "Leave now," her voice said, and she put her other hand on my back.

My entire body jerked into motion as if I'd been jolted with electricity, and I almost fell on my way past the three dead aliens sprawled on the floor. Behind us, the other rooms had caught fire. Black smoke filled the air, reaching toward us as we ran up the steps, me on two feet, Nonami on all fours. Behind us, the copper aging tanks in the cellars blew, one after another.

A pair of strong hands reached for me, keeping me on my feet. A vision of

Roberta's alien entered my mind, as if Nonami's soothing touch had placed it there, trying to show me where he'd gone wrong in trying to help Roberta. How some people — like Roberta — refused to give up their own anger and fear. How his contact with her had driven him mad. Nonami half-carried, half-dragged me through the steel double doors as the explosions behind us continued. I remember seeing the strange scars on the backs of her hands as well. Hers were two straight lines around a curly, spiral design.

As I held on, another vision filled my head, this time of a mountainous, black and gray landscape littered with caves under a cold, blue-tinted sun. The sun grew fainter and fainter with each breath I took, until the landscape fell away beneath me, and I couldn't get any air. I felt like I was flying, blasting off into space from a dying planet. I wanted to cry out at the sight of the planet shrinking below me, but I couldn't inhale.

We can never go back, Nonami's voice whispered in my head. Then we were outside and I could breathe again.

I wanted to ask her what it all meant, why that blue sun had scared me so much, and what Roberta's anger had done to the alien. But the crowds had already begun chasing the aliens away, waving fists, stun sticks, and broken beer bottles, and Nonami just disappeared. The brewery erupted a minute later.

#

Now everything has changed. I don't have a job, the brewery won't be rebuilt for another year or two, and almost all our money is gone. I gave in yesterday and talked to a Netstream reporter about what I'd seen the day of the explosions, and the cash card he gave me in return for the big story gave me the cash to get Toshera new lenses for her glasses. I told him enough about that day, but not everything. Nonami's visions I kept to myself.

Three days have passed since the explosions, and the aliens have been under constant surveillance ever since. And the police have been calling and stopping by our place at all hours. They want to know what I had to do with what happened.

I'd explain it all to them if I could.

Toshera and I have just enough money to get to Mom and Dad's on the bus. They live out in the country, near the Iowa border. It's not near as far south as I'd hoped, but it's a start.

I've got the tickets in my pocket, but there's one place I need to visit first. Toshera wanted to go with me, but I need to go by myself. I have to force myself to remember what the alien did to Roberta that day, and what he did to the three Wannoshay in the cellars, and how, two blocks away from the rubble of the brewery, they found his body frozen solid. But I also keep thinking about how much less angry Roberta has been since that day. How she's become almost human.

So I begin walking the streets of the neighborhood downtown where we lived before we had to move the first time, hoping against hope to find Nonami. Before I start asking her questions, though, I want to thank her. For getting me out of the burning brewery, and for getting me out of Milwaukee and headed south, even if it's not the way I'd planned on things working out.

Then — after I've thanked her, of course, and after she's told me her real name — we'll talk, woman to woman, about what *really* happened that day, and what will happen next.

WANTAVIEWER

Alissa Trang couldn't keep herself away from the Winnipeg slums, so she called in sick for her evening shift behind the counter at CanTechWorld once again and hitched a ride up Highway 3 into the city. For the entire ride from Sanford to Winnipeg, not wanting to be late, she had to keep her mouth clamped shut to keep from screaming at the old man driving the antique Saab to go faster. Faster. Everything in the world moved too slowly when Ally wasn't using Blur. And if the rumors about the aliens she'd been hearing were true, she might be able to find more than Blur in the city, so long as she kept her eyes open and her camera ready.

She leaped out of the car as soon as it stopped at the intersection of Portage and Maryland. Ally knew the elderly driver hadn't wanted to be caught in this part of the city, but she'd also known that he'd take her wherever she wanted if she let her skirt ride up higher on her legs, which were covered in black tights. As the old car sped off, Ally began to power-walk down the quiet street. She adjusted the fingernail-sized rectangle of her lapel camera and made sure the recorder in her pocket, connected to the camera, was still running. She smiled, knowing she'd gotten some great footage of the old fart checking her out while he gripped the wheel.

She hurried along the streets, her gaze moving without thought over the broken windows and the fire-scarred brick buildings that peppered the urban landscape. Keeping her vinyl coat zipped up tight, she wished she had her butterfly knife with her, but one of her housemates had borrowed it last week and lost it. To reassure herself, she touched the handful of explosive caplets of Mace in one coat pocket and checked that she had all five mini-DVDs in her other pocket next to her recorder.

Her coat rustling with each step, Ally hurried down Sargent Avenue and entered the main section of the run-down neighborhood. Boarded-up restaurants and businesses stared at her from below dark apartment windows, empty places that had simply given up in the past few years of recession. Jenae, her Blur dealer and occasional friend, lived above an abandoned bakery at the heart of the neighborhood.

Ally forced down her growing impulse to simply sprint like a madwoman down the street to her supplier's home. An electric car ambled past her, the black-tinted security windows hiding its passengers, and Ally edged closer to the rubble of the old pharmacy on her right. She calmed herself by thinking about how good it would feel to get a pink capsule of Blur in her, and to take a couple more back home to help get through the next day or two. With some Blur, she could face down a dirt-eating, two-meter-tall alien if she had to.

Now *that*, Ally thought, checking her lapel camera, would make a great flick.

#

Winded after rushing through the strangely deserted neighborhood, Ally at last stood outside Jenae's closed apartment and knocked three times. Jenae wasn't in. Or at least she wasn't opening her door, something she was prone to do if she was high or if the mood simply struck her.

Ally pounded on the dented, multi-locked door for another minute or two until she heard movement inside. She stopped, not wanting to piss off Jenae's upstairs neighbor. Milt was no one to mess with, especially at night, when he was cooking up Blur and God-only-knew what else in his apartment laboratory. Remembering that it was still on, Ally flicked off her tiny camera and gripped the cold metal of the doorframe. She contemplated banging her head on the door until someone answered.

The door popped open just as Ally was about to try it. It was Jenae. Without a word she pulled Ally inside. Jenae's usually pale face was flushed red, and Ally counted two facial tics before Jenae closed the door behind them. The skinny young woman was shivering as she strode across the floor to the couch, every movement exaggerated and too fast.

Jenae was whacked on Blur. Ally fought off a wave of intense jealousy and need.

Taking Blur was like a combination of the best, most addictive aspects of every other drug Ally Trang had ever taken. When Ally was on Blur, the rest of the world turned to so much fuzz while she zipped through the simplest of tasks at warp speed. Even peeling an orange became a race for the most dexterous fingers this side of the Red River.

The only things she didn't like about Blur were coming down from it — "flashing" — and the way the world crept in on her while she was sober, pressing down on her with its mundane weight and distracting her to no end.

And tonight Jenae had Blur, and as a result, tonight Jenae was Ally's hero. Ally already had her money card out.

"What's new up here?" Ally asked, pocketing the dozen pink capsules Jenae had sold to her for fifty dollars apiece. There goes most of this week's paycheck, Ally thought with a wince.

After snapping shut her metal box filled with Blur and tapping a few keys on the console to lock it, Jenae returned Ally's card to her.

"Cops," Jenae said. "We-got-'em-everywhere." Her words ran into each other as she rocked back and forth on the dirty carpet.

Ally swallowed a pink capsule and grimaced, the drug burning all the way down. "No way. They finally figure out Milt's operation upstairs?" Ally grinned, already feeling her pulse pick up. Finally. *Finally.*

"Nah," Jenae said. "Putting-up-a-show. Getting-ready-for-the-Wannoshit-invasion, y'know."

Ally gave a mock-serious nod. As she spoke, she felt her own words begin to pick up speed. "Oh, that's all. Thought we had something *serious* to worry about. But an invasion — shit. Nothing-to-worry-'bout."

They laughed, Jenae louder than Ally, cackling for ten seconds straight, and then she passed out. Her heels rattled on the floor as she trembled and quivered on her back.

The first time she'd seen this, Ally had panicked, thinking Jenae was having some kind of seizure. But she now knew better. She looked across the filthy apartment with its broken wallscreen and scarred furniture, looking up at the windows covered in masking tape, and then down at Jenae's skinny, trembling body. She waited for the drug to kick in. Jenae was on her own; Ally had just wanted to get her Blur and go out into the chilly March air to get some more footage. Unlike Sanford, there was always something good to see around here in the city.

#

Ally left Jenae's apartment with her vision tripled. She jumped down the steps and jogged to the next block of the dark, quiet streets, unable to move slowly anymore. She felt every muscle in her body twitch as if she'd been hit with tiny bolts of lightning. Ally wondered if she could make it back to her place in Sanford, thirty kilometers away, if she started running now. As usual, she hadn't made any plans for getting back home that night.

She paused for breath on a cracked sidewalk on Ellice Avenue. Trying to stand still was a little war raging inside her, but it kept the cold from affecting her. Just as she was wondering what had happened to all the traffic, a high-pitched squealing sound filled the air. Ally stood on the sidewalk, her arms shaking like loose wires, and held her breath for as long as she dared. The squeal grew closer, turning into a buzzing hum as the vehicle down-shifted. With a dull gnawing sensation in her stomach, she realized she hadn't seen any traffic on the street all night.

Cops, Ally thought. Something's up.

As the hum got louder, Ally finally ran and hid in the recessed entrance to an abandoned Thai restaurant. Sweat covered her face and dampened her armpits as she crouched in the darkness, peeking around the corner. The first electric bus pulled up a second later.

"Oh-shit," Ally whispered. "Oh-shit-shit-shit."

She pulled the recorder from her coat pocket with trembling hands and looked at the readout. The current disc was almost full. Ally knew she should've used the camera's wireless feature to stream the footage directly to her Netstream, but she hadn't been able to sit still long enough to learn how to do it.

The hum of the buses faded as first one, then another, and finally a third electric bus pulled to a stop half a block from Ally, who was desperately trying to reload her recorder. None of the buses had windows. When she got the tiny disk reloaded, she touched the sensor on her lapel and wished she'd brought the eyebrow unit from work. The footage from the piece-of-shit lapel camera always came out grainy and dark. And the light here completely sucked.

Her right foot tapped on the cold cement outside the restaurant when the doors to the buses opened. Ally's vision was tripling again as she fought the drug in her system, trying to will herself into sobriety, something that always made the Blur high even more intense.

The first to step off the three buses was a line of shadowy soldiers armed with rifles, their shiny camos and helmets blending into the dark green exterior of the bus. Once she'd gained control of her tapping foot, Ally leaned around the corner wall of the alcove, holding her lapel camera up and out. For the first time she noticed that the lights were on in the apartments above the closed businesses, and the "Open" sign was glowing in front of the old Howard Johnson's, details she'd been too busy enjoying her Blur high to notice before.

Something salty and moist tickled Ally's nose. At first she thought it was a bug or maybe the whiff of ozone left by the electric buses, but then she realized the smell was different. It was a scent she couldn't recognize, and it made her skin turn into gooseflesh. She was smelling . . . aliens. Wantas.

"Oh-my-God," she whispered, even before the first one stepped off the bus, a dark green Army bag clutched in its big hands. She couldn't see if the creature had fingers or not.

Just a delusion, she thought to herself. Nothing to worry about, really.

Most of the streetlights had been broken out long ago, keeping the creatures coming off the bus mostly hidden in shadows along with the soldiers. To Ally, they looked like regular people, but taller and less graceful than most humans. They walked with a strange swaying movement, and their legs looked too short. Some bent over onto all fours, which seemed a more natural position for them.

Ally felt a pang of disappointment at not being able to hallucinate something nastier, or at least something less human in nature. Their skin was pale, but with a bluish tint in the weak light thrown off by the running lights of the bus.

Ally found herself staring at their feet, her lungs full of icy air as she inhaled over and over again. Each bare foot had only four toes. Four toes as long as her fingers. She exhaled, her hot breath clouding up in the cold air.

That image clinched it for her — this was no Blur-addled delusion. These were *aliens.*

"Jesus H," she whispered, hugging herself tightly while recording everything she saw, "Fuckin'-better-not-erase *this.*"

She continued filming as the aliens filed off the bus, gathering together mostly in groups of five or seven, though sometimes just in pairs. Some teetered precariously, off-balance, while a pair of shorter aliens began pushing each other as soon as they stepped onto the street. The soldiers quickly separated them.

Including those on all fours, the aliens looked gaunt and spindly compared to the human soldiers next to them. Those that were upright walked half hunched over, like a tall person who was trying to look shorter. In complete silence, the aliens carried their bags off the bus and were led into the hotel by soldiers. They followed obediently, but occasionally one or two would look over in her direction, heads cocked to the side as if *smelling* her, even from over a hundred meters away. One of them stopped and looked directly at her, his or her — its — face hidden in shadows, and Ally had to clamp both hands over her mouth to keep from making a sound. The alien shuddered and crouched forward, clenching its four-fingered hands into fists the size of Ally's head.

Not sure if the strange ringing sensation inside her head was caused by the flashing of the Blur in her system or her closeness to the aliens, Ally held her breath and stared. Finally, the alien relaxed and straightened up with a crackling sound. The alien lumbered after the others, broad shoulders still twitching occasionally.

Ally forced herself to breathe again, and when she did, her heightened senses picked up movement off to her left. She peeked through the broken windows of the restaurant and saw a group of cops coming up the street on foot. They checked each doorway, and some of them disappeared into abandoned buildings. They were less than a block away.

Stifling a sudden urge to scream in frustration, Ally bit down on her bottom lip when she realized she was trapped: aliens on her right and cops on her left. She packed the recorder and mini-DVDs into the depths of her vinyl coat, keeping the camera running. The door to the restaurant was locked, but the window next to her was broken, backed up with plywood. Pushing against the plywood, Ally slipped into the restaurant as quietly as she could. She bit down even harder on her lip as she snagged her arms and legs on the shards of glass left in the window frame and dropped, bleeding, to the floor of the restaurant.

Short seconds later, a female cop wearing a black leather jacket and faded jeans stopped outside the door to the restaurant, but she left after trying the door and finding it locked. Ally touched the disks in her pocket.

The Wantas have come to town, she thought. And I've got it all recorded right here. The download potential was going to be huge, and she knew she'd make a killing from it.

Her arms quivering from the shallow cuts criss-crossing them, her coat and tights torn and wet with blood, Alissa nearly burst out laughing at her current state. But all the excitement and her burst of adrenaline had killed her Blur high. All over her body, her muscles began to ache with fatigue from the Blur and her power-walking.

She lay back onto the dusty floor, her vision going gray, and the cold late-March air washed over her. With a heavy hand, she reached up to turn off her camera so she didn't waste more disc space. With her arms and legs twitching in their own random dance, her breath whistling in and out of her mouth, Ally Trang lost consciousness.

#

A few weeks after her painful night spent on the floor of the restaurant, once her scratches had healed and she'd recovered from the bout of pneumonia she'd picked up as a result of that night, Ally was back in Winnipeg. She parked her newly-fixed clunker of a car on Toronto Street and swallowed a second capsule of Blur. The drug helped her remember the bits of the Wannoshay language she'd found on the 'streams, and she'd been preparing for this day ever since that cold night.

She entered the Winnipeg neighborhood flying high, but not so high that she wasn't on the lookout for soldiers or plain-clothes police officers (she knew who they were, try as they might to act like they were regular people). But the soldiers on Ellice Avenue seemed more interested in protecting the Wannoshay from anti-integrationists and cultists than they were with her presence there. They ran a wand over her, okayed her camera, and checked her ID card. Ally was allowed to walk unescorted through the neighborhood. The government had decided to keep the new Wannoshay dwellings accessible, thinking that would ease the fears of integration, but not *too* accessible.

She passed by the uneven rows of disposable Netstream cams dotting the buildings of the neighborhood, glued to the walls by reporters hoping to catch the first hints of any worthwhile Wannoshay news. She held up both middle fingers to the cams on her way past them. If she were taller she'd reach up, rip them down, and stamp on them. Bunch of amateurs, letting the cams do the work for you.

As her own camera recorded the renovations taking place in buildings that had been empty for over a decade, Ally was surprised to not see more aliens outside. The sun had been bright all morning, yet another uncommonly hot spring day, but clouds had gathered as she wandered up and down Ellice. With the sun gone, the air had turned cooler, and Ally saw three aliens walk out of the old Thai restaurant she'd hidden in on the night the Wannoshay came to town. The window had been replaced recently, and silvery holo-stickers were still stuck to the glass.

Up and down the street, more aliens came outside, sweeping off the sidewalks or picking up garbage that had blown onto the street. The three Wannoshay outside the restaurant were cleaning the new windows under the casually watchful eyes of the pair of young CF soldiers with rifles slung across their backs.

Ally's throat locked up when she was five meters from the aliens and the soldiers, and she stopped. Her legs wouldn't move her any closer. She could smell them, and she could hear their muscles creak as they scraped the stickers off the glass and washed the windows.

The aliens were tall and made her nose itch and her ears ring. Their long hair was thick and ropy, hanging partway down their broad backs. At the ends of their too-short legs, the feet Ally remembered so clearly from earlier were still bare, their long finger-toes clutching the concrete sidewalk like claws, as if they were afraid of being top-heavy and toppling over if they leaned too far one way or the other. They were well over two meters tall.

They wore second-hand clothes that didn't fit their bodies well — cuffed jeans held up with rope belts around their thick waists and T-shirts. Ally stared, wondering why nobody had attempted to make clothes for the aliens that actually fit their odd bodies. Surely there was money to be made in that area.

Thinking about the Wannoshay she'd seen getting out of the buses on that dark, Blurry night, Ally almost kept walking past the aliens hunched over their work, silent in their concentration. Then she saw a pair of 'stream reporters across the street, attaching more cams to a wall and searching for an alien to talk to. Gritting her teeth, Ally felt a burst of energy from the Blur, and her confidence doubled as she thought about how great some real footage by a real person, not some clueless hack reporter, would look on her Netstream. Lots of download potential there, and she needed the income — she'd already blown almost all the money she'd made from charging for the her footage of the aliens' first night in Winnipeg. She'd been rich with Blur for less than a month.

"Hello," Ally said, stepping up to the three aliens in front of the restaurant and making sure the tiny camera on her shirt was aimed at them. The Wannoshay towered above her, their long backs turned away from her. They continued working.

"Excuse me," Ally said. "Hello? Um, *huwatcha?*"

As soon as she spoke her last word, all three aliens looked back at her, their heads swiveling around impossibly far on their long necks. The ropy tentacles on heads of the two taller aliens quivered toward Ally as if smelling her. They appeared to be female, while the shorter, fatter one seemed to be male.

Their hair moves, Ally thought, her heartbeat tripling. She rubbed her nose, trying to get the salty-sweet smell out of it. Holy-shit-their-hair-moves!

"I'm—a . . . reporter," she lied, forcing herself to talk slowly and clearly despite the Blur in her system pushing her to go faster, faster. The lie came easily to her Blur-numbed lips. "I am working on a story. About integration. For your people. Could I talk with you? Um . . . *Allola?*"

She pointed at the sparkling clean glass of the window, then at the buckets, sponges, and squeegees around them. Ally had heard that the aliens knew a smattering of English — she'd been secretly hoping they'd learn French first, but the pushy Americans got their way, teaching them English, even those in Canada. She'd also heard that they often preferred communicating with gestures and tones. Which would be great for some quality footage, she figured.

Now that she was close to the aliens, Ally could see why speech wasn't preferable for them — their wide, lipless mouths weren't shaped the same as humans' mouths were. She made a waving motion with her hand in front of her mouth, trying to pantomime words coming from her.

Oh shit, this sucks, she thought, wishing she could take more Blur so she could recall the Wannoshay words better.

The shorter alien looked at her intently with his dark eyes, and then the sideways eye in the middle of its forehead opened. Ally swallowed a gasp; for an awful split-second it had looked like the gray-and-black-haired alien's forehead was splitting open. His hair quivered and moved like tiny snakes, but his tentacles were lighter in color and much shorter than the other two aliens next to him.

"Yesh, *allola*," the short alien said, pronouncing the word with a stress on the first syllable. "We talgh."

Ally exhaled and almost started giggling. The salt smell had been replaced by not unpleasant spicy scent. It was working.

The shorter alien was more hunched than the others, making him seem like the oldest of the three. Further setting him apart from the females, the third eye of the male was had flecks of white around the black iris, instead of complete blackness. When he set down his scraper, Ally saw a series of inter-connected triangles and one tiny circle carved into the back on his long hand.

He raised his right hand palm up, dipping his head forward as if to say, "After you." Inhaling a hint of vanilla along with the salty, spicy smells around her, Ally could have sworn she heard a voice say those words inside her head.

"This-okay?" Ally said to the two National Guard soldiers, who had taken a few steps closer to her and the Wannoshay. The soldier on the left nodded. "Great-thanks," she called to them, feeling her voice speeding up again. "Thanks-great."

The other two aliens were females, if Ally was safe in assuming the bumps under their T-shirts were breasts. Their skin was darker, more of a deep gray-black, and Ally caught the glint of metal in their jet-black hair. They also set down their cleaning tools. All three aliens squatted low, resting their backs against the brick wall next to the window. They were now exactly Ally's height.

Relax, she told herself. The hard part's over.

"Let's-start-with . . . " Ally took a deep breath and willed her hands to stop shaking and screwing up the camera's shot. "Let's . . . start . . . with names . . . ? I'm Alissa Trang. Alissa. My-gahawa-Alissa."

"A-issha," the aliens repeated. The older male's voice was lower than those of the two female aliens, though all three voices were deeper than a human's. Ally wanted to examine the scars on the back of their hands more closely, but they were looking at her now with intent black eyes, waiting. She'd have to watch the footage later for details.

"Close-enough," she said, swallowing. She pointed at the male and raised her eyebrows. "Your-name-is? Your *gahawa*?"

The male only stared at her, his oval face blank. The look on his face made her think of Marlon Brando, in his last movie before his death. Old Marlon had played a bald con man who faked Alzheimer's to fool his marks.

Feeling foolish under the gaze of those black eyes, Ally touched her chest and repeated her name. She did her best to ignore the two soldiers, who had stopped talking and were watching her intently, probably wondering if they'd slipped up by letting her inside, especially if she was some suicide cultist who had come to wreak havoc with the Wantas. She reached a hand up toward Brando's chest. He didn't flinch, but his middle eye narrowed and his spiky hair pulled straight back, away from her.

As the sun came out again, Ally raised her eyebrows and gave Brando her best questioning look. Stay calm, stay calm, don't get frustrated. One of the females snorted and twitched next to him, as if she were laughing.

"*Gahawa*?" she asked, nodding at him. She was starting to sweat.

"A-issha?" the male said in response.

The smaller female gave another snort and knocked her head against the glass of the window, her tentacle-hairs rattling against the window like hail. Her right foot kicked like Thumper from the old Disney downloads. Out of the corner of her eye, Ally saw the shadows of the soldiers inching closer, and the two reporters across the street had stopped to watch.

Ally sighed and wiped sweat from her forehead. "*I'm* A-issha," she said, her hands starting to quiver again. "My *gahawa* A-issha."

The aliens repeated her name and touched their chests, and Ally tried to come up with a way to get her point across, while the short female — Thumper — continued twitching and tap-kicking her foot as if in response to Ally's edginess. Ally fought the urge to tap her own feet in response, the Blur making her pulse race.

Before she could come up with a solution, however, Thumper's head dropped, her black hair now clinging protectively to her head. Her thick body shuddered in a wave-like motion, and when Brando moved closer to try to help her, Thumper pushed him back with a high-pitched squeal.

Brando took a half-step back before regaining his balance, and in the process, his hand brushed Ally's shoulder.

A fleeting image filled Ally's head, a vision of a mountainous, black and white landscape littered with caves under a stormy purple sky. The trees of the forest next to the caves were all dead, black fingers poking into the air, rimed with white frost. Inside the trees were the bleached white bones of deformed creatures that Ally couldn't recognize. The word "Late" echoed inside her head as the world fell away from her in a vertigo-inducing rush.

The vision ended as Thumper gave another screech as she spun away on her bare feet and ran off down the street, away from the soldiers. Ally almost fell over from Brando's touch and the vision that had come along with it. She sucked in air as she smelled the alien's odor of burnt toast, with something rotten underneath.

"Go!" one of the soldiers shouted. The other soldier sprinted after the female Wannoshay, while the first soldier glanced at the two Netstream reporters across the street. "Don't hurt her," he shouted after his partner, "just keep her from leaving the neighborhood. Use the—"

The soldier stopped when he saw Ally and the remaining two aliens staring at him. His fingers had been resting on a small green box clipped to his belt, but he dropped his hand from it as soon as he looked over at them.

What the hell? she thought, glancing again at the green box on the soldier's belt. Do they have some sort of devices attached to the aliens? Like GPS units, or stunners?

Ally watched the other soldier and the female alien until they disappeared around a corner. She barely had time to check to make sure her camera had gotten a clear shot of all the action. She closed her mouth, which had been hanging open. She was shivering, the Blur starting to flash in her system.

"Listen," the soldier said. The two reporters across the street were walking off, shaking their heads. The soldier stepped up close to Ally, his face pinched and tight as he lowered his voice. "You may want to come by some other time, ma'am. Sometimes the Wantas get that way, get a little out of control. Let's just keep that little outburst under our hats, okay? Don't put that in your news report, all right? I've got to talk to those two over there."

Ally nodded and flipped her hair out of the collar of her shirt so it covered the small camera attached to her lapel, hoping he wouldn't ask for her mini-DVD. But the soldier had already left her, calling out to the two reporters.

Her heart was still beating too fast for comfort, and without the soldiers watching over her, she felt exposed. Keeping her distance from the two remaining aliens, who were now squatting in motionless silence, she hurried back to her car. She drove back to Sanford shaking and giggling with the remnants of adrenaline and Blur, the image of the frozen forest of bones almost completely forgotten.

Ally had the footage uploaded to her Netstream in under an hour, and "Wantaviewer" was born.

#

On the last day of May, Ally Trang opened the door to her bedroom closet and was nearly swamped by dozens of mini-DVDs that had been piled at the bottom of her closet floor. They came spilling out at her like oversized coins in plastic casings. Each disc contained footage of her talks with the aliens she knew as Brando, Thumper, and Jane — she hadn't had the patience to successfully explain the concept of names to them, so she'd made up her own for them. With her hours of footage long since uploaded to her Netstream, Ally knew she should reuse some of the disks, but she couldn't bring risk losing her backups.

"Jesus H," she said, staring at the mess on her floor. She turned to her bedroom door and locked it, afraid her housemates would come barging in on her and her movies. "Where the hell did *they* all come from?"

She hadn't told anyone in Sanford about her Netstream, and she kept her real name hidden on the 'streams by using only "Wantaviewer." At first the need to hide her identity had simply been an instinctive, Blur-influenced reflex to keep all information from others unless forced to talk. The Netstreams were safe places for if you wanted to be anonymous, as long as you covered your tracks. But soon she came to like the name, and with the regular trickle of download fees, her 'stream was earning her almost as much as her day job did. The aliens had become a popular viewing alternative, preferable to the dismal, war-torn news on other sites. Even after the explosion in Milwaukee.

Ally had been keeping up with the explosion ever since it had happened a little over an hour ago. It was the constant flood of images filled with fire and smoke that led her back to her closet to find a couple hours of footage from an online friend in Milwaukee she'd backed up onto a disk. Sorting through her disks, she'd listened with a rising sense of disbelief to the stories about the three dead aliens who had just been found inside the brewery, and the almost two dozen missing humans. And another alien had been found a block away from the brewery, dead of some sort of shock.

A sick feeling grew in her stomach as she thought about her alien friends, and Ally jumped when her wallscreen screen beeped five quick tones, notifying her of a new download. She turned to her half-size wallscreen in time to see an image of a burning grain elevator, flames shooting up a hundred feet into the air despite the five fire trucks blasting water onto it.

"*What?*" she whispered. "Another one?"

The images flashed by faster, along with a voiceover. Very little was left of the elevator in South Dakota. Eleven men and women had been inside it when it blew, and eight of them had been killed instantly. Four Wannoshay workers were scheduled to be working at the site at the time of the explosion. All of the alien workers survived.

Ally looked over at the disks in her closet, a chill creeping over her despite the hot closeness of her apartment. As she stared at them in numb shock, she thought of Thumper's lack of stability, and the big muscles in Brando's thick arms.

"Evidence," she muttered, her throat aching for the burning sensation that came with swallowing Blur. "This place is full of fucking evidence."

Rubbing her face, trying to wake herself up, Ally knew she needed to make another trip to Winnipeg to see Jenae.

Skin prickling now, Ally jumped up and pushed all of the disks back inside, and then shut the closet door on them. After she collected her car keys and found her money card, she wasn't even surprised to note that, in a small corner of her fatigued mind, she was starting to believe that the aliens *did* have something to do with the two explosions.

#

Sitting on the floor of Jenae's hot and dirty apartment, Ally swallowed her second Blur with her fourth shot of lime vodka and came up gasping for air.

"Why would they blow up our buildings?" she said when she was able, her voice sounding too slow for her ears. "Especially with people and aliens in both of 'em?"

Jenae rocked on the floor next to her, her bony white arms wrapped around her knees. She'd been using all afternoon, and her shakes were bordering on convulsions. Her eyes were dark brown bruises in her pale face.

"Part-of-their-master-plan," Jena said. "Takin'-over, y'know?"

"Oh come on." Ally stared at the whitish residue on her shot glass, in the shape of her lips. "Why wait 'til now, after letting the CF treat them like such shit for the past half year?"

Jenae answered only by rocking faster. The Blur was making her sweat, and Ally could smell her unwashedness from five meters away. She grimaced and swallowed, breathing from her mouth as she waited for the Blur to hit her. She didn't like being sober like this — it made her imagine too many possibilities, none of them positive.

The two young women sat without speaking for a minute, until something rattled against Jenae's door. It sounded like skeletal fingers tapping on the dented metal, and it made a shudder run up and then down Ally's spine. Jenae was at the door and ripping it open before Ally could blink twice.

"Who-the-fuck—" Jenae shouted, but there was nobody there. A bitter smell floated into the room from the open door. Jenae looked up and down the stairs outside her apartment twice, her skinny body shivering as the Blur flashed inside her. Ally knew the feeling well: an almost orgasmic shuddering as the heart beat as fast as it could to push the toxic chemical of the drug out of the body. In fifteen minutes, Jenae was going to have a bitch of a headache, unless she kept the Blur in her system.

Ally still hadn't felt the drug hit her, and watching Jenae dance like a puppet on invisible strings on the landing outside her apartment, she wasn't sure if she *wanted* to feel it. Part of her was waiting for a gunshot or explosion to come from the other side of the door.

"Cold turkey," she muttered, and poured herself another shot of lime vodka. "I need to. One of these days, for sure."

Jenae spun and marched over to Ally as if she'd heard her. "Drink-up. We're-going-now."

Ally froze with the shot glass halfway to her lips. "Where?"

"To see those alien friends of yours." Jenae's voice was slow and deliberate. "My friends've-seen-you-with-'em, you know. Don'-know-what-you're tryin'-to-do, Ally."

Ally shivered as she swallowed the sickly-sweet alcohol. With numb hands she tried to set down the glass as Jenae filled her pockets with capsules of Blur. She ended up dropping the glass onto the bare wood of Jenae's floor. The shot glass bounced once and then shattered on the rebound.

"What," Ally started to say, feeling like she had a mouthful of glue as she spoke, "What're you going-to-do?"

"Expand-the-customer-base," Jenae said, her narrow face all angles and bulging eyes. She cackled as she spoke. "Wanta Blur, Alissa? Or should I say, *Wantaviewer*?"

#

There was a moment at the start of that hot, nightmarish night when Alissa Trang realized she could stop it all. She could have just walked away from the situation, taking Jenae's Blur with her, and nobody would have gotten hurt. Ally saw the moment with the perfect, unfettered clarity of an addict at the peak of her high. Jenae stood next to her, laughing and hugging herself as she shook her way through the Blur rush. The sound of Jenae's laughter was mean and sharp, like short, quick punches to the side of Ally's head. The soldiers had all disappeared.

Ally stared as Jenae held pink capsules out to the half-dozen aliens around them. Their skin was gray, but on many of their bare arms and faces were mottled patches of pink, almost the same color as the capsules of Blur. The aliens crept up to them like hesitant forest animals approaching a watering hole.

No, Ally thought. That's wrong. She'd talked too long with Brando to believe that. They're not animals. They're just freaked out because of the way Jenae was acting. They know what she's offering them. And they *still* fucking want it.

The warm night air was thick with the muddy, musky smell of the aliens.

One of the females, her squirming hair held back in a black metal clip, reached a short-fingered hand out to Jenae. Her long gray body rocked forward, and then back, as if she was trying to get her balance. The male next to her, wearing cuffed, second-hand jeans with holes and patches just like most of the other Wannoshay, also lifted a hand, palm up. His face wore a spreading stain of pink that ate away his gray coloring. Every vertical eye in the middle of each wide forehead remained closed.

The moment was there.

Ally felt her own hand move, poised to grab the capsules of Blur from Jenae's quivering hand and run. She could do it. She *had* to do it. Then she thought about the images on her Netstream, and Jenae calling her "Wantaviewer." All those disks in her closet to incriminate her, guilt by alien association. Jenae wouldn't hesitate to turn Ally in as an alien-lover if there was any hint of profit in it. Ally nearly bit through her lower lip as it curled up with fear and disgust.

The moment was there, but Ally allowed it to pass by.

Instead, the two Wannoshay took the offered capsules and, following Jenae's pantomimed movements, placed them in their lipless mouths. Their black eyes widened as they swallowed. Soon, more pinkish-gray hands reached for Jenae, the capsules quickly disappearing only to be replenished by the big pack on Jenae's skinny back.

"First time's free," she said, her voice going hoarse from shouting and laughing. "First time's totally free, no strings attached, Wantas. After that, though, we got to charge a small handling fee."

Ally watched the transactions, numb and paralyzed.

"Now you fucking did it," she muttered, and at least three alien voices repeated her words back to her: "Nah you fugg-hin' didh idh," one said, like a deep-voiced man with a head cold. "Fugg-hin' didh idh," echoed another, higher voice.

The screaming began less than a minute later.

Spinning and leaping up and down in a mad dance of agony, the first group of Wannoshay that had taken Blur broke free from the crowd and bounded out into the streets. Their skin was almost all pink now, whether from the heat or the Blur or both, it was impossible to tell.

Most drivers from the city knew to avoid Ellice Avenue, but a new hydro car with American plates flew up the road as if on cue and barreled into two

Blurred, madly-dancing aliens. The twin thuds hit Ally like hammer blows to her chest, and she tried her best to look away from the wreck. But as always, she had no control, no willpower. She looked at the broken bodies and screamed along with the others.

As the night wore on, hesitant Netstream reporters began to arrive in the neighborhood, collecting their cams now that a story here in Winnipeg was finally evolving. From what they thought was a safe distance, half a dozen began reporting on the madness in the wake of the explosion that day, talking into the cams they held out at arm's length from their faces.

Many of them never made it back out of the city once the aliens got their first taste of Blur. The drug seemed to activate the tendency for violent outbursts that the Wannoshay already possessed. Ally was the only person with a camera to get close enough to film Jenae, cackling and shaking and passing out Blur like Halloween candy.

Ally's only consolation, in the midst of the chaos, was that her three Wannoshay friends were nowhere to be seen. She'd spent enough time with them — shot enough footage of them — that she felt able to pick them out immediately in a crowd of aliens. Also, she couldn't sense that unique ringing feeling that occurred whenever Brando or Thumper or Jane was near, more of a tickle than a sound. Maybe it was the Blur, clogging her other senses of the aliens, but she couldn't see or feel her alien friends there that night, and that thought gave her a tiny sense of victory in this night of madness. The aliens danced and fought around her, big gray hands smacking into flesh every few seconds.

Amazed that she'd been able to get away from Ellice Avenue in one piece, Ally made it back to Sanford at half past midnight. She'd been sick twice on her way home, and the trucker had been nice enough to pull over to let her spill her guts both times. The driver didn't say anything when she climbed back into the truck, wiping her mouth. The big, gray-haired woman just looked at Ally with a look that was equal parts sadness and anger. Not at her, Ally knew, but at the deaths from the past week, and the Wannoshay.

Ally trudged toward her apartment from the gas station where the trucker had dropped her off. She cried silently, trying to cover her occasional sobs by humming a tuneless song. She felt the bag of Blur in her pocket, and a part of her wanted to throw the capsules into the sewer grate below her. Instead she pushed them deeper into her pocket and balled her hand into a fist. This was no time for drastic actions.

Casting her gaze skyward, Ally looked at the stars littering the sky. Somewhere out there was their home, she thought, wiping her eyes. She pushed the images of the burning elevator and the black smoke of the brewery from her mind.

Now they're stuck here with us, she thought, with no way to get back if they even wanted to.

The thought made her bend over and heave, but she had nothing left inside her. Sobbing in spite of her tightly-closed mouth, her body wracked with cramps and shooting pain, she finally made it to her apartment around one o'clock. Her housemate Darius was snoring on the couch, while Anita's bedroom door was closed.

Inside her bedroom, Ally opened her closet door and gazed at the five or six dozen mini-DVDs she'd never gotten around to organizing.

"Evidence," she muttered, her voice hoarse. She set a mint tab on her tongue and felt cool ice fill her mouth.

Just like the capsules of Blur in my coat, she thought. It's all evidence, linking me to the Wantas.

She'd left her wallscreen on, and she picked up her remote and surfed over to her 'stream out of habit. The home page for "Wantaviewer" appeared, and Ally felt her face grow warm at what seemed now like a childish logo and naive stills of Brando, Thumper, and Jane and the rest of their people in Winnipeg. She started up her most recent upload, and Brando's oval face filled the screen, forcing Ally to choke down a sob.

Looking away from the screen, she fumbled for an insta-flame on her cluttered desk. Ally pushed open her window and slid her metal wastebasket in front of it. After breaking the insta-flame in half, she used it to ignite the garbage inside the wastebasket. She was crying again, as much as she hated the tears. She'd flashed on the Blur long ago, and all she felt now was emptiness and the familiar pain in her muscles and joints.

"Damn it," she whispered over and over again as the fire grew and she began moving discs from her closet, making a pile next to the wastebasket. "Damn it all to fucking hell."

She dropped the first disc into the fire. Grabbing an old paperback dictionary she'd been using to keep her desk legs balanced, she ripped pages out to feed the fire. More discs followed, melting and giving off an acrid blue-black smoke. Ally fanned the smoke out into the summer air as best she could.

With the last disc in the burning mess of plastic and paper, she looked back at her wallscreen. Brando was sitting with his back propped against the wall of his furniture-less living room. He'd been trying to explain something to her yesterday, Ally remembered.

"Left them, Wannoshay," he was saying. His apartment had been cold enough to make his and Ally's breath steam, but he seemed to enjoy the chill. He pointed a stubby finger at his third eye, which had been closed all afternoon.

"Who-did-you-leave?"

Ally couldn't recognize her own voice at first, Blurred into high speed at the time of the recording. She listened to herself repeat her question, more slowly. She squinted at wallscreen, focusing on the unique design on the back of Brando's big, stubby-fingered hands.

Brando bowed his head in his version of a nod of agreement. His short tentacle-hairs wiggled randomly, like a field of thick grass teased by a small cyclone.

"They were . . . " He stopped, his face going blank as it did when he was concentrating, trying to find the words in English.

He put his right hand palm up, his signal that the game of charades was on. On the wallscreen speakers, Ally heard herself give a hissing exhalation that was half-laugh, half-nervous squeak.

Brando put both hands sideways in front of him, and then moved his hands over to his right, hands sideways again. The scar design on the back of his hands were clear: two triangles with one tiny circle in the middle of them.

"Um. *Next* to you?" Ally's voice said, filled with a patience that surprised her now, a day later. "Like-neighbors?"

Brando bowed his head again. "Next. And *late*."

His last word came out sounding like "lake," or maybe "light," but Ally had heard him say the word often in their recent conversations to know more or less what he meant. It meant something bad, she thought, something worse than just being tardy.

As the stink of burnt plastic began to fade in her apartment and most of the smoke had cleared, Ally held her speaker remote to her mouth again.

"Admin page," she said into the remote. "Password 'atrangviewer001.'"

On top of the image of Brando, lines of code appeared on the left side of the wallscreen. Tiny, moving thumbnails of all the screens of Ally's Netstream displayed on the right, scrolling downward.

What does it mean if an alien is late? she wondered, her gaze wandering over all the streaming digital movies she'd uploaded in the past month. There was the movie from the night the Wantas first came to Winnipeg, along with the dozens of interviews she'd done with Brando and Jane and Thumper since then. The footage of the warm day when Thumper took off running, leading the soldiers on a wild goose chase.

"Late," Ally whispered, fanning an empty mini-DVD case in front of her face, trying without luck to create a breeze in her overheated bedroom.

They were neighbors, maybe, she thought with a smile, thinking of Brando's earnest face and his strangely effective gestures. And sometimes neighbors were late, for one thing or another. Late as in tardy. Or late as in dead.

Ally looked at the image of Brando underneath the code and thumbnails of her Netstream. She wondered if he was hooked on Blur now, just like she was. Maybe someday they could talk about that, like old friends sharing their battle scars.

Maybe someday, she thought. Maybe if the Wantas don't kill us all, and we don't kill all of them. They were screaming for it, for the Blur, even as it fucking drove them insane.

Still smiling through the tears sliding down her cheeks, Alissa Trang began deleting every single one of her movies from her Netstream.

MUD AND SALT

Skin followed Georgie and Matt out of the pickup, his entire body shivering with cold despite the three layers of clothing he wore. Outside the truck, the early-morning November air was crisp, with just a hint of wind that seeped through his camouflage jacket. Skin felt Matt watching him in the semi-darkness, making his shoulder blades itch, until Georgie slapped Skin on the back and handed him one of his hunting rifles. Once all three were armed, they stood in an empty field a mile from the abandoned Omaha Indian reservation.

According to the guy in the bar last night, the alien had been seen in the area the previous afternoon.

"If it gets any colder, my nuts are gonna flash and go south," Georgie said. He rubbed his dark, sleep-bent hair, one of his fingers sticking out of a hole in his glove.

"Thanks so much for sharing," Matt said. "At least you have nuts, unlike our buddy Skin here, who won't even protect his own woman." He pulled out his military-grade field glasses and elbowed Skin in the ribs. Skin swallowed hard and checked his gun for the second time to make sure it was loaded.

The sun crawled over the bluffs of the Missouri River to the east as Skin glanced at his buddies, his heartbeat thudding in his ears in anticipation of the hunt. Georgie's boyish face had slipped into a grin, while Matt's chubby face frowned at the brown landscape from behind his expensive field glasses, his pride and joy, bought back before they'd all lost their jobs and spent most of the last few months on unemployment. None of them had ever killed anything larger than a deer before.

Georgie coughed and spit, breaking the sense of dread building in Skin. "Let's go."

Skin and Matt moved at the same time, forming a wedge with Georgie in the lead. The dead, frozen ground crackled under their boots, and the tree branches above them rustled in a sudden breeze. Pulling his jacket tighter onto his wiry body, wishing he'd been able to afford a new coat this fall, Skin glanced at the silent forest again. The Omaha Indians had left the reservation half a year ago, heading farther south to put more distance between themselves and the aliens. The Indians on the neighboring Winnebago reservation had followed them a few weeks later.

"Don't drop that new gun, Skin," Matt said, his jaggedly-cut blonde hair flipping into his eyes. He adjusted his field glasses on his nose and lowered his voice. "Of course Georgie gives me the shitty one. I know it's hard for you to carry a conversation, much less heavy weaponry."

"Shut up, Matt," Georgie whispered. "Someone's been through here recently."

They slowed, Matt glaring at the back of Georgie's head. Georgie pointed at some thorn bushes and matted-down grass, but Skin couldn't see any difference in the brown undergrowth. He knew they weren't going to find anything out here, but he liked hunting with Georgie. After walking around all day, freezing their toes and fingers, they'd all end up at Skin's trailer for home-brewed beer, chili, and football on the all-sports Netstreams that eastern Nebraska had finally gotten installed. They'd watch the game on the wallscreen Skin was still paying for, and would continue to pay for, for the next twenty months.

They continued walking north at a slower pace, closer to the abandoned reservation. Skin had only seen blurry pictures of the aliens, and he was pretty sure he didn't want to run across one today in the single-digit cold. By ignoring the stories on the Netstreams, Skin could just about forget that the aliens had ever come to Earth. Just about.

He inhaled icy air and held back a cough. His legs were getting tired already.

"So is Lisa going to be home tonight?" Matt asked under his breath, loud enough for only Skin to hear. "What's she going to be wearing? You know I like the curves on a pregnant lady."

"Don't talk about her like that," Skin said, regretting it immediately. He should've just shut up and taken it.

"O-ho! Now he's got an attitude! Where was that attitude last night, when she needed you?"

Skin shut his mouth and walked faster. Matt's soft laughter made his ears burn. He should've taken a swing at the guy hitting on Lisa last night, but Skin knew he would've gotten his ass kicked. Lisa had pulled him out of the bar and left Matt and Georgie inside, talking to the guy about hunting and aliens.

"Don't pull that macho shit with me, Tim," Lisa had said in the car on the way home, her hands laced across her round, tight stomach. Skin looked away from her belly and fought to see through the frosted windshield. "You're not Georgie, and damn it, you're not Matt. I can't *stand* that shit."

The sun stayed hidden behind the clouds all morning. The men moved gradually north, keeping to the shadows and stopping at every clearing so Georgie could look for signs of the alien's passing. At noon they stopped to eat a lunch of salted venison and stale rolls, but it was too chilly to stay in one place for long. Skin felt worn out from Matt's constant talking and the miles they'd covered, but he kept moving. The day grew overcast and dark as the noon hour passed.

For the first time since learning about the escaped alien last night at the bar, Skin thought about actually using the gun in his hands to kill it. He knew Georgie needed his portion of the reward money to help take care of his two girls, and he and Lisa themselves weren't exactly living like royalty lately, with the baby coming any day now. He had no idea what Matt, living by himself in his tiny apartment in Bancroft, would do with the money. Five thousand dollars was a lot of money, even in this day and age.

Caught up in his thoughts, Skin walked past Georgie, who was bent down on one knee examining the grass.

"I think we're close," Georgie said, his dark eyes squinting at the ground. Skin stopped, a thrill of fear and excitement replacing his guilt about last night.

Matt mimicked Georgie from behind Georgie's back, forcing his soft features into a fierce scowl. Skin shook his head and checked his gun again. It had one of the new safety sensors that was supposed to make it accident-proof, except Georgie hadn't explained to him how to use it yet. The fact that Georgie had lent him his best gun filled Skin with pride, too much pride to ask for instructions on its use. The sensor was dark, so Skin figured the safety was on. If they caught it, the alien could be strung out on drugs and unpredictable, so Skin had to be ready to shoot to kill if needed. He touched the sensor, turning it red.

Georgie began talking in a low, impatient voice. Matt nudged Skin and rolled his eyes. Skin knew from years of hunting with Georgie that this meant they were close to their prey.

"Huntin' and killin', ain't nothing better," Georgie muttered, walking slowly into the forest. "Got no room for graymeats, no Wantas, not in this country, not nowhere else." Skin remembered Georgie warming up for their high school's football games in the same chanting manner.

"Shh," Matt said. His field glasses had turned opaque, and he pointed at a large evergreen seventy-five yards away. Despite the lack of wind, the tree's branches quivered slightly. Skin never would have noticed if Matt hadn't shown the tree to them.

"Oh yeah, here we go," Georgie said. They spread out in a loose arc and stepped slowly toward the tree. Skin suddenly felt the cold weight of the gun through his insulated gloves.

When they were twenty yards from the evergreen, Skin smelled a lingering odor of wet, wormy dirt mixed with a burnt, bitter smell. They stink, Lisa had said. He turned to say something to Matt, but before the words could leave his mouth, a figure tumbled out of the tree. Like a gray and black blur, it righted itself and ran into the forest on all fours.

The air exploded with the sound of Georgie's gun. Matt and Skin, their own guns still resting on their forearms, stared at Georgie with wide eyes. The fast-moving image of the alien, if that was what it was, kept replaying in Skin's mind like a nightmare.

"Come on, Skin! Move it, Matt, you fat ass!" Georgie yelled from in front of them, sprinting after the creature into a stand of oaks. "I think I got him!"

Georgie fired his gun a second time, and then Skin heard him yelling in the forest, along with a strange, piercing shriek that sounded like an animal. Skin and Matt ran after Georgie and found him on top of a tall humanoid figure, holding it down with the weight of his body. The alien's stubby legs poked out from underneath Georgie.

"Yeah!" Georgie yelled, leaning over the alien. Bright, purplish-red blood dotted the tree trunks and bushes around them. Skin had never seen such a color before.

"Trying to get away from your camp where you belong, huh, Wanta?" Georgie's voice was harsh as he pressed his red face closer to the alien's oval-shaped, gray face. "Don't like your new home? What you going to do now, graymeat? Huh?"

Skin stepped closer for a better look.

"Come on," he said. His voice sounded like a bird's chirp. He coughed. "Take it easy."

The alien reeked of mud and salt. Thick tentacles moved like tiny, eyeless snakes across the alien's head, growing out of his scalp like hair. One tentacle beat helplessly against Georgie's midsection, giving off a tiny spark with each impact. Across one side of the alien's head was a purple slash where Georgie had shot him, but the flow of blood had stopped.

The alien's eyes — all three of them — were closed, and his narrow gray face was flat, almost peaceful, despite the dots of its own blood and his obvious discomfort. The alien's face was marred by thin white streaks that radiated out from his mouth, like scars or wrinkles.

Taking tiny steps, Matt walked next to them with his gun trained on the alien, for once not saying a thing. His expensive glasses were perched precariously on the tip of his nose.

"Okay, buddy," Georgie said. There was a change in his voice. His hand rested on the alien's back. Purplish-red blood stained Georgie's coat and the finger that poked out of the hole in his glove. "Let's get up."

Georgie held onto the alien's long arms as the alien rose to his feet. The alien's elongated torso and humped back made him look bent over when he stood upright. Judging from the blood on his khaki pants and too-small denim jacket, the alien must have been shot in the side as well.

Skin stepped forward to help him up, but he froze at the sound of Matt's voice.

"Let's take this thing out now, Georgie." Matt pushed his glasses up onto his forehead with a nervous hand. "It may have some disease. I've heard all about this shit they carry. Maybe it's on Blur right now and it's about to flash. It's got those junkie scars on its face. See 'em?"

Georgie brushed off the alien's ill-fitting jacket, gazing at the alien with calm eyes. Skin saw something pink and small fall to the ground.

"Be quiet, Matt," Georgie said, staring at the alien. His face was almost blank, as if the wild adrenaline rush from the hunt had melted away, leaving him devoid of all emotion.

Skin couldn't take his eyes off the tall, gray-skinned being in front of him. The hunched gray creature was almost as thin as Skin was, and he didn't look dangerous at all. For the first time in months, Skin wondered if the explosions at the brewery and the grain elevator had simply been freak accidents.

"We got to take you back, man," Georgie said.

"*What?*" Matt cried, lifting his gun. "What are you talking about, Georgie? The reward was dead or alive. I'm not fucking around with some alien that's whacked on Blur."

Georgie continued talking over Matt's shouts. "You have to go back to your camp." Georgie's voice was gravelly, like an old man. "Do, you, un, der, stand, me?"

Swaying slightly, the alien straightened up and opened his eyes. Matt stopped yelling. Despite the cold, a trickle of sweat started from Skin's armpit and ran down his side. His mouth felt so dry it hurt. Deep black, unshining, with no whites at all, the eyes of the alien stared right at him. Skin backed up, bumping into Matt.

"If you're not going to kill it," Matt said, "we'd better get it tied up so we can haul it back to the truck."

The sky was turning dark blue, and Skin watched his own breath leak out of his mouth in a cloud. Georgie didn't move.

"Come on, man, let's go!" Matt said. When Georgie didn't respond, Matt poked him in the back with the butt of his rifle. Georgie jumped, and his eyes fluttered.

"God damn graymeat," he whispered, wiping one of his blood-stained gloves on his coat, keeping his other hand on the alien. He looked like he had just woken from a deep, dreaming sleep. Turning toward the alien, he reached for his gun. "What did you do to me?"

The alien immediately dropped to all fours, dotting the frozen ground with blood. Almost faster than Skin could follow, the alien reached into his jacket and pulled out a pink capsule, which he stuffed into his mouth. His gray arm blurred back into place on the ground. Skin wasn't sure if his eyes had moved fast enough to see it all happen.

"What the hell?" Georgie said. "Spit that out, Wanta." He bent over the alien, but his hand stopped an inch from the writhing tentacles of the alien's head, as if he expected the alien's touch to shock him. Three tentacles reached up toward Georgie's shaking hand.

"Get over here and help me!" he yelled at Matt and Skin.

Skin took a slow step forward, his gaze fixed on the alien. "What do you want me to do, stick my hand in his mouth?" he asked Georgie. The alien began to shake, his strange hair-tentacles quivering like a handful of garter snakes. From the middle of his forehead, his third eye winked sideways at Skin.

"Shoot him."

Georgie's voice was flat. Matt moved next to Georgie, rustling the dead weeds. Skin's eyes took in his old high school buddies on his left, and the gaunt, trembling alien on his right. Everything else — the cold, the bare trees, even the weakness in his arms — faded into the back of his brain.

"He's got Blur in him," Georgie said, his calm voice floating into Skin's head like a light wind. "He's gonna flash on us and we won't be able to bring him in. He'll be moving so fast it'll be like trying to hold on to five aliens. You know how strong these Wannoshits are."

Skin moved closer to the alien as Georgie spoke, until the alien's smell filled his nose. The muscles of the alien's face contracted wildly, like a mask of moving gray flesh. His wide shoulders rocked back and forth, and his stick-like arms vibrated with energy. The wound on the alien's head began to bleed again. Skin lifted the barrel of his gun a few inches, but he didn't point it at the alien.

Accidents, he thought.

"We did our parts," Georgie said. "Matt spotted him. I took him down. Now it's up to you to finish it."

Skin looked down at the rifle in his hands. No, he thought. I can't.

Turning it around, he aimed the butt of the gun at the alien, then glanced at the safety sensor before swinging it. When his eyes left the alien, the alien leaped. In two seconds' time, the rifle was knocked from Skin's hands and he fell back. The gun hit the ground, discharging. With three rabbit-like leaps, the alien disappeared into the trees of the abandoned Omaha reservation.

"Damn it, Skin you let him get —" Matt yelled, then stopped.

Numbly, Skin looked over at Matt, then Georgie. Georgie wasn't standing anymore. He was on his back, his head at an awkward angle against a tree trunk. Blood oozed between his fingers from a hole in his stomach.

"Fuck," he said. "You fucking shot me, Skin."

"Oh Jesus," Skin said.

Georgie jerked away from Skin's touch, then screamed. When he stopped, he looked at Matt. "Get that son of a bitch."

Skin ducked his head instinctively, waiting for the butt of a gun against his temple.

Matt swore and yelled, "Not you, idiot. He means the alien. Let's get it."

"We'll never catch him," Skin said, looking away from Georgie at the darkening sky. "Plus we can't just leave him here."

Matt looked at Georgie without any expression on his face. "He'll be all right. We'll be back soon, anyway."

"Yeah. Go get the fucking Wannoshit," Georgie said calmly. He ripped off the bottom of his shirt and touched it to his midsection. "Go on," he said, and then added quietly, "Don't let me down, Skin."

Skin's arms dropped to his side as he watched Georgie's blood drip onto the ground. Matt picked up a pink capsule from the ground where the alien had stood.

"Here," he said, biting the capsule. He held half of it out to Skin. "Now we'll make up for lost time."

"*What?*" Skin whispered. "We don't know what this'll do to us, Matt."

"Take it." Matt grimaced as he swallowed the drug. "Take it, or I'll shove it down your goddamn throat."

Skin set the gelatinous capsule in his mouth, its bitter contents almost burning his tongue. Blur was supposed to do evil things to a human's nervous system, but since the camps had started, the aliens had adopted it as their drug of choice. Somehow the Blur dealers had gotten the Wannoshay hooked on the drug, even before the camps ever started. Skin swallowed the Blur at last and ran after Matt into the thick trees that hid the alien's escape route.

The drug worked fast. Skin's pulse quickened almost immediately, and the cold air felt warm on his flushed face. He ran after Matt, pumping his tired legs faster than he'd thought possible. His eyes flicked over every shadowy inch of the forest. He felt liquid and gloriously strong.

They ran deeper into the trees. The alien had bent branches and torn up the hard ground in his mad flight, and his trail was obvious in the dying light, even to Skin. Matt's panting sounded like small screams as the big man pushed his out-of-shape body ahead of Skin. Skin's hyper-sensitive ears heard the panicked hooves of at least four deer, running a mile to the west.

"There," Matt shouted, pointing with a shaking hand at a clearing ahead of them. The remains of an old fire and the bleached bones of a cow were scattered across the circle. Bisecting the grassless clearing were the oval prints of alien feet and hands.

Matt slowed, panting hoarsely, and entered the circle. Skin followed, his arms and legs shaking with the need to keep moving. He felt ready to jump out of his body at the slightest provocation.

"Something's wrong here, man," Matt said between gasps of air. His field glasses had fallen off somewhere in the forest, and his face looked naked and vulnerable without them. He took another step into the clearing. The woods rustled suddenly, and a gray and black streak hit him. Matt was knocked off his feet without making a sound.

Skin's Blur-enhanced eyes caught the figure of the alien for a split second before the creature disappeared into the forest again. He didn't have time to raise his gun. Without checking on Matt, he chased the alien deeper into the forest, his body moving before his brain had a chance to make sense of anything. Images of Matt on his back in the clearing and Georgie holding his bleeding stomach swam through his head. His leg muscles began to cramp and burn. Skin suddenly wondered what he would do when he caught the alien.

He barely finished the thought before the alien stopped, flattened, and covered his head. Skin tried to pull up, but was running too fast. He tripped over the alien's body and crashed into the trunk of a tree. The world went black for a few seconds.

When he opened his eyes, the alien was bent over him, inches from his face. An earthy, salty sensation filled Skin's mouth and nose. The flat black eyes of the alien watched him in the gray darkness. Swallowing hard, Skin felt his throat constrict and his chest tighten. His breath caught in his lungs. He tried to talk, but the alien held him fast in his black gaze.

This isn't a human in front of me, Skin realized with a strange shifting in his mind. The world spun around him.

The alien stepped back, almost blending into the grayness of the forest, but he didn't try to run. Lifting his gun, surprised he still had it in his hands after his fall, Skin looked up into the alien's eyes.

"You're not supposed to be here," he whispered. Pointing the gun at the alien from the ground, Skin fumbled for the safety sensor. He tried to focus on the reward money.

"Everything's wrong now, ever since you came here. This is our home." His arms shook as he aimed the gun. "You don't belong here."

The alien took a step back, his elbows jutting out and his long back straight. He looked like he was getting ready to do a formal bow to Skin. The wind suddenly picked up, rattling the bare tree limbs above Skin's head.

"I have to—" he began, but his mouth wouldn't cooperate with his mind. He couldn't breathe.

Random images hijacked his brain: Matt and Georgie, pregnant Lisa, the single thick strand of alien hair he and Lisa had found at the ruined elevator, the white vans, the internment camps, and the reports of the reward money. Trying to aim down the barrel of the trembling gun, Skin squinted into the darkness, his lungs burning. The alien dropped his long arms to his side, made a whistling noise, and the forest fell silent. Skin tried to take a breath, but could suck no air into his lungs.

The alien lifted his chin in what would have been a gesture of courage and defiance in a human.

"Home," the alien said in a deep, clear voice.

"Have to take you . . . " Skin mumbled. The cold ground was seeping into his body, numbing him. His finger touched the trigger of his gun, and a leaden weight filled his chest. He didn't want to let Georgie or Lisa down.

"Our home, too," the alien said, pointing at the trees around him. "*Nee-brash-yah*."

The way the alien said the word was more beautiful than anything Skin had ever heard.

"Home," Skin whispered, his mouth dry.

More images filled his head. Lisa, on the verge of tears last night. The detainment camps hidden behind high walls and electric fences. Georgie joking with the loud-mouthed guy at the bar. The buses of aliens on their way to the newly-built labor farms, then back to the camps. Matt's face red with laughter. His friends, his home.

Skin lowered his gun and cracked it, dropping the shells uselessly to the frozen forest floor. Finally, he was able to take a breath, and he nearly fell over backwards from the shock of the icy air in his lungs.

Ignoring the creature in front of him, he got to his feet and began walking back toward the clearing where he'd left Matt. He stumbled, and the alien reached a hand out to him, palm up. Without stopping to think, Skin touched the alien's thick hand with his own. Numbing electricity coursed through his body, and Skin fell to the ground, his body rigid. The last image he saw before losing consciousness was the colorless depths of the alien's black eyes.

It was completely dark when Skin opened his eyes again. His back spasmed for an instant as he sat up on the hard, cold ground and tried to make sense of where he was. He worked his way back to the clearing where Matt had had gone down and found him on his side, breathing deeply, as if he had fallen asleep instead of being knocked unconscious by a flashing Wannoshay.

"Matt, it's me," Skin whispered. He put a hand to Matt's head, and he realized that his fingers weren't even cold. "Can you walk?"

Matt's lips moved, but no sound came out. All Skin could hear was air rasping in and out of his mouth. Skin helped him up and guided him through the forest.

Georgie was raving by the time they got back to him. A flare stick sputtered weakly next to him, covering him in flickering pink light.

"Gray, gray, get the graymeat," Georgie mumbled in a hoarse voice, turning his head back and forth.

"Shh," Skin said. After the short pain in his back, he'd felt no other pain there. He was shocked to realize he felt no more fatigue in his arms, legs, and back. He should have been exhausted, but instead he was electric with energy. "This is going to hurt, Georgie, but we've got to get you back."

Bending down, Skin eased one hand under Georgie's neck and slid the other under his legs. With a grunt, he lifted the big man like a child and balanced him in his arms. Georgie groaned and pressed his hands on his stomach, but he didn't scream.

"Did you get it?" Georgie whispered. "Did you get the Wanta?"

Matt looked at Skin, the same question on his face. A soft wind rattled the deserted trees of the reservation, carrying with it a hint of mud and salt. Skin allowed himself a long inhale and exhale before answering.

"He's where he belongs," he said.

With Georgie in his arms and Matt leaning on him, Skin turned away from the forest and walked through the cold November darkness toward the pickup.

CROSSING THE CAMP

At the west entrance to the detainment camp, government workers string another layer of wire against the wall. It uncoils through human hands like a metal snake without a head. I tell Jaime Mundo, my new trainee, that the fence will be electrified by the time we leave tonight. He nods, fingers twitching for rosary beads that aren't there, and I force a smile his way. We pass the guard house and enter the camp. He's going to have to learn quickly.

The people have been in camps for almost two years now. After the brewery accident in Milwaukee, followed almost immediately by the explosion in North Dakota, they have been under constant supervision in camps like this one. The Department of Defense insists the accidents were sabotage. I try not to let what happened in the past affect my work, yet the facts are always there, like a dull ache or a dry mouth.

I have to force myself, on this gray November morning, not to dwell on the squalor around me. It reminds me of the worst sections of Chicago's south side: the discarded ration boxes in mud puddles, the broken bottles on dead grass, the clothing limp on the line. All that's missing are high-rise tenements. Instead, here we have government-issued Quonset huts and a landscape scraped clean of all trees.

The cold air has numbed my ears already, and our breath forms a cloud in front of our faces. I catch myself starting to believe the few remaining priests left at the Minneapolis rectory who claim that the camps were built to remove the burden of guilt from the people. Many of them are convinced that the people, working as unskilled labor as part of the government's hastily-constructed integration plan, somehow caused the explosions at the brewery and the grain elevator. They tell me again and again that the camps are a way of ensuring safety for us and atonement for the people. Penance through imprisonment.

The sun pushes out from behind some clouds, warming me slightly through my black coat. Jaime slows down next to me, his dark eyes scanning the road and the shadowy entrances to the huts on either side of us. He has barely spoken all morning.

In front of us, young alien voices approach, growing louder. Jaime pauses in mid-step, then sets his foot down.

"When a child comes close to you, don't jerk away," I whisper in his ear. "Just relax."

A band of five children slide out from behind a hut and gallop toward us, using their long, thick arms like front legs. Fat hair-tentacles bounce on the children's narrow heads. They'd look almost human if it weren't for the tentacles and the third eye, sitting sideways in the middle of their foreheads. And if they didn't run towards us like small horses, on all fours. The clump of their hands and feet on the dirt road is loud in the morning stillness.

"Favvyer Yotchooa, Favvyer Yotchooa!" they call to me in bird-like voices as they stand, wobbling. Next to me, Jaime inhales suddenly.

"Good morning, children," I say slowly. The alien smell of rich dirt and salty sweat is strong, but with the children it is easy to overlook. Our greatest hopes lie with the young. We need to reach them before they see the labor farms, the Blur dealers, the violence and hatred outside. "This is my new friend, Father Jaime. He'll be working here, too."

They step back to examine him. Most of them are already taller than me, almost as tall as Jaime. The adults, when they walk upright like humans, are nearly seven feet high. "Favvyer Yaimye," a boy in the back whispers, and the rest of the children giggle with chittering voices. Their gray skin, flushed bright pink in spots from running, is covered in a light sheen of sweat despite the cool air. Ezra's fore-eye opens and closes, giving Jaime a crooked wink.

Jaime rubs his hands together, touches the square of white on his collar, but to his credit, he meets their gazes and smiles. Bless you, Jaime.

When I look back at the children, Lucas, one of the bigger boys, has dropped to all fours and started hitting the child next to him. Lucas's open hands pummel the smaller child mercilessly until the other runs off on all fours, howling. When I touch him, Lucas screams and sprints after the first child.

The people, especially the young, are prone to outbursts like this, senseless and violent. Nobody knew about the outbursts until the people began working in the factories and grain elevators and breweries. By then it was already too late. Annina, the camp doctor — and the only other human in the camp — claims it is a combination of a chemical imbalance and a hypersensitivity to the emotions of others. Next to me, I hear Jaime's sharp intake of breath once again.

The rest of the children scuttle away as well, hands and feet barely making a sound on the dusty road. They leave an almost-sweet scent of mud and salt behind them. We walk past the Quonsets and the grassless front lawns. Everything is quiet, since most of the healthy men and women have already left for the labor farms. They can do the work of three humans, and the farm owners no longer have to worry about migrant workers and green cards.

I don't say anything about Lucas. Some things Jaime will simply have to learn on his own, without me.

Off to the right, old Noah balances an armload of garbage, and a newsletter slips from his grasp when he waves. I can barely make out the slash marks and jagged scribbles on the paper. When the sun moves behind the clouds again, the camp gradually comes alive with the young and old. Blankets used as doors are folded open and fastened with wire, letting in the cool air that the people love so much. The cool air that reminds them of their home.

It had been less than a year ago, during one of the coldest winters ever, when the first reports of the ships began flooding the news channels and Netstreams. Across the empty fields of southern Canada and Minnesota and Wisconsin, almost thirty of their dainty, tired-looking ships crash-landed. Their arrival turned the world inside out, sparking protests and mass paranoia.

I turn to Jaime. "See how pale their skin is? Sunlight can burn their skin to a horrible orangish-red color. And overexposure can kill them."

Jaime shivers, as if suddenly aware of the chill in the air. The lack of warmth barely fazes me anymore, even though I still feel the congestion in my head from the night I spent outside the church doors almost two weeks ago.

"The people place great importance in their sense of touch," I say, continuing my lesson. "It took me half a year before anyone would get close enough to touch me, much less give me a hug. Hopefully," I gesture at Jaime's white collar, black shirt and black pants that mirror my own clothes, "they'll trust you sooner."

I swallow and stop in mid-lecture. They may have no choice if I agree to Father Miller's offer.

The tired-looking Quonset huts are arranged along the road in rows of five per side, and many have been painted and reworked by their inhabitants. Some give hints of the world the people escaped: synthetic black vines cover curving roofs, white-gray patterns on the walls give the corrugated exteriors depth and the appearance of caves. Others have been left unchanged. We approach an olive drab hut and step inside.

"Good morning, Eli," I say, shouting to get the attention of the old man dozing in his kitchen. A meal of wilted lettuce and an unrecognizable chunk of brown meat sits uneaten on his foldout table. His chair tips precariously as he jerks awake, but he doesn't fall. Eli has been almost deaf since a brutal fight with another one of his people during an anti-integration demonstration in Minneapolis. Many of the people's ships were destroyed by mobs during such demonstrations. That was after the grain elevator in Fargo blew, a month before the first camps. Even the Canadian government agreed to place the people in camps temporarily, "for their own good."

"Favvyer Yosh!" Eli exclaims. Still sitting, he takes my hand in his stubby, short-fingered grasp. His hands are cold and scratchy. "Was bad weeken' for her," he shouts, then sighs, his muddy odor tickling my nose like a mosquito. With a crackling sound, Eli stands, and his long torso ripples. He rubs his stubby fingers together and touches the thin scars on the back of each hand before bending to all fours. "She look worsh."

"Let's go," I say, needing to keep in motion. The hospital is always at the top of our list of stops, I want to tell Jaime, but I think he knows where we're going. Hopefully he's been studying the camp maps I made for him. Like the fifty other of its kind across the plains of northern America and southern Canada, the camp covers six square miles, row upon row of scraped earth and old Quonsets. A young priest fresh from seminary can get lost quickly here.

"Keep five feet away from the sick, Jaime. Some of the elders aren't used to being this close to humans." I squeeze his shoulder. "Or maybe it's my red face and big nose that scares them." Jaime smiles and picks up the pace.

The camp hospital is a two-story cinderblock fortress that I had to lobby for six months to get built. When I first arrived here from Chicago, the people were bringing their sick to a huge tent ringed by four Quonsets. Most of them died in that tent.

At the front desk, we pass Annina, the camp doctor. Her long black hair hangs down in her eyes as she signs a chart on her handheld computer. She nods at me as I lead Jaime toward our first patient. Eli is already in Sarah's room.

Sarah is a shriveled-up woman, but her nobility is obvious in her proud chin and clear black eyes. I can barely smell her. She smiles, unveiling a row of slightly-pointed teeth that are bright white and spotless. Her long body barely fits on the standard-size hospital bed. There are three long, narrow scars on each of her hands, symbolizing — to the best of my knowledge — her connection to Eli.

"Favvyer," she whispers. I feel a sharp stinging sensation deep inside my chest, but this is more than a physical pain. I see a hollowed-out teenager in her face, for an instant, then the human visage is gone, replaced by the familiar, the alien. Jaime stares at Sarah's wasted body. Outlined under her sheet are the elongated ribcage and the curved spine that distinguish her people.

"You are looking especially beautiful today, Sarah," I say, trying to focus. She should never have left her home planet, to die here. Even if their planet had, according to the stories, grown too hot for them to continue living there. Father, watch over her, my mind manages to whisper. The rest is silence.

We leave Eli standing awkwardly at her side, his thick hands cradling her slender, scarred hands.

"This is what the camps are all about," I begin, but the words fade like my prayer. I want to tell Jaime about the anger that courses through me at night, when my head is filled with images of Sarah and Eli and the rest of the misunderstood people. I want to tell him about the unholy hatred I feel at the blank-faced Blur dealers lurking outside the camp walls, waiting for the labor trucks to pass by. I want to tell him that the administrative job Father Miller told me about would be an answer to my sleepless nights. I want to tell him to leave this place now with his soul intact. But again, I say nothing.

An hour and a half later we leave the hospital. I usually stay longer, but I can tell that Jaime is close to sensory overload. I don't think he sees the people as living, sentient beings. He couldn't even stay at my side for the last three rooms.

Outside, the clouds are burnt away and the sun beats down on empty brown streets. The wind skips around the huts and throws dirt on us, streaking Jaime's black pants. On our way past another row of houses, I wonder about Ruth. She passed away late Saturday night, succumbing finally to her respiratory infection. I'd hoped to anoint her body and ease her transition to heaven. Ruth and I had talked about it last week, and she had agreed, but her body has already been removed from the hospital. The people do not bury their dead, and I try to grant them some amount of privacy and dignity by not asking about her.

"The people have a very loosely-organized culture," I say. The people take care of their own, I continue silently, wondering what exactly had happened to Ruth's body. Who am I to try to change their beliefs and customs?

"But everything here is so . . . " Jaime's voice cracks. He coughs.

"So structured? Yes, but it's not their choosing." The schoolhouse looms over the huts next to us, built by volunteers from the people during my first week in the camp. At the time, I couldn't believe how quickly it had been built. I've learned in my time here about the strength they possess and their drive to complete a task once it's started. I wonder, also late at night when sleep won't come, why they don't use that strength to pull down the walls like my namesake from the Bible. Again, I know it is not my place to ask.

As we enter the drafty schoolhouse, I feel another pang of guilt. If I leave, I will miss the children the most. They restore my faith on an almost daily basis.

Half of the children show up for their language lessons on time. The rest straggle in without apologizing, and Thomas and Elizabeth come in half an hour tardy.

"Loosely organized," I say under my breath to Jaime. He taps his pen on the Bible in front of him.

We use scripture passages to teach English to the people. They learn quickly, despite the problems they have with pronunciation. Today's verse is from Saint Matthew. Jaime speaks a line from the Bible, then the children try to repeat his words. Most of the children have difficulty with their t's and j's and other hard consonants. I am content with being known as "Yosh."

Jaime fiddles with his collar as he repeats the lesson at the front of the classroom. His Mexican accent thickens, and the children giggle at his rolled r's and clipped endings. I watch for any sudden movements by the children in their seats, any bursts of energy or violence. Jaime starts to sweat.

"*Shovinosh*," I say, with an edge to my voice. Elizabeth claps a hand over her mouth, and David's fore-eye snaps shut. The room is quiet. I turn to Jaime. "It's a good idea to learn their language as well, Father Jaime. Continue."

As they recite, I am reminded once more of the sound of birds who cannot sing. They try so hard to learn our language, yet what have we done for them? Locked them in a walled fortress, surrounded them with miles of electric fence.

Father, give me strength. I don't know how much longer I can do this.

Elizabeth peeks over her Bible as if reading my thoughts. She blinks all three eyes at me in succession until I smile. I point at her Bible with what I hope is a stern expression, then walk over to Ezra, who has started beating both hands slowly against his desktop. I put my hand on his shoulder and keep it there until he stops.

Ten minutes later, Jaime dismisses the children with a weak wave and a hesitant "*Wanniya*," which roughly translates to "goodbye." David's quick, hiccuping laugh echoes through the room as he and the other children push each other on their way out the door. They leave papers scattered on the floor and across their desks.

"They like you," I say to Jaime, who is still gripping the lectern. "But they feel your nervousness. Just relax. They're used to disorganization, and they'll take you for a ride if you let them."

Jaime drops into a chair and crosses his legs in front of him. His brow furrows, and he gives me the look. Eyebrows slightly raised, mouth half open. I've seen it on four previous trainees.

"How can you maintain your spirit here?" he asks.

"Don't you enjoy doing the Lord's work?"

"*Sí*," he answers with a quick smile, then his face tightens. "But there were all those deaths from the attacks. You cannot deny the fact that they had something to do with it. They were the only ones working at the grain elevator the night before it blew up. That was not an accident." He shakes his head slowly, looking at the papers littering the floor. "And the way these children act sometimes, all this hitting and fighting. Maybe the government tried to integrate them too fast. We're supposed to forgive the grayskins, I know, but they are aliens, and . . . "

I stand up and move the desks back into straight rows. The metal feet of the chairs scrape against the floor.

"You'll see, Jaime. The people live and breathe and feel just like you and me. They're misunderstood. We're all trying to learn." I slide the last desk into place. Safety for us and atonement for the people, I think, forcing another smile onto my face. "Let's go see our next parishioners."

Jaime follows me outside. I can hear my voice, speaking, informing my potential replacement about more belief systems of the people. But my mind is elsewhere, thinking of the day the first ship crashed thirty miles south of Winnipeg. A few hours before the news broke I had been mugged in Grant Park. The thieves had taken everything and broken two of my ribs. In the emergency room, when the newscaster repeated that the downed ship was indeed an alien ship, and more were on their way, something shifted inside of me. I didn't care if it was an invasion or not, though I somehow knew in my heart it was not. I felt the second calling of my life that winter day, a stirring that began as the deepest emotion I'd ever known. I've been here for half a year now, though lately I've felt the strength of my calling eroding day by day. The boy I met outside the camp wall twelve days ago only confirmed my need to leave this place.

He walked up to me outside the camp, his eyes bloodshot, his hands constantly moving. I didn't think he was using anything — I wouldn't have been able to see his hands moving at all if he were on Blur. He told me he was starting over, getting off using and selling. He walked with me all the way back to the church, telling me how he sold only to the people, bartering with them through the walls and on the labor trucks, because Blur was more addictive to the people than humans. How Blur hit the user like a mix of cocaine and speed, with a little morphine thrown in to ease the harsh edges. By the time we got to the church doors, I'd made up my mind. I couldn't let him in. Not after all he'd said and done. I spent hours talking on the front steps with him as if to compensate for not doing my chosen duty and offering him sanctuary. Then his so-called friends came looking for him just before dawn. I let them take him.

"Father?" Jaime turns to me. We stand in front of a heavily-vined hut. The sky has become dark again, promising snow. "Should we knock?"

I nod, trying to clear my mind of everything but the Lord's word, but all I can remember is the look of betrayal on the Blur dealer's face. Jaime's knock is drowned out by the wail of a siren cutting the air. I feel my chest tighten. The sound rises and builds until I glimpse the red lights of a police car.

"It must be in the square," I tell Jaime. We leave the hut and run five blocks, following the siren. I gasp for breath at the center of the camp. The huts flash red in the spinning lights of the Minnesota state police cruiser. Two officers in black helmets and thick body armor ease their way out of the car. One swings a shotgun back and forth in an arc while his partner pulls two bodies from the back seat. They leave the bodies in the middle of the road and drive off, engine fading as they rush back to the camp gates.

I forget about Jaime and the police and run up to the bodies in the road. They are just boys, too young to work in the fields, and they are covered in their own purplish-red blood. Deep bruises and jagged cuts crisscross their gray skin. Just boys. They are alive.

"Get Annina from the hospital," I yell at Jaime, "and come right back here." The smell of coppery blood — so much like our own — makes me want to gag, but instead I pull out my handkerchief and wipe the thickening blood from the closest boy's face. Under the swelling, I recognize Matthew, who should have been off at the labor farms. At my touch he moans deep within his long chest.

"Shh," I say. He has too many wounds for me to stop the bleeding. I loosen his clothing and straighten his long body in the dirt. I move to the second boy, but I don't recognize him. "Hold your hand there," I command him, but instead of obeying he opens his hand and swings at me. His strength is gone, though, and his arm falls back to the ground.

I sit between the two boys and take their hands in mine. I try to clear my mind to pray, but no words form. Help me, Lord. Nothing comes to me but the words of the young Blur dealer, shivering from the cold and detoxification: "We all act like we're going to live forever, so we take the drugs and we sell the drugs, but all it boils down to is not hurting anymore, and not dying."

I look down at Matthew. "Where were you? Who did this to you?"

"Fence off this morn'," Matthew murmurs through broken teeth. He was one of my first students, and his English is strong. He loved his new name when I gave it to him. I couldn't pronounce their real names, but I realize now how arrogant it was for me to rename them from my Bible. "Went to city. Wanted to fight. Men chase us, catch us."

Footsteps echo through the square. I hope it's Jaime and Annina, not any of the people running up on all fours. Matthew's thin lips move, but no sound comes out. His fore-eye opens wide, stretches taut, then closes. His hand slips from mine.

Annina runs up and begins working on the two boys. She spits obscenities under her breath as she touches bruises and welts. I step back to give her room. I'm covered in purplish-red blood. Alien blood. There's nothing else I can do.

The wind blows on me again in a blinding burst of anger. There are no tears in my eyes, and the only thing I can feel is a deep ache on the left side of my chest. Jaime brushes past me, a dark figure that floats across my vision. I glance up and see aliens, standing upright and inching closer on every side. I can't see over them. This will be my last day here in the camp.

"Joshua," Jaime whispers from the ground. "We can't just leave them." Without realizing it, I had taken two steps away from the bodies. Jaime kneels, taking Annina's place next to the boys. I look down at him. There is a tiny drop of blood on his collar. Dark red soaks into pristine white.

"We couldn't save them," I say.

One and a half years. It took that long to open my eyes and see the truth.

Looking up at me, Jaime's eyes tighten at the corners. It's a tiny movement, but I see it. "If we can't save these boys, we can at least help them in our own way."

The crowd of people moves back when Jaime pulls a vial from his shirt pocket. Matthew's mother is there, and she nods stiffly at Jaime. His brown finger anoints Matthew's forehead with oil, above the third eye, then the boy's lips and chest.

Whispering the prayers, Jaime's voice hums with an ancient rhythm. He repeats the sacrament over the nameless boy. The humming is picked up by the people gathered around us. The air vibrates with alien mourning mixed with one human's words of prayer. Within minutes, the wordless throbbing is deafening.

Jaime crosses himself, his hand trembling the slightest bit. He leaves the two bodies at rest and touches the dampness at the corner of his eyes.

The alien voices continue rising to an impossible pitch, an inhuman sound of sorrow and pain. My eardrums feel like they are about to burst, and I want to scream. Before I can, my eyes squeezed shut tight, the song ends. I open my eyes again. We are surrounded by the people, a wall of gray, alien flesh. Annina has already walked away from the crowd, abandoning us. For the first time ever in the camps, I feel a flickering of danger, of fear.

With my ears ringing, I pull Jaime out of the circle. Energy builds as we pass by old and young, male and female. The hair on my arms and the back of my neck stands up. An ageless female voice begins to sing. The words are lilting and almost indistinguishable from one another in the people's exotic language. I stop outside the circle of energy to listen. Jaime listens as well, a look of peace on his face.

The only words I can make out are life, death, sorrow, and a word that I've heard before but never quite comprehended. Now, in context — in *song* — I understand it.

Forgive.

They had been listening to what I'd been teaching them. The lone voice is joined by soft female voices and low male voices. I smell hints of incense and ozone. I try to turn away but I cannot. My fear is gone; I need to listen.

The two bodies in the middle of the circle glow with a wavering light. The light grows stronger as the song speeds up. The words blend together. I see young Lucas, the bully from this morning, and he is unmoving, free from his fits of aggression and mindless violence. I take Jaime's hand and pull him to the ground, onto his knees next to me.

"Pray," I say to him, my final lesson, but his head is already bowed. Pure white light fills the camp, pouring from the two bodies in the middle of the circle. The alien energy swirls around like the wind and lifts the bodies. Before I close my eyes, the bodies begin to dissolve into the air as if melting into the people encircling them. I whisper a fervent prayer that I hear only in my mind.

"Father, let me have the spirit to continue my work here." The wind blows hot onto my skin. "Father, let the walls crumble so one day the camps will be no more. Father," I whisper, "give me the strength and the grace to endure, here in the camp." I finish my prayer with dust in my throat as the wild energy of the people spills onto me, and I open my eyes.

BLACK ANGELS

In an abandoned graveyard on the outskirts of a small midwestern city, on his ninety-seventh birthday, a slender man stood in front of a slab of concrete and wished for death.

He pulled the hood of his gray coat tighter around his head, hiding his unlined face. Tomorrow the workers would tear out the slab, all that remained of the obsolete cemetery. He stood in front of the statue's base as the sun turned the cloudy sky red, then purple. All too well he knew the legends surrounding the statue that had once rested on this slab, but that had not kept him from returning for a final visit to the Black Angel.

In the center of the block of cracked concrete, three inches of blackened copper remained, in the shape of bare feet. There, on the outside of what had once been the left foot of the statue, were three tiny white marks. Fingerprints.

The ninety-seven-year-old man reached out and, for the second time in his life, he touched the Black Angel.

#

Tom Arneson was betting he could get Mercy to the cemetery by telling her the story of the Angel. And unlike his run of bad luck in the past two years, he was positive this bet would pay off for him.

"It came to Iowa City from France," he said, his voice quivering from a mixture of excitement, nerves, and need. He handed Mercy a beer and stuffed three cans into his jacket. "Took a team of four horses to deliver it to Oakland Cemetery, back in 1911. And get this — the statue had started out white, but it turned black during its first Halloween in the cemetery."

Mercy gave Tom a long look as she pulled on her leather jacket. Having met her only two days ago, Tom didn't know her well enough to really understand what that look meant. And after tonight, he would never get another chance to learn its meaning.

"You want to go there," Mercy said. It wasn't a question. "Tonight."

"You got it," Tom grinned.

"I think I liked the metal-goth club you took me to last night better. Or do you always take girls to the graveyard on your second dates?"

"Ah, come on," he said, hoping he didn't sound like he was pleading. "It'll be a blast," he added.

They left his apartment and walked north. Tom finished one beer and started another, tossing the can onto a gravel driveway. Leaving campus behind, they walked past unlit houses and empty lots in the older part of town. A rusted-out Ford Escort puttered past, filling the air with the stink of burnt oil.

To keep Mercy from getting suspicious, and to keep himself from losing his nerve, Tom told stories about the Angel.

"Now, the base of the statue was supposedly cut from the same rock that they rolled from Jesus' tomb Easter morning. And the Angel takes a flight every Christmas at midnight, returning before dawn — like Santa," Tom added with a barking laugh.

"And you waited 'til it was *dark* to show it to me?" A flash of anger showed in Mercy's brown eyes like a hint of lightning. She shook her head, her curly blonde hair falling around her shoulders in a way that made Tom's heart ache.

No, Tom thought, even as he leaned closer, inhaling Mercy's smell of cloves and roses. I have to do this, repay my debts. Otherwise, I'm going down. Hard.

He hadn't told Mercy about the Angel's black eyes that would cry tears of rusted silver for lost souls, and most of all, the danger of touching the Angel if you were impure.

"Oxidation," she said as they passed through the gate outside of Oakland

Cemetery. Her eyes were closed, and she seemed to be smelling the crisp autumn air around them.

Tom closed the creaking gate with a wince. "Huh?"

"Copper oxidizes." She opened her eyes and tapped on his chest, twice, and Tom felt like his heart had stopped. "That's why the statue turned black."

Tom looked at her as they walked down the path of uneven bricks embedded into the ground, passing blocks of grayish-white concrete on either side. Had she been able to see his eyes then, he knew he'd have his thoughts displayed in them like a neon sign. But his face was hidden by the darkness, and the Black Angel was just ahead of them.

#

A silver coin, almost hidden in the grass, sat right in front of Tom's shoe, but he wasn't looking down. He was looking up, at *her*, staring like a kid at wings he could barely make out against the night sky. He'd seen the statue before, of course, but she still stole the breath from his lungs. As he stared, he'd felt something drop in his gut, as if he'd just dropped ten floors in an elevator.

Falling.

The Angel was taller than a human, and on her slab of concrete she loomed over Tom and Mercy like a nightmare. Her bare right arm was held up as if to ward off a blow from above, while the other arm reached out parallel to the ground as if for balance. Lifted up to the sky, the Angel's starkly beautiful face was streaked with lines of gray rust, like tears.

But the realistic details of her face, the implicit threat of that upraised arm, and the imposing height weren't what gave Tom the shivers. It was the massive, seven-foot-long wings — one nearly touching the ground, the other spread to the side like a feathered awning — that made his mouth go dry.

Falling, his mind whispered again, then he shook himself out of his reverie, sloshing beer onto his arm. I have to do this.

When he looked down at his shoes to make sure he wasn't dropping through the earth, he saw the coin. A silver shekel, to be exact. He'd looked it up on the Internet, and this was one. Tom picked up the coin with his free hand, touching with his thumb the coin's upraised eagle perched on the prow of a ship. Just as promised.

Tom looked away from the coin to find Mercy staring at him.

"Tom," she said. "Where did *that* come from?"

He shrugged and slid the coin into his pocket. It was rough-edged and surprisingly heavy. It had to be genuine.

Mercy's face dropped, as if in disappointment. Then an explosion rocked the night.

#

The explosion was unlike anything Tom Arneson had ever felt in his life. There was no sound, only the numbing blast of wrongness. The shock wave knocked the half-empty can of beer from his hand and burst the two beers inside his jacket.

Dripping and shuddering with cold, Tom grabbed Mercy and pulled her to the ground behind the statue, almost touching the statue above them in the process. Panicking, he probed his wet shirt. He wasn't bleeding, just out of beer.

"What was that?" Mercy spoke directly into his ear. "Tom?"

He swallowed, trying to get his ears to pop. Something hot and wet trickled from his left ear.

Concussion, he thought. Fuck.

Another explosion shook him, and Mercy lifted herself halfway up behind the statue before Tom could stop her. A second later, she slid back down next to him, eyes wide.

"What is it?" Tom peeked around the statue.

Mercy answered by pointing toward the brick path leading to the Black Angel.

Tom's first reaction was to check to make sure he still had the coin in his pocket. But he suppressed the urge and stared hard at the dead grass and white crosses around him. As he squinted, he wondered at the warmth of Mercy's hand in his left hand. She wasn't even shaking.

"There," she said into his ear, her whisper like a scream as his ears finally popped. "Catch it in the corner of your eye."

Following her gaze, Tom again saw nothing. He tried to smile, but just as he was about to say something about it, a third explosion knocked him off-balance.

Three? Tom felt true panic overtaking him. The agreement had been for only two. Not three.

His upper body drenched in Old Milwaukee, he was shaking with cold when he saw the shadow of a two-foot-tall headstone *move*. The shadow lifted up, unfolding like a man rising from a crouch. It grew legs. Arms. A head.

Another explosion lacerated his ears, then another and another. Before he could blink, his eyes became unfocused with fear. In that instant of unfocusing, Tom saw *inside* the blackness of the moving shadow in front of them. He saw narrowed black eyes, a greasy, dog-like nose, and sharp yellow teeth in the depths of the moving shadow. As he stared, two other shadows pulled themselves together and flanked the first.

This, Tom Arneson wanted to scream as Mercy wriggled out of his grasp, was definitely not part of the agreement.

#

The agreement had been simple: thirty pieces of silver in exchange for Mercy.

Tom hadn't known anything about the silver coins before two o'clock a.m. the previous night, immediately after he'd gotten home from his first date with Mercy. Ears throbbing from the music of the night club they'd just left, head spinning from Mercy's kisses, he didn't know until he'd closed and locked the door behind him that he had a visitor.

Standing behind Tom's second-hand chair in his combination living room and bedroom was a short, thin man in a dusty gray overcoat. The man held a battered leather pouch, shiny with use. Before Tom could do or say anything, the brown-skinned man opened the pouch. Tom's voice died at the sight of the coins inside.

"You and I need to talk," the man said. "Have a seat."

Completely unnerved by the man's presence, with the taste Mercy's lipstick still clinging to his lips, Tom did as he was told. He heard himself offering the man, who smelled of hemp and cheap wine, a cold beer in exchange for another look at the silver coins. The man refused the drink.

"We've been looking for a sturdy young man like you," the man said, fingering a purplish scar that wound its way around his thin neck. He wouldn't sit down, but kept pacing around the piles of laundry, beer cans, and empty fast food bags of Tom's apartment. "My people have found someone they need to contact, someone that you seem to know. Call me the middleman. Just like you, my boy. We can both profit from these circumstances."

Tom was still staring at the thick coins in the pouch next to him on the end table, thinking of how much they had to be worth, aching to touch one of them. The man stopped pacing.

"We know of your new friend," he said. "We've been looking for her for quite some time, though she proven to be quite elusive. In exchange for one simple task, the Nephilim and I are willing to pay you with the contents of this pouch. My employers would have come here themselves, but their movements are a bit limited, and they tend to make slightly, ah, shall we say, dramatic entrances."

"Right," Tom said. He was still staring at the coins. "What the hell are these things, anyway?"

"These are silver shekels, boy, made in the coastal city of Tyre, the only coins accepted at the Jerusalem Temple. In such pristine condition as these, *one* of these shekels would be enough to pay off your debts. And I'm offering you more than one."

"Who told you about my debts?" Tom tried to stand up, but he felt a weight on his chest, keeping him in place.

"I have my sources," the man said, rattling the coins in the pouch. "Mr. Valerio is getting quite impatient, by the way. His boys are quite big, and they never get to see much action these days. There was mention of broken limbs to help speed up the loan repayment process. Broken limbs, plus interest."

Tom stared up at the man standing over him. Gazing into the man's dark eyes was like falling into lightless tunnel.

"What do I have to do?" Tom said.

The man nodded. "I knew," he said with a faint smile, "that I'd found a kindred spirit in you."

#

In the cemetery, behind the Black Angel, Tom Arneson was counting backwards.

There had been six of the silent explosions. *Six.*

"Tom," Mercy said in a calm, almost resigned tone of voice. "Who the *hell* have you been talking to?"

He glanced at Mercy, her long hair in her face as she huddled closer to the statue. She was beautiful in almost distracted way that Tom had immediately noticed when he walked into the off-campus tavern where she was tending bar. He'd never been to the tavern before, but all of the bars on campus had refused to let him come back until he'd taken care of his stack of unpaid bar bills, so he'd come to the Half-Dollar Tavern. With his last bit of money, he'd bought twenty scratch-and-win lottery tickets from Mercy, convinced he'd get a winner.

When he'd scratched off an entire set of losers, Mercy had smiled at him and poured him a beer, and they began talking. At the end of the night, when all three of his credit cards came up invalid, she shrugged and paid for him, then went home with him.

Now, two nights later, Mercy stood next to him with her face cast into shadow, her eyes hardened with some emotion Tom couldn't decipher. Anger? Fear? Resignation?

Tom looked away, and the shadows caught his eye again.

Inside the first shadow glimmered a man-sized beast made up almost entirely of yellowed, sharpened teeth. The teeth lined its mouth, as might be expected, but they also rippled up and down its shadowy arms and chest and legs. They moved, opening and closing up and down the creature's body, as if it were covered in hungry mouths. Tom squeezed his eyes shut.

I have to do this, he told himself, touching the cold coin in his pocket. I *need* to do this.

When he opened his eyes again, the two other shadows had spread out, with the first in the middle. They moved as one toward the statue of the Black Angel. Two more shadows coalesced on the other side of the brick path.

He forced his eyes open and reached for Mercy. Her breathing was shallow and forced.

"Tom," she hissed. "How did they know we were here?"

Wiping a line of blood from his face, Tom searched the gravestones and walkway for the sixth creature. If they brought three times their promised number, that must have meant they wanted both him and Mercy. Or they were expecting some kind of fight. Maybe Mercy was more powerful than Tom could've imagined.

"How did they know we were here?" Tom said, responding to her at last, his eyes still unfocused. "They know because I—"

Before he could explain how he'd told the shadow creatures to meet them there on that night, his words were drowned out by a sizzling burst of light, like lightning that eradicated the darkness for a few seconds of daylight brightness.

"They came," Mercy said, loud enough for Tom to hear her. "I don't believe it. It worked."

Tom slid down to the ground, deafened once again as well as blinded. He rested his head against the base of the statue and thought, I'm a dead man.

Moments later, after his eyes and ears recovered, he saw that the cemetery was filled with a white, strobing light, accompanied by the roar of battle from all sides. Mercy stood up next to him, only partially shielded by the Black Angel's wing.

Tom pulled her down out of the combat zone. Even when she was next to him, her face remained dazed, with a slight grin. The battle paused as voices shouted from the flickering shadows around them. The newcomers must have seen Mercy and pulled back. Spinning dots of light glinted in the starless sky above them, as angry, gutteral words assaulted Tom's aching ears.

"What is that?" Tom hissed. "Greek? German?"

"Latin." When she finally looked at him, her eyes were red-rimmed, on fire. "Surely you know Latin, don't you, Tom?"

Above them, five figures of light dropped from the sky, followed by a sixth and seventh. While the shadows had pulled together to form the creatures made up of teeth, the creatures of white energy hovering above the cemetery seemed to suck the remaining light from the night and bring it into themselves. Their glowing faces were devoid of all detail. Standing in a semi-circle around the statue, the creatures of light outnumbered the shadow-and-teeth creatures by one.

"They came," Mercy said again.

Tom touched the cold, heavy coin in his pocket one more time as arrows and spears of light began flashing past their hideout behind the Black Angel.

No coins are worth all of this, he thought. I should've known this deal was screwed when that skinny bastard tried to kiss me before he left the apartment.

Silent now, the surrounded shadow creatures formed a defensive circle, crouching back-to-back in front of the statue. They reached out and formed weapons from the shadows surrounding them. With a surge of mad screeching, they leapt up to attack the figures in white.

Tom realized they were screaming the same thing, over and over again.

"What are they saying?" he asked Mercy.

"*Mine*," she said. "Like kids, fighting over a toy. *Mine*."

Tom swallowed. "They're protecting us?"

Mercy put a hand to her forehead, as if massaging a headache. Tom felt something shift inside of him, and his face grew hot with guilt. She looked at him with red-rimmed eyes.

"You could look at it that way, I guess."

I don't know this girl, Tom thought. I'm just here for the silver, that's all.

Battle raged around them as the creatures in white took to the air again, flinging their missiles of light at the shadow beasts. The air was filled with a horrible popping and grinding noise as light met dark, and the weaker of the two canceled out, sometimes dark, sometimes light.

Next to him, Mercy rose to her feet. She began walking toward the fighting creatures with her arms uplifted.

"*Stop*," Tom heard her say. A shadow beast and a winged man fought not five feet from her. Tom couldn't muster the strength to reach for her even as she reached out to the two fighters.

"*Stop!*" Mercy screamed again.

A heartbeat later, the night sky tore open. A winged man dropped to the earth like a falling star, directly in front of the two creatures. He held his hands at his side, as if for balance, and Tom was reminded of the Black Angel above him.

Who else was coming to this little soirée? he thought madly. Jesus? Moses?

The shadow beasts screamed and fell back into the darkened cemetery, melting once again into the shadows. The other creatures in white dropped onto their faces.

A name filled Tom's mind. Not Jesus or Moses, but *Saraquel*.

"Oh, fuck," he said.

In his mind was a vision of a stone being rolled from the front of an ancient tomb by a giant man with wings longer than Tom was tall. The same winged man stood in front of them, beckoning to Mercy. The hints of eyes and a nose were slowly coming into shape on the man's white face, and his wings flapped gently, the sound like a huge bellows.

"Why did you come here, Mercedes?"

Tom touched his ear, but the blood was gone, along with the ringing. That voice was too beautiful not to hear clearly.

Standing again, Mercy shuddered in her thin white shirt. She had wriggled out of her leather jacket, and it sat next to Tom, forgotten.

"Did you not realize?" the winged man continued. "Did you want to be caught? They cannot touch you anywhere but here."

"Maybe," Mercy said, standing shakily and rubbing her bare arms. "I may have wanted that, Saraquel. The borders *are* weakest in cemeteries. And I know how much angels hate to lose."

The man in white shook his head. He was so beautiful Tom wanted to cry, or dash his head on the stone in front of him.

"I saw you fall like lightning from Heaven, Mercedes. We know of your sin, of your compassion for the failings of mortal flesh. But Heaven needs its Angel. We shall take you back."

"You'd do that? After I deserted you?" Mercy waved a hand at the destruction around her. "After I left you, for *this*?"

"We shall take you back into our fold. For rehabilitation." He smiled. "For our Angel of Mercy, we can show you the same."

She shuddered again, but stepped away from the statue without a look back at Tom. As she walked away from him, Tom felt a small part of himself die.

The creature in white took Mercy's hand, and immediately the air was filled with the stink of burning flesh. Mercy's blonde hair burst into a yellow-white flame at the creature's touch, yet Mercy didn't even flinch. Instead, she smiled.

The coin slipped from Tom's nerveless fingers, hitting the cold earth without a sound.

"*Nephilim!*" shouted the angel holding Mercy. "There will be no *rekullah* tonight. Mercy is not a commodity to be bartered for and traded for among traitors and hellspawn such as you. Remember the Word and the judgment."

The creatures of blackness screamed, their ragged voices like the sound of enormous chains, but they dared not pull themselves again from the sheltering shadows.

"Mercy?" Tom said, reeling.

"Tom," Mercy said, her skin melting into light. Her face was fading and filling with light, as if she was being lit up from the inside. "Don't question anymore. Heaven has rehab for Fallen like me. I'll be safe there. In case you were worried."

Mercy hugged herself, as the outline of a pair of wings took shape around her. "Though it won't be much fun at first."

They were gone in a flash of energy that left Tom blinded.

#

"Fuck."

Blinking hard, Tom stood all alone next to the Black Angel, Mercy's leather coat next to him like a crumpled bag. His sight was coming back to him, slowly. He grabbed the coat and held it close, trying to inhale the last traces of Mercy before her scent was gone forever.

His solitude lasted a few more seconds before the shadows began to reform again around him. Sharpened, jagged yellow teeth grinned at him as his eyes tried to adjust to the darkness.

"Nephilim!" His voice broke as he repeated the name he'd first heard two nights ago. "Remember the deal!"

Harsh laughter answered him.

Tom tried not to let his eyes go out of focus, but they betrayed him. Two of the monstrous teeth men stood on his left, one on his right. The creature in the middle, the largest, approached him. The big one was limping from the pitched battle of short seconds ago. It gave Tom a wicked smile that spread across its monstrously long face. Before his eyes snapped back into focus, Tom could see the sharp yellow teeth covering the creature's entire body. Those teeth looked hungry.

"*Deal?*" Its voice was the sound of chewing gravel. "The deal, our *rekullah*, just abandoned us and left with the fucking angels, dog-boy! With *Saraquel*," it spat. "Saraquel the tomb-robber, the stone-mover, the dead-raiser, Saraquel-the-fucking-archangel!"

The shadow creatures pressed closer, and Tom stepped back, unable to breathe. The sound of rattling chains filled the air.

"The wandering Jew betrayed us all," the creature said. "We should have hanged him when we had the chance." It moved closer with a heavy rattle of metal and the chattering of teeth. "No, we came here for a soul, dog-boy. We won't return empty-handed."

With nowhere left to run, Tom reached up to the statue. With his fingers frozen to the Black Angel, he waited for the teeth.

Frustrated screams burst inside his head. Through his eyelids, another show of white light had erupted. As before, the light came from above. The same senses-shattering explosions that had started the night's madness began, but in reverse, as if something was being sucked back into oblivion instead of being spat out from there.

After long seconds had passed, he opened his eyes. The biggest of the shadow creatures remained, though it shimmered and faded in and out of focus without Tom having to adjust his vision. It looked to Tom as if the creature was still there only through a sheer act of rage and willpower.

"You have a *guardian*," the creature spat. It raised his shadowy, teeth-infested hand until its forefinger touched Tom's chest. Something black and spiky was lodged in the teeth of that infernal hand, and Tom writhed like a worm on a hook.

"Tonight you will live," the teeth-beast continued. "But not even she can protect you from my curse. My vengeance against you is this: you shall live forever. That way we won't have to deal with your betraying soul in the underworld. Ever."

The shadow beast disappeared with a sucking un-explosion. Tom fell back against the base of the glowing statue, which was already fading, its light losing its power.

"Live forever?" Tom asked the night sky when he was able to breathe again. He saw the flash of silver on the dead grass. "What kind of curse is that?"

A grating voice scratched its way into his mind. "You may change your mind in fifty years, boy. Ask your good friend *Judas* how it feels. Ask him if he ever tires of *his* wandering."

Tom looked behind him at the Black Angel. Fresh tears of rust covered her cheeks, and the imprint of his handprint glowed on her left foot. He bent for the piece of silver, but the coin held the profile of John F. Kennedy now.

Fifty cents for Mercy's life. Fifty cents to sell his soul.

Swearing under his breath, Tom grabbed Mercy's leather jacket, and walked off into the night, determined to prove the shadow beast wrong.

#

The old man let go of what was left of the Black Angel statue, his ninety-seven-year-old hand still smooth despite the years since that night eight decades ago. The wind was turning cold, but he didn't bother fastening his coat. He'd lived in countless small towns and villages around the world during the past eight decades, gambling away fortune after fortune. Always he was able to find money, somehow. He could not starve.

The old man was tired of the constant guilt that fed his loneliness since that night, the nightmares, the fear of shadows. He wished for rest.

Or at the very least, though he knew he did not deserve it, Tom Arneson wished for some kind of mercy.

"I am a fool," he whispered to the four acres of land scraped clear around him. The people of this new era had beliefs Tom could barely understand. They saw land as too valuable for planting the dead; this cemetery would be a landing strip for the inter-city shuttle in half a year. The Black Angel was probably already melted down and awaiting new life in some nano-factory.

Tom stepped away from the base and froze. He thought he'd heard a familiar voice, calling his name.

"Mercy?" he said, his heart clenching. Was it her voice, he wondered, or the rattle of chains? "Is that *you*?"

He tried to form words of apology, but they lodged in his throat. He toppled forward, reaching for the base of the statue, but he missed it. The earth rushed up to meet him, pain convulsing him so quickly he had no time to cry out. He was dead before he hit the ground.

The only answer to his question was the sound of ancient, powerful wings.

THE DISILLUSIONIST

I was a day behind him, riding west as fast as my horse would allow. He held my future in his rotting, trembling hands, though neither of us knew it then.

Until my deputization just fifteen days ago, I had been flailing and floundering with the direction of my life like a tired man in deep water. I left Kentucky years ago, traveling to Orleans and Illinois, searching for something more from life, knowing I needed to do my part for my country. This nomadic life came hard on the heels of my defeat for the Illinois General Assembly, which in its turn followed the nightmare of the Black Hawk War. It was the summer of 1834, and I was twenty-five.

I rode west, followed hard by spirits. Everywhere I looked, I could still see their faces — not those of my political opponents, but those of the dying redskins. To be honest, I had no qualms about volunteering to help with the Indian troubles in my adopted state of Illinois. I was elected captain of my company, though we did little fighting, and my men reminded me to duck to avoid making such a large target. I would respond that, despite my height, I was too thin to hit.

The sudden appearance of Chief Black Hawk leading his hungry people across the Mississippi back to their ancestral lands near Rock Island to plant their corn created a panic. The Indians were driven by the militia into Wisconsin and slaughtered like wild animals. I could hear the gunshots in my head, as if my skull was empty and the bullets still reverberated inside it.

Since that battle, I'd been rootless. As spring drifted into summer, I again considered running again for the legislature. Part of me knew that if I brought in the killer with the strange nickname, I would have an easier time of being elected.

I pushed those prideful thoughts out of my head as I read about the disillusionist, spreading madness and death across the Great Plains: he would enter a town in the morning, plant posters at noon, and perform in the evening. By midnight he was gone again, leaving most of the townspeople dead in his wake.

I decided that my future in civil service could be put on hold until this madman could be stopped. I volunteered to bring in the disillusionist.

#

According to the stories of the survivors, the previous night's show commenced at nine o'clock.

Despite the late hour, all were welcome, including the children. Every row of chairs in the town hall, which also doubled as the courtroom, was filled with expectant farm families dressed in their Sunday best. The town elders sat off to the right, in the front row. The smell of hay and sweat was reputed to not have been strong enough to squelch the odor of something rotten coming from the man standing at the front of the hall.

The posters he had distributed had done their job, filling the town hall long before the church bells sounded nine times. I myself had seen his posters, and I had to admit, they *were* attractive, with their bright colors and elegant calligraphy proclaiming his arrival, trumpeting his Feats of Truth.

"If you care not for the Truth," the man at the front of the hall announced, a skeletal hand pointing at the exit, "if you care not for the dissolving of Lies and Illusions, I show you the door. You may leave now, if you please."

He stood on the stage, arm still upraised and aimed at the exit. Not a single soul stirred from the chairs.

The witnesses described his performance as starting badly, and fast becoming painful to watch. His voice was so weak that the entire audience spent the first half of the show craning their necks closer to him. But the people of the town rarely had entertainment, and they were willing to endure just about anything to take their minds off their crops and their chores.

Foregoing any preamble, he asked for the mayor's watch and without pause, smashed it with a tiny hammer he pulled from his sleeve. Shards of glass and metal flew as far as the third row.

The man in black never tried to undo his damage. He simply held up what was left of the watch, mostly springs and bits of metal, and then dropped it to the warped wooden floor, looking at the audience as if to say, "What were you expecting? Magic?"

While the audience sat stunned, he continued his act. He pulled a dead rabbit from his top hat and threw it behind him onto the empty judge's desk. Setting the fouled hat back on his head, he pulled a mirror from his breast pocket and procured a thick golden coin in his right hand.

"Behold the magic doubloon," he whispered in a voice similar to the pulling of bent nails. "It goes up, yet never comes down. At least not where it is expected."

Walking the coin down the cracked skin of his gray knuckles, he held the mirror so it caught the light of the lanterns on either side of the audience. He threw the coin high into the air. Wiggling the mirror, he pulled an identical coin from the brim of his hat with a guilty brown grin.

"Presto," he hissed, even as the first coin dropped to the floor and rolled into the first row, where the mayor's wife squeaked as it touched her shoe. "The mirror distracts, while a second coin is produced. What a Feat! How like magic it is!"

Two teenaged boys from the middle of the crowd began to boo, and they gained confidence when no adults scolded them. "Boo!" they cried, though their voices broke when the yellowed eyes of the man in black came to rest on them. One of the survivors who sat near the front claimed that the man's eyes gave off a smoky light as he stared the boys into silence.

I did not disbelieve such stories. I only reported what I heard; it was not my place to doubt the witnesses' testimony.

Ignoring the interruption, the man continued talking in his soft, raspy voice, as he performed more failed tricks. By this time, more of the audience was beginning to boo and hiss, careful to do so behind their hands or when the man at the front of the hall was not looking.

Finally, the man in black held up both hands, silencing the crowd. He bowed with a smile like a grimace, and then he announced his final Feat of the evening. Sarcastic applause and cheers rippled through the crowd, but when he turned his smoky gaze on them, every person in the hall fell silent.

What followed was next to impossible for the survivors to describe.

Some told of the way he threw all of his props into his slim pack, even his dead rabbit and the corpse of the broken watch, and then faded from sight. Others described how his voice grew louder and his eyes brighter as he talked about the nature of Truth. How he claimed that every person, young or old, male or female, carried within them countless fabrications and falsehoods, created on a daily basis.

"And now, tonight, I'm *taking* them," he said. "I'm taking each and every one of your lies. I leave you with only . . . the Truth."

The effect was instantaneous. Removed of all falsehoods, from harmless fibs to long-hidden indiscretions and nasty secrets, the people of the town turned on one another. Mrs. Smithfield saw the affairs of her husband as plain on his face as the wart on the tip of his right eyebrow. Janey Recker learned that Little Jim Fickling had meant to throw that rock at her and split open her chin. Paul Wandrey discovered that his best friend Matthew Tildmann had been selling him bad feed and overcharging him for it for decades.

Friend attacked friend, husband on wife, wife on child. No one in the audience was left unscathed as secret affairs, untold grudges, simmering hatreds, and so many more falsehoods were stripped away by the whispering man in black.

"I am exactly what you see before you," he was reported to have said over and over again as he went through purses and pockets and coats, dodging swinging fists, booted feet, and biting mouths. "I would never lie to you about who I am. For I am solely what you see, nothing more."

His pack stuffed full, he took the best horse from the mayor's stable and rode west out of town. The town hall's walls were stained with blood, the chairs broken underfoot like so much kindling.

The disillusionist left no trace of himself, just the damage he left behind.

#

I thought I knew this disillusionist, at least enough to understand him.

He thought of himself as a sort of truth artist, this disillusionist. He knew the magic words that could never be heard by the human ear, the words that cut through the falsities of our lives. He worked in piercing and dissecting lies in much the same ways as a poet or a politician works in creating them. The true irony of the disillusionist was that he himself was a walking falsehood, half-man, half-corpse, alive only to spread death and harsh reality like a sweep of paint across canvas.

I knew him, and I would stop him, if only I could catch up to him. He was always a day ahead of me, always a town beyond wherever I stopped. Nobody could say with any certainty where he had come from. There were rumors that he had pulled himself from Lake Michigan during a lightning storm like a drowned corpse, too dead to realize he was no longer alive, seeking revenge on the living for his own murder. Others claimed he was a fallen priest who had seen firsthand, during his own personal rapture, that the Bible was wrong, and the knowledge had driven him mad. Still others claimed he was half red-blooded shaman and half demon.

I scoffed at such stories. I would discover the truth about the disillusionist. His trail was filled with corpses, and I was learning his methods. In his methods I could see his weaknesses. It was only a matter of time before I caught up to him.

#

I found them the next afternoon, their pockets and purses emptied and blood on their dress clothes. Only a very few battered and torn spectators, eyes like war veterans, lived to tell me about the disillusionist's performance. Just a handful of adults and most of the children of town, along with the sick and elderly who could not make it to the showing. The survivors. They told me all that had happened, their eyes still wide and unbelieving.

"He cleaned us out, boy," a toothless old man told me, shaking his cane toward the west, where he'd seen the man leave town. "Cleaned us out of our best people and all their valuables. Like a human tornado, he was. Damn his face and curse his path."

"No need for such language, sir," I said, my own voice rising to match his. "Take heed of the Good Book and pray for help. And don't forget to lock your doors behind you."

I left the emptied town and rode west. I set out on his trail, riding for another long week following his tracks until the night I finally caught up to him, at the start of another show.

#

Though I could have filled my ears with wax to protect myself from the sound of his uncompromising truths, I entered the town hall with open ears and unfettered hearing. The strength of arm that I'd inherited from my father gave me the ability to hold myself back as the show unfolded in front of me like a nightmare skit. Over and over I told myself that I would not fail. I was a man of the land, after all, and a devout Baptist. I would not be stopped by lies, even as the gunshots from the redskin massacre continued to echo in my mind.

The disillusionist was over halfway through his act. "You see before you a man cut in two," he cried from atop the rickety stage, his angular, discolored face framed by his black locks and curling sideburns. In his own way, he was handsome under his dusty top hat. "I harbor no illusions from you about this. I show you only the *Truth*."

With his final word, the man in the shiny black suit pulled himself in half at the waist.

The audience was shocked into silence. I'd heard of this trick before, not from the last town but from the survivors in the many towns to the east, but it still did not stop my jaw from dropping like a drawbridge. I could feel the coarse hairs of my beard on my neck, tickling my adam's apple. Flecks of something dark fluttered to the floor in front of the split disillusionist, fluttering slowly to the floor like slow-moving moths, or scales from a snake.

I closed my mouth when the man let go of his upper torso and set it back on his waist, straightening his vest to hide the separation. On the table in front of him sat his hat, turned upside down. Something with whiskers twittered inside of it, trying to distract the audience. He saw our interest and laughed softly, like wheezing, and then his eyes met mine.

I felt my will being tested. I again saw the Indians trying to surrender as the guns of the militia blazed. The guns that had never stopped going off in my head ever since that battle. My own courage quailed as the sound buffeted my ears, and I knew I was not the courageous soldier I thought I was. I was just a man holding a gun, standing far removed from the actual fighting. My destiny did not lie there. My eyes felt hot with shame for myself and pity for the dying redskins. Gunshots echoed in the distance, growing closer.

The man in the black suit, the disillusionist, stared at me. The rest of the audience was frozen.

"Who are you?" he whispered, but the words did not enter my ears. The man seemed to be inside my head, whispering to my mind like a snake in a tree.

And then I was released. My eyes fell shut, and when I opened them again, my back was sore and a dead rabbit, a golden doubloon, a broken watch, and a pack of smoking cards lay scattered on the makeshift stage in front of the disillusionist. I had been lost to the world for longer than a single blink of the eye.

Guns roared again in my ears, and bullets hissed past my jutting ears. At that moment I realized that I'd never asked what I was to do with the man once I'd caught up to him. I couldn't very well pull my pistol and stop him in the middle show, could I? Or should I, before it's too late?

"And now, instead of any further Feats of Truth," the disillusionist mumbled, and the audience leaned forward, "we will skip ahead to my final, and most prestigious Feat. I will need total silence from the audience please. Not a sound." His voice softened, losing volume, until all I could hear was a hypnotic whisper. "Do not dare even to breathe. I want to show you all something. I want to acquaint each and every one of you with an old, old friend of mine. The *Truth*."

The mix of booing and snickering voices stopped at the sharp clarity of the man's voice. He waited until complete silence fell around us, his black eyes scanning the audience like a surveyor. He gestured at himself like a man showing off a new suit. "Look at me. I am only an illusion."

As he spoke, I reached into my coat for my gun I'd been given at the start of my quest. My long arm moved as if it had been soaked in molasses. Each inch closer was a tiny victory.

"I am not a man at all," the disillusionist continued. "I am only here for you, to show you the error of your ways. To show you the folly of your falsehoods."

I could feel the cold metal of the gun, but my arm would not move to pull it out of my coat. That voice. It felt so real, so honest, that I wanted to listen and believe.

"And now, tonight, I'm taking them," he said. He inhaled with a long, wrenching sound. "I'm taking each and every one of your lies. I leave you with only . . . the *Truth*."

He snapped his fingers, a hollow sound. The lanterns flickered and my ears popped, as if the pressure had changed suddenly in the barn. I saw myself, in that moment, lying in a pool of my own blood, next to an ornate balcony chair as an unknown, somewhat homely woman sank to her knees in shock next to my lifeless body. Though my head was filled with the roaring aftermath of a gun's explosive force, I could hear a man cry out something in Latin far below me, followed by the sound of mad footsteps. And then the image was gone.

"Mary," I whispered, though the name meant nothing to me then. I knew no woman of that name, other than casual acquaintances. I realized that I was holding onto my chair with both hands, barely able to stand even as the people in the hall fought like dogs with one another. The floor was miles away from me.

The disillusionist stopped emptying the billfolds and purses of the raging audience members long enough to look directly at me with his lightless, yellowed gaze. His face was twisted in rage.

"Why does not the truth drive you mad?" he hissed. The people around him continued fighting, fingers in the eyes of their neighbors, knees in the groins of family members. The disillusionist stepped closer, the top half of his body shifting as if it would somehow slide off his pelvis and fall to the floor of the meeting hall.

My mouth was dry, and the sudden silence unnerved me. A mother and daughter rolled across the floor in front of me, screeching like hawks in mid-hunt. I opened my mouth to speak, closed it, and tried again. All I could think of was my defeats, in my run for office as well as the loss of my courage and innocence during the Black Hawk War.

Gunshots. Always more gunshots. And the Mississippi turned to blood.

And then, when I thought I would never be able to speak again, words filled my head like rain. As always, words had been my salvation, whether I was telling a story down at the post office, or giving a speech about improving the quality of the rivers in Springfield, or exhorting the armed men under my command to not lose faith. The words came to me and cleaned my vision of the harsh light of the disillusionist's intentions.

"I have been familiar with disappointments," I said, my voice a whisper to match the disillusionist, "too familiar to be very much chagrined these days. And I hold no illusions. All I have is my own honesty. And my hopes for the future."

The disillusionist looked long at me. His eyes were dead, like the corpses we had buried on the eastern shore of the Mississippi back in '32. And then he snapped his fingers again, so hard that flesh fell from his bones. The sound echoed in the barn.

"You will not take me in," he said. "I cannot be captured."

"I will," I answered. The gun was out of my coat and pointed at the disillusionist. His snapping fingers and scratching voice could not touch me now. I knew the truth and faced it willingly. "And you shall. *Sic Semper Tyrannis*," I added.

Thus always to tyrants.

In the meantime, the townspeople were still doing their damnedest to tear one another apart. I held the man in black in my sights, but I could not pull the trigger. I had vowed, at the resolution of the Black Hawk War, never to kill another man, regardless of his race or wrongdoings. Instead I pointed the gun at the ceiling and pulled the trigger.

The explosion of the pistol broke the disillusionist's hold over the townspeople. Battered and bloody, they helped one another to their feet, weeping now as their rage was overcome with fear and disgust. They emptied the hall and ran off into the night. I was left with the disillusionist and his bag of failed tricks. He gave me a cold smile.

"So the farmers and their pathetic families live for another day. Do not think you can stop me from moving on and continuing my work. My *art*."

I nodded at the blood on the chairs on either side of us. "That is not what I would call art. I would call it malice and cruelty." I walked closer to the man in black. With each step he seemed to shrink, while I grew taller. Or perhaps I simply imagined it all. I was, after all, taller than almost any other man I'd ever met. Uglier too, many have whispered, when they thought my big ears were out of range.

"It is true art," the disillusionist said. "True realism. I give them the world, without the false tint of prevarication."

The money he had been clutching in his hands fell to the floor along with more chunks of his rotten flesh. He backed up until he was at the far wall. He bent for his bag, but froze in the act when I cocked the gun.

"We all need our illusions," I said, and stopped. My breath caught in my chest as I thought of the slaughter of Indians all around me, and not just in the Black Hawk War. I saw everything, all the injustices of our young country that we visited on one another. The Negroes bent over in the fields, the burning villages of the Indians, the unknowing townspeople who had run off only moments earlier. We were a cruel, cruel people.

"And you think you can change all that?" the disillusionist said. I knew, in that moment that he had seen the images flashing throughmy head as clearly as I had.

I aimed the gun at the man's heart. It would be so simple, I thought. And it could end here.

The disillusionist, sensing his advantage, stepped closer, still talking.

"You? You with your dreams and aspirations? Do you think you could make amends to all that has gone before?" He paused and inhaled, exhaled loudly. "I see the dreaming future — the lie — you have built for yourself, my gaunt, bearded deputy. Would you be our greatest leader and end all that?"

I lowered the gun. I saw him clearly now, his eyes dead like the men under my command after the Blackhawk massacre, and I heard the fear in his voice mix with the gunfire in my mind.

"I will try," I said. "That is all any of us can do."

The disillusionist looked down at the gun, aimed at the floor, as if disappointed. "You won't kill me?"

"I'm not sure," I said, pulling out the handcuffs I'd been given upon my deputization, "that you *can* be killed, friend."

Raising his nearly fleshless wrists, the disillusionist focused his gaze on me. The sound of guns made me clamp my jaw shut.

"*Who are you?*" he asked again.

I stood up straighter and looked down at him, this half-dead man with his fancy mustache and bloody top hat. I heard one final echo of gunfire, and then the guns fell silent. My jaw relaxed. The eyes of the dead had finally closed inside my mind.

"Who I am," I said, "does not matter." I wrapped the cuffs around the man's wrist, careful to avoid contact with him. "All that matters is that you will not kill again."

With the snapping of the locks, I saw my future open up before me, free of false hopes and wrong-headed pride. There would still be time to prepare a run for the General Assembly this fall. As soon as I brought this creature in to justice, I would pursue my dreams until they were within my grasp, and I would succeed. Of that I had no illusions.

COAL ASH AND SPARROWS

Lina Seymour had been putting off going into the barn all day. Less than a week ago, the doctor had come to tell her, her mother, and her younger sister about her father's fall from the church roof. Daddy had been working with a crew of three other men, trying to finish shingling the roof of the new Petersburg church before a storm blew up. The rickety old wooden ladder on which he'd been standing had given way when he reached for a fistful of shingles. He lingered for almost four days, his face and body swollen and unfamiliar in the back room of the doctor's office. Then two days ago he simply let out a long sigh and never drew in another breath.

One of the few coherent sentences he'd mumbled to Lina during those awful hours had been something about a ship, a train, and three strange words.

Still wearing her black dress, Lina crept into the barn the day after her father was buried and found the book. It was barely bigger than her hand, with an unadorned white cover and only the number four printed on the spine. She would have missed the book completely if she hadn't reached down to wipe her dusty hands on her late father's old fleece-lined hunting jacket. When she let go of the jacket, the book slipped onto her bare foot. Young Lina let out a tiny meeping sound: the small white book was icy cold to the touch. In the years to come, she would never be sure if she actually found the book, or if the book found her.

Shivering in the drafty barn, she pulled her mother's shawl closer around her thin shoulders and stared at the book that had presented itself to her like a gift. In her right hand she held the sheaf of documents her mother had sent her to the barn to find. She'd found all of them neatly stacked in the dusty steamer trunk her grandparents had given Daddy years ago. The hand-me-down trunk was a kind of good-natured joke with the family. As a farmer in northeastern Iowa, her father had rarely traveled; the cows and crops demanded all of his time, not to mention that of his wife and two daughters. For all Lina knew, Daddy had never left the state.

Lina had always wanted to fill that big steamer trunk with her own souvenirs from around the globe. Unlike her father, she wanted to *see* the world and travel more than an hour away from home. She had once ridden with her father to Dubuque, a painful ride on their wagon that seemed to last forever, but once they had arrived at the Mississippi River, all of Lina's hurts disappeared when she saw the great paddlewheel boat pass by, heading south. Her dream of crisscrossing the world, however, ended the moment she touched the white book.

Lina gently set the papers on top of the steamer trunk and turned up the wick of her lantern. At some point night had fallen outside the barn window. Mother will be looking for me soon, she thought, though her mother hadn't risen from bed all day. The house was too quiet and dark without Daddy's voice filling and lighting it as he sang nonsense songs with Lina and her sister and laughed at their stories. Mother was too sad, and neither Lina nor Jenny felt like singing ever again. In the now-cool barn, Lina covered her legs in her father's hunting coat and picked up the tiny white book.

Another shiver ran through her at the book's touch, and a puff of her own breath clouded around her face as she exhaled. She opened the cover with a trembling hand, realizing in the back of her mind that the book was no longer icy cold, but almost warm, inviting her to lose herself in its thin pages.

She whispered the ornately-written word on the first page of the tiny book: "Magic?" Her thin voice echoing in her ears, Lina Seymour settled in and began to read.

#

Joseph McAndrew was the first boy from his orphanage to volunteer to ride the trains west. At ten years old, he was already bigger than most of the other children in the rambling white house south of the city. He knew that his chances of being brought home with any of the few prospective parents that came to visit the orphanage were slim, and probably none. With his unruly black hair and dark eyes, he also knew he was not adorable like the other Irish children with their milky skin and brilliant blue eyes. Joseph was a realistic ten-year-old. An orphan train was his only chance to escape.

The Children's Aid Society and the Foundling Hospital, along with a few clergymen and dealmakers in New York City had dreamed up the so-called orphan trains. The facts were simple: Families in Nebraska, Missouri, Iowa, Illinois, and Michigan needed extra hands with the harvest and the endless chores on their farms; orphanages were overflowing with immigrant children and waifs abandoned in the city. The first orphan trains began their westward journeys in late fall of 1854, and Joseph was determined to be on one of them. I could be like Father John Murphy at Boolavogue and Vinegar Hill, he thought, traveling into the great unknown to do battle. His mother would have sang a song about him, if she had survived the voyage from Ireland.

Behind the front desk of the orphanage, arranged like mailboxes or tiny safes for the rooms in a hotel, were stacked dozens of small, square boxes. Each cardboard box belonged to a different child in the orphanage, stuffed with the child's belongings and papers. The orphanage provided them with donated clothing — rough woolen shirts and scratchy cotton pants, two pairs of socks and undergarments, all faded browns and grays — so their boxes held all that mattered in each child's life. Once a week, the children were allowed to look inside their boxes.

Until the day he left on the train, Joseph skipped his time with his box. He had already memorized the three pieces of paper inside of it, though he never let on to the others that he could read. In the months before his mother and father took him to the shipyards of Dublin, his mother had taught him his letters and read with him every day. As a reward, his mother would sing about Ireland and the heroes of the land. Joseph had learned quickly.

Along with his birth certificate, his passport, and his ship's receipt from the *Odessa*, the box also contained a small white book. The book was a gift from his eccentric great-uncle, a great black-haired bear of a man who was well known in their small Irish town as a world traveler. Joseph had only known the man as "Mo," though he was sure — despite the fogginess that filled his brain any time he tried to remember specific details about the man — that "Mo" was not his great-uncle's real name. Joseph doubted that Mo was even his great-uncle; the big man certainly didn't look Irish with his dark skin and big brown eyes.

Great-Uncle Mo had given the book to Joseph three years ago back in Ireland, without his parents' knowledge. Joseph had told nobody about the book, and he hadn't ever seen Mo again. On the unending, seasick ship ride on the *Odessa* from Dublin to New York City that had taken the life of his mother by pneumonia and nearly killed his father from dysentery, Joseph had filled his days with the words of the white book he'd been given by his great-uncle Mo.

That changed upon his arrival in the orphanage five months later, after his father had forgotten about him and could only remember his last and next drink. He had tried to put the book and its contents out of his thoughts. In his cot next to the forty-two other boys in the sleeping room, the contents of the book had given him nightmares, blurry visions of white-blue lightning and arrows of unholy green fire. I am not the hero I thought I was, Joseph thought, waking from his dreams with tears in his eyes. He left the book in its box, never revisiting it.

Of the strange words in the book — *Words*, he always thought of them, like proper names — Joseph would remember only three, and they would come back to him only once, sixteen years later, his mouth dry and tasting of coal ash.

#

Nine-year-old Lina Seymour held the book in small hands that no longer shook. The lantern had burned low, almost out of fuel, and she could hear her mother calling her name, but she could not stop reading.

The book was proving to her something that she'd always thought, always *wished*, was true: that there was more to life than cooking for a hungry, weary husband, more than scrubbing floors, clothes, and dirty childrens' faces. More than a hardscrabble life of working the land, following the lead of a man like her dead father as they scraped through another season. The book told her what she had always longed to know.

Lina forced her gaze away from the tiny print of the book and closed her eyes. She saw brilliant green and blue flashes under her eyelids as she thought about those words.

I must be dreaming, she thought, blinking her eyes in the gloomy darkness of the barn. There's nothing extraordinary here on our farm, and especially not inside me.

"Lina?" her mother's hoarse voice called once more, with finality. The screen door to the house slammed shut. Lina heard but did not register the sounds. She was reading again, her thin white lips moving with each sentence, all doubts erased by the small words in the book she held inches from her face. The author was right there, inside her mind, filling her with a steady diet of insight, potentiality, and desire. Words passed from her unblinking eyes directly into her imagination faster than the beat of her heat.

Magic existed, the book repeated over and over, *and it was inside of her.*

She wanted to shout it to rafters of the barn. This knowledge was better than any trip to see the Mississippi, more wonderful than watching a paddle-wheel float past. *Magic!*

Determined to learn more, Lina Seymour remained in the barn for the next one hundred and thirty-one years.

#

Joseph sat on the first passenger car behind the coal car, his lungs full of ash and his mouth painfully dry. He held his small valise on his lap the entire trip, afraid to let it out of his sight and risk losing his ticket and the paper containing the names of his new mother and father. Also inside his valise were a change of clothes and his three pieces of identification folded into his small white book. Right before leaving, Joseph had thrown the square cardboard box that once held his entire life so far into the orphanage fireplace. I'm ready for the Camolin Cavalry, he thought, walking out of the orphanage to meet his train.

He fought the temptation to slip the white book out of his bag and read to pass the long, swaying hours of his train ride west. But a deep, laughing voice filled his head every time he even thought about pulling out the book. "It is not yours to read any more," the voice said. "You've already read it on one trip. The book must go to someone else now. One journey is all you get in this life, my boy."

Joseph closed his eyes and let the rhythm of the metal wheels on the smooth iron rails below rock him to sleep. He dreamed he was back on the

Ellis-Island-bound *Odessa* and his mother was still singing about Irish soldiers defending Erin's lovely home and his father hadn't started drinking and stopped caring. Their laughter brought tears to his sleeping eyes.

When he woke he was in Iowa, at a station in the river city of Dubuque. He pulled himself painfully from his seat, his legs asleep, and stumbled out of the ash-filled passenger car to meet his adoptive family. His first vision of his new life was the slow, muddy Mississippi framed by the brown banks of Illinois to the east and the skeletal railroad bridge to the north. Joseph caught himself wishing for the familiar desperation of the orphanage walls. Luckily, the sensation lasted only as long as it took him to walk onto the platform to meet the strangers who had paid for his trip west.

The Seymours, his new family, lived on a farm outside Petersburg, forty miles west of Dubuque, and all of them spoke German, and German only. The ride home in the horse-drawn wagon took four hours, and Joseph was close to crying from the violent jouncing of the wagon on the dirt roads. His ears were full of harsh-sounding, foreign words, though the words were spoken by gentle people who smiled at him often and gave him food to eat.

The sun was down by the time they arrived at the big white farmhouse, and for a bad moment Joseph thought he had returned to the orphanage, the two big buildings looked so much alike. Then his vision cleared, and he saw dark, flat fields on either side of him and blue sky stretched above him instead of rows of apartments and distant factory smoke clotting the gray air. He went inside to clean up, sleep, and begin his new life. He never thought about the orphanage again.

Five years passed in the blink of an eye.

Joseph left school at fifteen, married his neighbor Anne-Marie at sixteen, and was a father at seventeen. By the time he was twenty, when his first daughter Lina was three and his second daughter Jenny was walking and talking, he felt like he'd accomplished much in his life. He spoke both English and German fluently, and he lived with his wife in a house he and his father and three brothers had built fifty feet away from the big farmhouse. He attended church weekly, prayed daily, and though he was not like the heroes from his mother's songs, Joseph felt that his was a life that had been blessed and was full of light.

Six years later he would be pounding nails into the roof of the new church, balancing shingles on a borrowed ladder as a storm approached.

#

Lina talked to her father while she slowly lost her mind during the rest of the nineteenth century and all of the twentieth century.

"I forgive you for wishing I was a boy," she said, whispering words in the stuffy barn that she'd never been able to say to her father while he was alive. Tears filled her eyes as she twisted strands of hair around her fingers and pulled. "Someone to carry on the family name and a strong back to help with the work. I'll make it up to you, Daddy. Just watch me."

When she ran out of words, Lina was left with the world of the barn and the contents of the little white book.

The barn itself held untold mysteries. Two stories high, the interior felt as if it took up more space that it appeared to on the outside. Lina could walk for close to an hour and never retrace her steps or cross her path. She avoided the shadowy areas, especially the corner where the rusted tools sat like a death waiting to happen, and spent most of her time in the loft. Up a sturdy ladder, the hayloft ran the length of three-fourths of the barn, leaving only a rectangular gap in the middle where the ladder was positioned. If she climbed to the top of the stacked bales of hay, she could see outside through the hole that a woodpecker had knocked into the wall by the roof. Only half of the loft was filled with hay, and it was in this half that Lina spent most of her time, reading.

The first thing she learned from the book was how to make sparks fly out of her fingertips. Luckily she hadn't burned down the barn with that trick, or its more advanced counterpart, lightning bolts. The hay had been damp from a recent rain in spring of 1873, though dates no longer mattered to Lina. For her, a year passed as quickly as sneezing or breaking wind.

Lina also learned how to levitate — chapter five — and how to catch small animals in a net of binding energy — chapter eight — for her meals. Spark-roasted rat and sparrow were her usual delicacies. The energy she expended catching and cooking her meals exhausted her, and she would sleep for at least half a week after eating. Life in the barn, Lina thought on the rare occasions she let herself be distracted from her book, was good.

Just before the turn of the century, another family bought the farm from Lina's younger sister Jenny, who had never married and had become a sour old maid at the age of thirty-five. Neither Jenny nor the new tenants had ever paid a visit to the barn, which was barely visible to the outside world (unless it was foggy and the temperature was between fifty and fifty-five degrees Fahrenheit, and even then it was just a red blur next to the cow pasture).

In the last month of 1899, Lina had her first visitor.

She had been taking a break from the book for a few months. After searching its pages endlessly for a lesson on how to fly, she'd thrown the book at the wall in frustration. That four on the spine haunted her. Were there three other books? Or even more than that? Maybe book five talked about flight. It sure as blazes wasn't in Book Four. Lina had glared at the book lying on a pile of rotting, half-burnt hay, and began chatting again with her dead father.

"On the day the doctor told us the news, Jenny and I had been skipping our chores, Daddy." She wiped tears from her face with a hand that was thin and spidery, unfamiliar in her clearing eyes. Everything for the past decade had been a blur. She blamed it on too much book-reading. "Mama was so mad at us. She said we'd have to tell you about it when you got back from roofing the church. But we never got a chance to."

Lina trailed off on the one hundred and eighty-ninth time she'd confessed this to her father's memory. Against the far wall of the barn, above the pump where she drew water from a well that had yet to run dry, a sparrow perched on the steamer trunk and stared at her.

Lina tried to remember the Words of Binding from the book, but she couldn't recall if it had been chapter five or eight. She hadn't eaten in over a week. Then she realized the book was on the other side of the barn, sitting where she'd thrown it. Before she could stand up and get it, the sparrow began to talk.

"I heard you were here," the sparrow said in a high-pitched, stuttering voice. Its last word was repeated five times — "here-here-here-here-here!" The sparrow stretched its short neck closer to Lina, as if inspecting her. "You're not much to look at, are-are-are-are-are you?"

"Come closer," Lina said, fighting the impulse to inch toward to the bird herself. She remained very still, holding her breath.

The sparrow cocked its head to the side as if smiling at her. "Your great-great unc-unc-unc-unc-uncle's shade told me you'd be close to this barn. Didn't tell me you'd be *living* here-here-here-here-here!"

"I like it here," Lina said, inching closer. The Words of Binding had come back to her, even though it had been weeks since she'd last practiced them. Her blood began to swirl hot and cold through her veins as the power vested in the Words filled her. She was hungry. "It's safe here. Even if I fall, like my Daddy, I'll always land in hay. Come closer."

"So you've been reading the book-book-book-book-book?"

Lina was ten feet from the sparrow. A bitter, ashy taste filled the back of her throat. "Who wants to know? Whose business is it but mine?"

The sparrow gave its cocked-head smile again and didn't answer. It gave what to Lina's eyes looked like a nod, and then gestured with its dirty beak at the book on the far side of the barn. "It's ev-ev-ev-ev-everyone's business, miss. You must keep that book safe until the right-right-right-right-right person comes looking for it."

Lina was having trouble following the sparrow's words. She was so very hungry. "I'm going to have to ask you," Lina said, her muscles shaking as she prepared herself to leap, "to leave now, Mr. Sparrow."

The sparrow remained sitting on the trunk, watching her. It lifted one leg and set it back down, then did the same with the other, never taking its black eyes off the tensed woman on the other side of the barn.

Lina couldn't wait any longer. She dove at the bird, shouting Words of Binding. But already the bird was gone, twittering loudly as it flashed past Lina's bird's-nest hair. The sparrow gave her a good peck on the back of her head before arcing toward the hole in the ceiling. Thunder rumbled across the sky, and rain began to fall against the dirty barn windows.

Lina put her right hand on her wounded head and screamed. Sparks flew from her left hand, catching the sparrow just before the bird made it out through the hole to safety. Cackling, Lina caught the bird before it hit the hay-covered floor and shoved it into her mouth. Two feathers puffed out of her mouth and into the air, but Lina caught them and swallowed them as well. She chewed, a thoughtful expression on her dirty, lined face.

"Nobody's business but my own," she said, swallowing. "Not ev-ev-ev-ev-everyone's business."

The bird had tasted like mud, accompanying the bitter, ashy taste the Words had left in her mouth. There were coarse hairs on her tongue when she burped. She spit out as many hairs as she could and dropped to the floor for a nap as her lunch digested. Rain spattered on the roof and dripped through the hole in the ceiling. The rain fell on the book and bounced off harmlessly. The book was safe.

Lina wouldn't have another visitor for a hundred and two years.

#

Joseph had always believed in hard work and giving of his time and his strong back, so on that windy day in October, 1870, he found himself balancing a hammer, a bag of nails, and a sheath of shingles on a forty-foot ladder on the church roof of Petersburg.

He'd never been afraid of heights, but, being a man of the land and crops and dirt, he'd never been higher than the second story of his barn. Eyes focused on the section of roof directly in front of him, Joseph calmed himself by thinking of his girls. Jenny's giggle and Lina's high-pitched, bird-like voice filled his head, and he smiled. She'd sang him "Ring Around the Rosie" that morning after he came in from the milking, before he left for church. The girls had danced around him while he ate his breakfast, falling giggling to the floor at the end of the song.

The morning passed and the rows of shingles slowly crept up the side of the church roof like a growing shadow, one shingle at a time. Keeping his weight forward on the ladder, fighting the harsh pitch of the roof, Joseph wielded his hammer with five times the care than he'd use if his legs were planted firmly on the ground.

When he ladder started to tremble under him, he felt as if the moment he'd been waiting for all morning had finally become reality, just by his trying so hard to avoid it. As the wooden rung under his feet cracked, Joseph saw three small words — Words, his panicked mind had corrected him — in front of his eyes. He shouted the Words with all his energy, scrabbling for the roof with his hands. He began to fall, and his hammer, the nails, and the shingles he'd been holding all fell to the hard dirt below.

"Ring around the rosie," Lina and Jenny's voices sang in his head.

Joseph remained hanging in midair over a ladder that was now lying on the ground in two pieces. His mouth went dry, and he tasted something harsh and bitter, like coal ash, on his tongue.

"Pocket full of posies . . . "

Joseph was levitating. Just as the book said he would, if he said the Words properly. His heart hammered in his chest, the throbbing like the engine of the ship he'd felt on his cot in the *Odessa*, lying on his stomach as he read the tiny white book from his great uncle, over and over. Joseph was levitating. Just as he had once levitated in the ship, a full two feet above his cot. Until his father walked in the door and whipped him, all the while cursing Mo's name.

"Ashes, ashes . . . "

I don't believe this, he thought, his legs dangling under him like useless pieces of scrap wood. With a childish laugh, he kicked out as if he were swimming in mid-air. His worn-out left boot slipped off his foot and fell to the ground below, hitting with a dull thud. He looked at the church roof, five feet away from him, and the broken ladder on the ground under him.

"I forbid you to ever read this book again," his father had shouted that day in their tiny room on the *Odessa*, ripping it from Joseph's hands. He took it to the deck and threw it overboard, but the next morning the book had reappeared in Joseph's valise.

As if the memory of his father's anger made him realize that what he had been doing for the past five seconds was impossible, Joseph Seymour felt the magic drain from his body. No longer levitating, he dropped to the unforgiving ground forty feet below.

#

When Lina turned sixty-five, unbeknownst to anyone else around her — her family having forgotten her after her disappearance, as if she'd never really existed in their world at all — she made her first attempt to leave the barn. She'd been thinking about Jenny, singing songs with her, and she wanted to give her mother the documents she'd been sent to retrieve decades ago.

The sheaf of yellowed, brittle documents in her hand, Lina opened the door and was greeted by a dozen sparrows. All of them stared at her in the same curious way as the first sparrow had all those years ago, moments before she ate it. Two of the sparrows had darker feathers than the others, brownish-black in color.

"You are the guar-guar-guar-guar-guardian," the first black sparrow said.

"You can't leave-leave-leave-leave-leave," the second black sparrow said.

"Oh yes," Lina said, her breath coming to her in short bursts as the bright sun hit her skin and blinded her for a heartbeat. I am no simple guardian, she thought. I've read the book and learned the Words. I am a sorceress. "Oh yes . . . I can . . . "

"Your journey is not com-com-com-com-complete!"

Lina paused and looked up at the sparrow talking to her, a twin of the brown bird she had eaten years ago. "What journey? I've been nowhere, nowhere but this barn!"

"One journey is all you get-get-get-get-get."

More sparrows joined the first row of mud-colored birds as she struggled to lift her now-heavy legs. She had yet to cross over the threshold of the barn and enter the yard. She lifted her leg to step closer to the outside world. Nowhere but here, she thought to herself.

The birds took to the air, blocking the bright rays of the sun, turning day into night. They flew up as if of one mind and body and turned on Lina, who stood with her foot still suspended in the air. They flew closer, and she screamed. She scrambled in her mind to find the Words that would dispel the sparrows, but nothing came. Finally able to move, she slammed the door shut before tiny beaks embedded themselves in her skin, instead thudding harmlessly off the wooden barn door. In the barn, she was safe.

Never again will I try to leave, Lina thought, shaking hands searching for the comfort of her plain white book. The yellow documents from her father fluttered to the floor, forgotten. Never again.

#

Moammar had always had a special place in his heart for his great-nephew Joseph. Though he knew the boy would never truly *understand* him or the way he could never stay in one place for longer than a few weeks, still Mo had taken a shining to the boy. With the thought always in the back of his mind that Joseph could be the next One, he did his best to make the boy's life special.

Like the time Mo had taken Joseph and his mother to the ocean to watch the dolphins race, and Mo had let a piece of Joseph go out toward the salt water and enter one of the dolphins for a few wondrous seconds. Moammar went out with him into another dolphin, and the waves touched his and Joseph's new bodies like caresses. They kicked their tails and dove out of the water as if they were both filled with lightning. When Mo brought Joseph back to himself, he watched the boy with an intense smile, one not unlike the smile made by a curious sparrow years later.

This could be all yours, my boy, Moammar had thought — but not said — at the time. Joys like this, and so much more.

On another visit weeks later, a much less relaxed Mo pulled his chair close to Joseph the instant Joseph's parents left the room. Joseph had been seven years old at the time. Moammar was rushed for time, and he hoped his voice would not betray him.

"Joseph," Mo said. "I have something for you."

"What?" Joseph said, unable to contain himself. "What did you get me, Mo?"

Mo answered by passing him a book. The older man stifled a grin as Joseph tried to hide his disappointment from his great-uncle.

"A book?"

"Not just any book," Mo said, tapping the small book's plain cover. He forced himself to speak slowly and not rush. "A book of power. More power than you could imagine. Think of swimming with the dolphins last month. This book holds secrets like that, and more. And I want you to have it, my boy."

Joseph's small hand shook as he reached for the book. "Why me?" he squeaked. "I'm just a boy."

"Time is short, Joseph. Just read the book, let the Words enter your mind, and remember them." Running his big hands through his beard, Mo gazed out the window at something in the distance. A puff of dust had been raised on the dirt road coming from Dublin. Mo felt his face tighten, and his words came faster. The Sorcerers of the Fist may be sending someone to get me, he thought with a shudder. It had been a long time since he'd had to do battle, and he knew he'd have to fight his former colleagues who would be using their new magic. He cleared his throat and looked down at the waiting boy next to him. "Just remember that the power of the book can be fickle. It may fail you when you need it most, or if you show the slightest doubt. And it will always look to find the most powerful person around, abandoning you if you appear to be weak. So be confident and strong, and you will be our next hero."

"What . . . "

Mo shook his head. "No more questions. Just be confident and strong, Joseph, and remember what you read in here."

Joseph looked at the small book in his hands. He slid his dirty hand down the front of the book, but his finger left no track on the white cover. In a few seconds, Joseph was engrossed in reading, his mouth slightly open and his eyes wide.

Moammar slipped out of the house without a look back at the boy and his book.

Short minutes later, the tall man with the black-and-gray beard and dark complexion let out a long breath and set his knapsack onto a park bench four miles away. An instant later he collapsed onto the bench himself. Someone had been calling to him for the past month, a familiar voice from his past, an old acquaintance from the long-ago times. Before Moammar Grayson Avitular had given up on that life, as part of the Sorcerers of the Hand. And now that old friend was calling him back. Back to Stonehenge, where the Druids had began their teachings about magic, before magic split into two competing factions.

Moammar didn't want to go, but he had no choice if he wanted to help close this rift.

He had made his last stop before his ship left Dublin for England. He hoped he'd done the right thing. If the magic of research and knowledge that he had always believed in was to continue, the Sorcerers of the new, more aggressive magic could not be allowed find the book or its counterparts. The five books had been spread to the corners of the world, their final destinations hidden to all other Sorcerers. Moammar's old friend Ishi had confided in him that the users of the new magic were calling it the Fist. The name was an insult to the teachings of the Hand, and a good portion of the hopes of the older magic rested with the young boy Moammar that had just entrusted with one of the books of magic. It was a massive responsibility for a boy so young as Joseph, but again, Mo had no choice in the matter.

Digging a box of mud and a square tin of horsehair from his bag, Moammar clucked and shook his head. Joseph would never have been his first choice, but there was something in the boy, even if he was only seven, that gave him hope. And in times like these, beggars couldn't afford to be choosers. If only he knew for sure that Joseph, or even Joseph's descendants, could handle this task and not let the book fall into the wrong hands. And there were the other four books to consider as well.

Moammar rolled a handful of mud in horsehair, and began shaping the mud into a tiny, bird-like figure. He'd check back on Joseph when he could, after he returned from Stonehenge. Setting the tiny sparrow made of mud and horsehair on the bench next to him, Moammar stood. Until then, just like the sparrow he left behind, Joseph's future was out of his hands.

The mud sparrow shook itself once, then took off toward the west, in the direction of the McAndrew house. Moammar would never again see Ireland or his great-nephew again while he was alive.

#

In May of 2001, at the age of one hundred and forty, Lina Seymour sat hunched over the pristine pages of the white book of magic that she had been reading for most of her life.

Her black dress had been worn away to next to nothing, and her father's hunting jacket was wrapped around her waist, now part of her dress. Half of her white hair lay scattered around her on the floor, and what remained on her head stuck up at wild angles that formed identifiable shapes. She weighed less than eighty pounds, and her mind was quite gone.

She lifted her head and squinted out the upper window. Someone was approaching the barn. A young, dark-skinned girl with a determined crease in her forehead carrying three small white objects clutched to her chest. As Lina watched, the girl slipped the square objects with great care into the backpack she was wearing. They were *books*, Lina realized.

Lina lifted herself from the wood floor and caught herself crying. She didn't know if it was with relief or fear. And were those books, she thought, for me?

"I have a guest, Daddy," she whispered. "I hope you don't mind if I go out to greet her."

Scurrying down the ladder from her second-floor roost, she let go of her own white book, which had turned cold in her gnarled hand, and covered it with hay. Gasping for breath, she pulled the steamer trunk in front of the pile of hay.

"Now stay there," she said to the book, even as her small hands ached for the comforting weight of it again.

With a shaky breath and an unsteady stride, Lina Seymour opened the barn door and, having skipped all of the twentieth century, stepped into the twenty-first. She pulled the door closed behind her. No sparrows were in sight, and her mouth was filled with the taste of coal ashes. She made it half a dozen steps before facing the young girl only five feet away.

"Why are you here?" Lina said, raising her voice but still sounding like a bird's cheeping. The girl stopped, looking past Lina through the open door of the barn.

"I think you know what I came for, ma'am," the girl said.

Lina squinted at her. The girl couldn't have been more than thirteen years old. Her skin was dark, like Daddy's coffee blended with a touch of cream, and her long black hair was thick and curly. In all of her life Lina hadn't seen anyone who looked like this, and she stared, mouth open. Then she remembered the book, hidden behind the trunk.

As if reading her thoughts, the girl nodded. "There's something out there that's bigger than both of us. It's called the Fist, and I need that book of yours to fight them. They've been gathering forces for longer than either of us has been alive. I'd rather fight them than fight you." The girl gently set her backpack onto the long grass in front of the barn and stepped closer. "I hope you understand, ma'am. I can't leave here without that book."

Tears slipped from Lina's eyes even as she began running the Words through her mind. The calm voice of the girl in front of her threatened to unnerve her. She caught herself in the act of turning back to the barn to retrieve the book for the girl. A sparrow fluttered to the ground from her right and sat on a tree stump a few feet away, as if watching and waiting.

I can't let you take the book, Lina thought, the wild rush of magic flowing through her ancient body. She answered the girl at last with the most powerful spell she knew: lightning bolts.

The battle waged that day lasted less than three hundred seconds. Witnessed only by a growing crowd of brown sparrows, the two women threw bursts of blue lightning and white energy back and forth across the Iowa countryside at each other, scorching the sides of the old red barn and digging deep divots into the black earth. Lina Seymour fought with all she had, but her strength and her ability were not enough.

By the time Lina realized the painful truth, that her destiny had never been Sorcerery, it was already too late. Her incomplete knowledge of magic and her untrained skill could only carry her so far. She thought of the three Words her father had whispered to her on his deathbed. He body racked with pain from the magical attacks of the young girl combined with her new knowledge of her misspent life, she spoke her final Words on this Earth.

As Lina began to lift gently from the ground, the girl tried to stop her final, fiery attack, a blue globe of flame intended to subdue the older woman. The ball of magical fire slammed into Lina, who was laughing and crying as she levitated two feet above the ground.

Her final thought had been that she was finally — after so much time spent reading her book — *flying*.

Through his sparrows, the shade of Moammar had witnessed the battle that had been over a century in the making, and he was inordinately proud of both of his descendants. The young girl, the great-granddaughter of the illegitimate son of Jennifer Seymour, Lina's sister, not only walked away with the fourth book, but she also knew where to find the fifth and final book of magic (which, among many other procedures, detailed how to fly). Before he could rest in his stony grave just outside Stonehenge, his final act as a benevolent spirit was to enfold the brittle soul of the book's guardian, Lina Seymour, close to him.

"Lina," Moammar said to the thin woman levitating between death and life. "Your life was neither wasted nor misspent." He held out a hand to her. "Come travel with me, at last."

Lina looked at him with surprise and a hint of recognition. He was dressed in white robes containing bits of mud and clumps of horsehair. She gave a tiny nod as her ears filled with the soft voice of a woman, singing about Ireland.

Yes, she thought, tasting coal ash on her tongue. I deserve this.

After nearly a century and a half of life, Lina Seymour's great-great-uncle Moammar guided her into the afterworld, and they were accompanied by a flock of chittering, mud-colored sparrows.

AN OUTRIDER'S TALE

After the short, lopsided battle, as the younger warriors hauled the dead bandits out of the old castle, the man known only as Seeker carried a bottle of dark wine over to where the outrider known only as Fist sat, alone. Though the Code forbade him to ask the history of another outrider, Seeker needed to know the man's story. Now that the fighting was over, his goal was to loosen the tongue of the big, scarred man.

Night had fallen, yet the moon shone brightly through holes in the ruined roof of the tower. Seeker's eyes had been trained, in his first life, to see perfectly in pitch-black night, but when he stepped up next to where Fist rested, he doubted what his eyes saw.

The big man was cradling in his hands a perfect red rose.

Seeker turned to leave, chiding himself for even approaching the other man. He would drink his bottle of wine by himself and try to forget the way Fist cradled the rose in his hands like a tiny animal.

As he was moving away, a voice stopped him: "Wine?"

He looked down at Fist again. The rose had disappeared.

"From the black grapes of Southland." Seeker handed the bottle to Fist. "Enjoy."

Fist stared at Seeker so long with his mismatched eyes, one brown and one blue, that Seeker nearly let the bottle slip from his fingers.

"Will you join me?" Fist said.

Seeker exhaled. "Of course."

Fist took the bottle and removed the cork. After a long drink, he grunted with appreciation.

"So," the big man said. "You want to know about me."

Seeker cast his gaze around the darkened tower, hoping none of the others had overheard. Something shifted high above him, at the top of the ruined tower.

"Of course not," he said, trying to smile. "That's not our way. *One man's history is nothing to an outrider*, of course."

"Would you try to stop me if I attempted to tell you anyway?" Fist's mismatched eyes glittered in the moonlight.

Seeker felt a chill fall over him. Out of the corner of his eye he caught movement above them, inside the castle proper. But when he turned to look closer, the movement was gone.

"Of course not," he said, motioning for the bottle.

"Good," Fist said. "For I have need to tell my story. Tonight."

Half of the other outriders had pulled out their sleeping rolls and settled in for the night in the newly-cleaned tower, though three others, like Fist and Seeker, remained sleepless. Seeker pulled a flask from an inner pocket — Fist had already finished most of the rich Southland cabernet. After a quick mouthful of the sturdy moonshine, Seeker nodded.

"So. Tell me."

"I know this castle well," Fist began. "I was once the lord of this keep, years ago. Until, only moments after I was given a new life, I killed my beloved."

Seeker knew he had control enough over the muscles in his face and body to keep from flinching at the man's words, but it had been a struggle. He nodded slowly at Fist.

"She was named . . . Teresa. In my youth I rode with her father. We were two young men from neighboring fiefdoms, dreaming of the day when we would rule our own land, the adventures we would have before then. We even talked of becoming outriders, leaving responsibility behind and swearing by the Code."

Seeker smiled with sadness. He vaguely remembered what it was like to be a boy.

"Yet I knew we were deluding ourselves. My father and my uncle had both relied on me to carry on the leadership of this valley." Fist waved an arm about him. "As you can see from one glance at this desolate town, I have disappointed the legacy and the memory of both men. I would never leave this valley, I thought as a young buck, wishing for a life of adventure and danger."

As he waited, Seeker watched something flicker off to his left, a snatch of white that could have been a reflection of a distant fire or moonlight. He touched his daggers and kept his eyes on both Fist and the broken walls of the keep around them.

"The summer before my seventeenth year, before my life of responsibility was scheduled to begin, I was exploring the caves west of this valley with Teresa's father, Timoth. We left our horses hobbled in a grassy field and climbed to the caves with the enthusiasm of our youth, and soon we were deep inside the darkness, searching for the fabled drawings left by the Early People. We found one —- a two-headed beast devouring a fawn — when we heard the horses nicker, followed by the sound of hooves.

"Timoth, as was his nature, bolted from the caves, sword in hand. There had been word of horse thieves in the area, and Timoth would never be — by losing his horse to them.

"I entered the clearing ten steps behind him, just in time to see both of our horses disappear. Timoth gave chase, and he caught up to them, easily. He leapt into the midst of the three thieves, knocking the first rider from his own horse and breaking the man's neck when they both landed on the rocks below. I often wonder how Timoth's and my lives would have turned out if there had only been the three thieves that day. But of course, there were more thieves — there are *always* more thieves — and Timoth's shouting brought them upon us. Half a dozen more rushed up from the other side of the pass to help their allies.

"I killed two of them myself before they ran off, but Timoth was badly wounded by the thieves' daggers. The thieves rode off, leaving our horses, and Timoth survived, but barely."

Seeker saw the flash of white again, this time off to his right, at the top of a ruined stairwell. He nearly got up, but Fist's hand flashed out and grabbed him by the shoulder.

"Calm yourself," Fist rumbled. "I see it too."

Fighting a surge of anger, Seeker sat down again.

"When he was well, Timoth offered me half of his family's land as reward.

He claimed I had saved his life, and I couldn't refuse: it was a Life Vow. While you may not have heard of such a thing, in my time a Life Vow was not something to be taken lightly. On top of that, the land was also in the midst of what would turn out to be the first season of the Dry Spell."

Seeker looked up sharply at the other man. The Dry Spell had taken place long before Seeker was born.

"I refused to take such a gift, for doing so would have ruined them. Yet, as a result of my refusal, Timoth changed from that day on. He grew distant and watched me with a burning look in his eye. In the meantime, the Dry Spell continued, and people began leaving our land and the neighboring lands. Almost two decades it would last, no rain for nineteen growing seasons.

"One night, a year after my refusal, Timoth challenged me to a night of gambling with his brothers. I thought nothing of it at the time, and left my sword at home, taking only a handful of coins and three bottles of wine. You can probably guess what happened next. We played cards — mad sixes, five-hand draw, witch's cat, queens, and dead jacks, all the old, forgotten games — for most of the night and into the next morning. The entire time I could not stop winning Timoth's money.

"When I realized what he was doing, I folded up my hand, drank the last of my wine, and gathered up only the coins I had brought with me from the piles of gold in front of me.

"'Good night,' I called to Timoth, right before he dove onto me, screaming that I would not insult him again by not accepting his Life Vow. We scrambled through the castle, into the kitchens, where the morning cooking had already begun. It was there that Timoth drew his sword on me, outside the hot furnaces of the kitchen.

"He drew his sword on me. Even now I can barely believe it.

"His crazed swinging backed me further into the kitchen, my eyes never leaving his sword. I didn't see the pot of hot cooking oil until I lost my balance and fell backwards, my head striking the hard metal. The pot overturned onto me.

"The oil burned off most of my face, but I thank the gods that I only lost one eye. I was healed as best as their herbs-and-alchemy man could heal me, and the seeping wound that was my face was covered in skin taken from a newly-dead man. Despite their valiant efforts, the pain has never fully left me.

"Timoth was devastated by what happened. He rode off to the clearing outside the caves where he was convinced I saved his life, and fell upon his sword.

"This need not have been so.

"Timoth had always been one to live by his emotions, to explode into action before stopping to think. He was a good man — don't even begin to think otherwise — but he was also consumed by helplessness as his own land died and not even his wife and newborn child could divert his thoughts. In his last days, I know that when he saw my face, he was reminded of his failures.

"This need not have been so. For I healed quickly, though the scars, as you can plainly see, will remain until my death."

#

Seeker could feel the numbness from the wine and his moonshine filling his extremities. As Fist spoke, Seeker had three more times caught glimpses of white inside the castle, and he was convinced it was a person. He saw the figure only in the corner of his eye before it melted back into the darkness.

"So that is your story," he whispered, exhaling, careful not to speak too loudly. His gaze kept returning to the uneven, grayish flesh on Fist's face, the flesh of a newly-dead man. Willing his hand not to shake, he raised his flask. "I toast your strength in healing and enduring, and I thank you for your tale."

Fist only stared at Seeker. Shuddering, Seeker looked away and saw a flash of white, like a drape or curtain in the wind. He squinted into the darkness inside the castle. At the foot of a broken staircase, a pale face came into view.

Moving his head slowly, he was able to see that the person appeared to be watching the two men and listening, despite the distance between them. He blinked, and the face was gone again.

"But there is more," Fist said. "I haven't even told you of Timoth's daughter. I haven't told you of my sweet Teresa."

"No. There is no sense in reliving it."

"You don't understand, little man." Fist held the rose in his hand again, though Seeker hadn't seen the man pull it from the folds of his cloak. "I must tell you this. For I have need of your aid, before I can find my final rest. You must listen."

Seeker settled back onto the hard tower floor, forcing his pulse to slow. For once, he wanted the person he was interrogating to stop talking, but that was no longer an option.

"Continue," he said, his voice a croak. He knew if he attempted to leave now, the other man would kill him. "Please."

Fist glanced at the broken stairway and his eyes closed for a moment. He opened them slowly as he spoke in his gravelly voice.

"After Timoth's self-inflicted death, I threw myself into saving both my land and Timoth's, by whatever means necessary. At the same time, my uncle was killed by bandits, and my father grew sickly and frail — hardship seems to always follow hot on the heels of hardship. I knew the responsibility of keeping the crops alive and the people happy would soon fall upon my shoulders. I wanted to have a land worth inheriting, not the dust-filled fields and empty buildings I saw on my rides through my fiefdom.

"I searched for new wells to bring more water to the land, tried to find new methods of irrigation, and even attempted to reroute a river with blasting powder and the help of two-dozen strong-backed criminals from our jails, armed with shovels. None of it brought the water we so needed. Without rain the land baked and burned, and each year my head hung lower, until my back became hunched from attempting to hide my shame and my scarred face.

"My disfigurement, despite the efforts of the herbalists and alchemists of Timoth's land and my own, was my only companion during much of the years of the Dry Spell. When Father passed on, I felt myself grow as dead as the land around me. Years passed.

"My redemption came in the form of Teresa. Twice a month I would visit her and Katherin, Timoth's wife. Even when Teresa was a baby, Katherin would let me hold the child. My face never scared Teresa. She would reach up a tiny hand to touch my ragged cheek or uneven chin, and she would smile, and . . . "

Fist stopped for a long moment and turned his head toward the castle. Seeker listened to Fist's labored breathing and waited. He didn't dare look.

"But that was then, and neither mother nor daughter knew of the Death Vow Timoth had made with his adviser. More binding and permanent than any other vow, this was Timoth's third and final attempt to repay me for saving his life all those years ago. He knew I wouldn't dare deny this vow, as it was made just before he left this world.

"I was given his daughter, Teresa.

"At the start of her fifteenth year, she became my property. The young girl with the curly brown hair, the smiling child with her father's eyes and temper, the always-growing Teresa I'd visited during the long years of the Dry Spell, was now to become my wife. No one could refuse a man's Death Vow. On her fifteenth birthday, Teresa arrived at this castle, before it fell into its current state of disregard.

"Growing up without a father made Teresa stronger than most would have guessed upon first sight of her. She was a small girl, somewhat pale-skinned, but her eyes were sharp and piercing. She had a short temper, like her father, and was quick to act and speak her mind. Never once did she complain. She simply took the news with a cool smile and began packing her belongings. Her only regrets, she would tell me later, were having to leave her mother behind, not getting the opportunity to select a wedding dress, and not having a proper wedding ceremony.

"I gave her the entire southern wing as her own. I would not allow her into my bedroom as my bride. I put off organizing the wedding ceremony. I could not let such a beautiful, intelligent girl wither away with me in a forced marriage. We would carry out her father's binding Death Vow in spirit, if not in detail. In my own way I loved her, but not in the manner her father intended.

"Two events during the next year changed those feelings. The first was a visit from a traveling circus to my fiefdom. Those who remained in my land in spite of the Dry Spell were somehow able to find the means to pay the small fee to watch the magicians, the painted-faced men and women, and the horse riders in their battered tents leaning in the town square. Any distraction from the heat and the dryness was worth the expense, and this circus did not disappoint. They even had a thin, bony elephant that would bow for a handful of peanuts. Teresa went without me, and she came back with her cheeks flushed red, straw in her hair, and a book of alchemy.

"I should not have been surprised to see her with the book — Teresa was always one for knowledge. She could read even the densest book of science, or the most arcane journals perused by my advisers, or even the printed version of the ballads of her favorite tales of dragons and warriors, and the words would remain with her forever. During the circus's brief stay, she most enjoyed the tent of the so-called Sorcerer. She watched him make iron coins disappear and reappear as gold, observed how he pulled eggs of bronze from the mouths of audience members, and stared in amazement as he turned corn silk into ropes of silver. It was he who convinced her to buy the book of alchemy.

"If I had known the evil that book was to bring into my land, I would have burned it and killed the Sorcerer myself."

Again the man across from Seeker stopped himself and looked away. His big shoulders shook again, but no sound came from the man's mouth. Seeker looked away.

That is the face of regret, Seeker thought to himself. He had seen such regret in the broken men in the many windowless, underground rooms scattered throughout the land, moments after he had wrung a confession from them. He'd seen it briefly in the pale face of a young man, right before the boy's eyes clouded over with madness.

I know too much of regret, Seeker thought.

"But I did none of those things," Fist continued. "Instead, I let Teresa keep the book, and a week later I picked it up, hoping to find something of use for the land, which was still dead after all the years of the Dry Spell.

"What I found, to my shock, was a chapter that dealt with enchantments, written in the Ancient Language. In those few pages written in the nearly-forgotten script, the only chapter in the book that used the Ancient Language, I learned I could give objects power over certain aspects of our lives.

"An enchanted coin could suck the bad luck from a cursed piece of land. A stick filled with enchantment could hold the ability to crack the earth. And a perfect rose could remove . . . But I am getting ahead of myself.

"I sent riders after the Sorcerer, but he eluded them all and was never found. Knowing that Teresa was unable to read the language — Timoth and I were the last of our generation to have to learn the Ancient Language, and it had been an arduous process for us both — I began to learn all I could about enchantments. At first, all I wanted from the book was to learn how to pull rain from the sky.

"Surely it would have ended there, and I would never have become an outrider, if the first rains hadn't come to my land in almost two decades.

"This rain was the second element in our shared downfall. The first cloudburst hadn't been much, only enough to wet the dust and keep the dead crops from blowing away. But for the entire next week, the hard rains came. The Ancient enchantments had worked. The parched earth drank deeply, and those remaining in my land began to have hope once again. Plants began to grow again, including the roses in my courtyard.

"Free from my worry over the land for the first time in two decades, I realized there was something I wanted to do with the knowledge I found in the book. I told myself I wanted to do this for Teresa, but I was only deluding myself. I realize now I did it for selfish purposes.

"According the chapter in the book, it would be quite easy. All I needed were the proper words, the proper hand gestures, the proper time of day, and the proper receptacle. One of the roses blooming in my garden would work perfectly for this, I knew.

"I kept myself distant from Teresa during this time, and practiced the words until they were etched into my memory. She was constantly at my door, but I kept the locks thrown and would not see her. Her curiosity was surely getting the best of her, and her words were harsh and suspicious.

"I do this for you, my Teresa, I would think, ignoring the pounding of her fist at my door.

"At midnight during the new moon, I performed the alchemy, the reddest rose from my gardens in my hand, its thorns biting into my palm and fingers. As I spoke the words, the rose turned black as the scales of the scar tissue melted from my face. Blurry vision filled my dead eye, slowly clearing, and within five heartbeats I could see from it again. Just as the book predicted, the perfect rose absorbed my misshapen form.

"I did not dare look into a mirror until the sun came up the next day. When I did, I couldn't contain my joy, and my laughter echoed through my chambers. I was whole again. Even my hunched back straightened with the pride in my appearance. I felt, at last, that I could ask Teresa to be my bride.

"But before I could ask her, she came looking for me after hearing my rare laughter. She stopped at my desk, as if afraid to come closer after she saw my face.

"'My love,' she said. She plucked the blackened rose from my desk and gripped it in her hands. 'You read my book, didn't you?'

"I couldn't answer her. All I could see was the delicate, withered flower in her hands. I was whole only as long as the enchanted rose remained whole, and I couldn't let the rose come to any further harm. At the same time, I couldn't stop running my hands over my smooth face.

"'Father taught Mother the Ancient Language,' she said.

"'Teresa,' I said, my voice barely a whisper. I didn't even think to ask her about the words of the book, and how she knew them. 'Give me the rose.'

"'And Mother taught it to me as a way to remember Father.' Teresa shook her head. 'Don't you know, my Samuel, that I love *you*?' She held up the rose and looked at my new face with a grimace. 'That face is not yours. That is not the face I grew up with as a child, the face of the man I love.'

"I thought I understood our relationship, but when I saw her eyes, I saw Timoth's instead. And they were looking at me with a grim satisfaction as she began crushing the rose in her hand.

"'I want the *true* Samuel,' she said. 'Not the creature I see in front of me now.'

"I didn't even have time to scream. The burning pain of the hot oil from years earlier entered my face and boiled away my eye all over again. My flesh bubbled and shriveled up into its old shape. I'd been whole for all of seven hours.

"When I looked into the mirror, feeling the dead skin on my face again, I felt my back hunch over with rage. I saw at last how Timoth had punished me for saving his life, cursing me three times over with his death, my disfigurement, and now with his daughter. His strong-willed, headstrong daughter, holding the crumpled rose that was blood red once again, free of the ugliness I had forced into it. And Teresa dared to smile at me in my grotesquerie, repeating what her father did to me years earlier.

"For the first time in my life, I let my rage overtake me. I struck her."

#

Seeker could sense the sun beginning to rise even before the night sky had begun to lighten. During and after his five years' entrenchment as the Royal Interrogator, when he'd learned how to earn the trust of the guilty and get them to confess their crimes to him, he'd never heard such a story.

"I was to marry her," the big man continued. "I would have been a lord with his lady, and we would have ruled our rejuvenated lands together. But my rage had given me inhuman strength. Teresa never recovered.

"She was buried in her mother's wedding dress, a garment she never wore while alive. Wearing that dress, her ghost watches us from the castle tower, in the wing where she can no longer leave. It was not luck, nor was it your tracking skills, nor the whispered gossip of the townspeople, that brought us here today. It was Teresa. She calls to me."

Seeker lifted a heavy hand to rub the back of his neck, where his flesh had turned cold and prickly. Movement flickered in the corner of his eye. It may have been a woman in a white dress, slipping behind a column in the southern wing of the castle. Perhaps she was clad a wedding dress that had never been worn while the wearer was alive.

"Teresa," Seeker said, swallowing hard. "She's still here?"

Fist nodded. "She waits for me."

The big man stood, and Seeker lifted himself painfully to his own feet, his legs cramped from sitting for so long. Fist reached out and dropped the red rose into Seeker's hand. Through the stem had been slightly bent, the petals were still soft and almost moist. Fist motioned for Seeker to follow.

The two men walked in silence through the outriders assembled in the tower. Those who slept moved in sudden pain as Fist passed, and those who could not rest felt the traces of a nightmare fill their minds. The moment passed, and they stood inside the southern wing of the dead castle. They were not alone.

"Teresa," Fist said. He held his gaze down, focused on his big, clenched hands. "Forgive me."

Seeker felt his knees waver as soft footsteps approached in the darkness. Despite his night vision, he was unable to see with any sort of clarity who was approaching. All he saw was a woman dressed all in white, wavering in his peripheral vision. He felt her sadness, mixed with a hint of rage and, strangely, relief.

"My Samuel," the woman said in a rough, whispering voice. "You came back for me, at last."

Fist's eyes were locked onto something just behind Seeker. The big man held a dagger to his own neck. The hand holding the dagger never shook.

"As soon as this is done," the big man said, his emotionless voice raising on Seeker's arms. "I want you to burn my body and this accursed rose. Neither of us will be free until this rose is destroyed and its enchantment is removed."

Fist looked away from Seeker at the shimmering young woman in white a few feet away. "I also ask that you remember my story. Remember *our* story."

Seeker nodded, and Fist's dagger moved. No matter how man times Seeker heard it, his ears could never grow accustomed to the sound of metal upon flesh.

The perfect red rose in his hand began to wither and darken, and the small, pale girl in the white wedding dress made a sighing sound. And then she faded away, taking a chill breeze with her as she passed. The ruined castle was again heavy with silence.

#

As dawn broke, the man known only as Seeker — who in a previous life had been a King's operative until the day he interrogated a suspected criminal too long and made the boy lose his mind — began retelling to himself the story of the beastly man called Fist and Teresa, his beauty.

He sat whispering to himself in the darkness, eyes closed, until flames began to turn his eyelids orange. He opened his eyes and looked off into the distance. Somewhere in the kingdom a young man was locked in a jacket with his arms tied tightly to his side, and Seeker owed that boy, the last suspect he ever interrogated, this story. There had to be a middle ground between hard truth and a happy ending, he thought. For the disfigured man lying on the pyre in front to him, for a headstrong young girl and her father, and even for an outrider like Seeker, seeking justice on the winding roads of the King's lands.

The color of the rose had faded to a dark red that was almost black. The story fresh in his mind, Seeker threw the rose onto the fire, and yellow-orange flame swallowed it.

I will keep this vow, he thought. This Death Vow.

He told the story over and over to himself as his fellow outriders rose and prepared their horses for their next campaign. This version of the story, the one he would tell others, would end with the hero's return to the arms of his beloved, followed by a reunion with a wayward friend. They would walk together in their shared lands and rejoice in the green grass and healthy croplands. As far as stories went, it would not be far from either truth or happiness. Or so Seeker hoped.

NATURAL ORDER

They picked me up outside Wilmington, North Carolina, just before the rain began, but not before the gale-force winds blew the cigarette out of my mouth. In the dark, I touched the fresh pack of Camels in my coat pocket with relief, feeling more tired than usual. But as long as I had my smokes and my ride, the wind and the rain didn't bother me. That was just my nature. In a matter of speaking.

In the shotgun seat, Mrs. Thompson was bent double, her tiny black hand holding the seat forward at a sharp angle. I pushed my way into the back seat of the mint-green 1972 Monte Carlo. The interior light was dead. I could just make out Missy, a young girl with brownish-blonde dreadlocks, squirming impatiently behind the steering wheel and revving the car's big engine. I'd have to fix the light tomorrow, on our way to the next job.

The front seat dropped into place as I fell toward the back seat, but instead of the cool, welcoming bucket seat I was expecting, I landed on top of something hard and furry and muscular. Sudden barking filled my ears as yellowed teeth flashed in front of my face.

"Down!" Mrs. Thompson shrieked, her voice carrying over the wind and rain. A coiled umbrella shot past me to hover an inch from the muzzle of the long-nosed dog glaring at me. Mrs. Thompson's black face was a perfect circle of pinched mouth and squinted eyes as she shook the umbrella tip at the dog.

Bob? I wondered, trying to shift my exhausted body off the long-legged dog taking up most of the back seat.

"Put that thing away!" Missy shouted, swerving as the Monte hit water and hydroplaned. "You're gonna put us all in the ditch, old lady."

It wasn't Bob.

The umbrella retreated, and I eased back onto the blanket-covered back seat. The thin, stretched-out looking animal eyed me in the green light of the car's massive dashboard, and the smell of wet dog filled the car. Where the hell did they find another one? After all this time?

Missy punched the accelerator, and the dog and I were both thrown back against the seat. The Monte flew up the onramp leading back onto I-40, just ahead of the storm. I was too tired to push the dog off me, fur in my face. It had been a while since I'd had to share my space in the back of the big old car.

"Meet Walt Whitman," Mrs. Thompson said, trying to relight her pipe with a cheap red lighter. She'd left her window open again while I'd been working, and the rain had drenched most of her right side, including her ancient carved pipe. The two entwined hands that formed the bowl of the pipe were dripping with tobacco-stained water. "He's our new flame."

"Put up your window, Tee," I said, leaning forward to take the wet pipe and lighter from her gnarled fingers. My arms shook as I blew a puff of air onto the pipe, then lit the tobacco again with the cheap lighter. It caught on the first try.

"I could've done *that*, showoff," Mrs. Thompson said, winded from working the crank on the big passenger side window, looking as tired as I felt. She snatched the pipe from my hand and sucked on it greedily.

After pulling out a rawhide chewtoy wedged under my left butt cheek, I reached into my pocket for another cigarette. Next to me, Walt Whitman the dog kicked his legs once with a final growl and curled up into a surprisingly small ball. Only after my eyes had adjusted to the gloom did I see the numbers tattooed in each ear. I lit my Camel.

"At least you got a racer," I said. "Did he win many?"

"He's won his share, down in Florida," Missy said. Her gaze remained glued to the road. Red lights flashed up ahead as we approached the evacuation roadblock. Wind shook the south side of the car, hurling droplets of rain against the windows.

"Twenty-two wins this year alone," Mrs. Thompson said, pulling on her big glasses to peer at a rumpled sheet of paper. "Over eighty in his career, according to the Bosses. He's a flame, all right, our Walt Whitman is. He's . . . "

Her voice dwindled away to a low buzzing for a few seconds. I opened my eyes and exhaled the smoke I'd been holding in. I must've blanked out for a while there, still recovering.

Missy downshifted as she pulled into the median of the interstate to avoid the state troopers and the mess of traffic-snarled cars attempting to leave the coast too late. I tried not to look at the panicked faces inside the cars, lit by the headlights of those behind them. All waiting to escape the storm. Just like us, but powerless to move — to *phase*, if needed — the way we did. Sucking on the cigarette, I slid lower onto the wornout springs of the back seat. Slowly I pulled my gaze away from those we were leaving behind.

One thing I learned from Oklahoma: if I thought about the people too much, I'd be worthless.

The car bounced hard on its way up the other side of the median, the Monte's ancient shocks working overtime to compensate. My head hit the roof and I glared at Missy, to no avail. Wind slammed the rear of the car as if trying to push us west faster.

With an effort, I stroked the thin fur along the back of the dog next to me, only to evoke a low growl. "Dog's all skin and bones, for shit's sake," I mumbled, just to keep conscious.

"Don't talk bad about the dog," Mrs. Thompson said.

"You could've at least talked to me about this," I said, blowing smoke toward the steering wheel. We had the empty eastbound lanes all to ourselves, with all the signs facing the wrong way. I blinked hard twice, barely able to keep my eyes open. "Consulted me, you know," I said, and passed out next to Walt Whitman.

#

A day later I was leading Walt Whitman on a jog around a 7 Eleven parking lot south of Davenport, Iowa. At the car, Missy filled the tank while Mrs. Thompson loaded up on Slim Jims and mineral water. A cool breeze, growing stronger, blew in from the northwest across a darkening sky. Two storms in as many days. El Niño and La Niña were tag-teaming our asses, and had been for years. We'd driven all night, leaving behind hurricane John on the Atlantic seaboard, pushing hard to make our next appointment. It was Tee's turn to shine, so she was loading up on carbs and lots of saturated fats. I'd forgotten to do that yesterday.

I watched the way the fawn-colored greyhound trotted over the asphalt and concrete of the parking lot. He had his own loping grace, very little wasted movement as he padded around dusty pickups and idling eighteen-wheelers. Only his head bobbed side to side, his big eyes taking in everything around him with what looked a shit-eating grin pasted onto his narrow snout as he puffed efficiently next to me. I was still beat from last night.

We slowed, but I kept my eyes on him. Just as I was beginning to admire Walt's streamlined figure, he lifted a hind leg and aimed a stream of urine toward my boots.

"Stupid dog," I muttered, stepping back and letting his leash out another foot. He proceeded to piss onto his left front leg, then his right. Great. I couldn't wait to spend the next two days in the back seat with him and his piss-stained paws.

Walt Whitman kept right on smiling up at me and whizzing away until a sharp whistle stopped him in midstream. Missy stood at the pumps, glaring at us while she whistled again. Tee was already buckled into the shotgun seat, tossing greasy wrappers onto the dash as she ate. We took our time walking back to the Monte.

"What *are* you two doing?" Missy said, voice spitting from her young lips like venom. She pulled at her faded Depeche Mode T-shirt. "Watering every fire hydrant in sight? Let's *go*."

"I needed to check his legs," I said. I dipped two paper towels into the water used for cleaning the windshields and rubbed both of Walt Whitman's front legs. "When he's not pissing on them, that is. I want to make sure he's got what it takes."

"Don't trust us?" Tee shouted from inside the Monte Carlo. Her voice was thick with Slim Jims. "Don't think we've been at this long enough to know what we're doing?"

I watched Missy as I threw away the soggy paper towels. "He's no Robert Frost," I said. "I can see that already."

"Would you rather go back to us doing it on our own, without a flame?"

I shuddered before I could stop myself.

Missy turned and slipped into the car, her slim body moving without a trace of awkwardness in her eternally teenaged body. "That's what I thought," she said, starting up the car.

I felt a familiar pressure start to build in my ears as I led the dog around to Tee's side of the car. According to the atlas, it looked like we'd be out in the country, far from too many people. Lucky, I thought, then caught myself. What we did was a necessary service, a balancing act with nature, really. It had nothing to do with luck.

Walt and I slid in behind Tee, who was already beginning to hyperventilate. Her dancing slippers were now hidden by empty bottles of Evian and Slim Jim wrappers. Wind whistled through her partially-opened window like the world's angriest flute solo.

Missy's jaw was set in her typical way whenever she got word of the need for her skills. According to the Bosses' message on the radio, we weren't needed in LA until Friday. I wanted to remind Missy of that, but I bit my tongue. Ever since we lost Bob, she'd gotten tense about her work. As if she thought it was all her fault.

But now wasn't the time nor the place, I thought, lighting up a cigarette once we were safely away from the noxious fumes of the 7 Eleven. Tee was breathing deeply now, as if she were asleep. I patted Walt on the head, feeling the delicate bones of his skull under my hand. This was Tee's moment, and I wasn't going to let Missy ruin it for her.

#

The first time I ever saw Mrs. Thompson dance, Robert Frost — Bob for short — had been alive, and I'd broken down into tears at the way she'd moved.

Under a thick black sky, we raced south for another two and a half miles, then parked outside a field far from any farmhouses. The late summer soybean plants rippled and shook like dancers on speed. A tractor roared past on the gravel road, not five feet from the car, the tractor's driver hunched over the wheel with his gaze raised to the clouds massing overhead. I could see his fear, an animal fear. I fought the urge to hurry him out of the way of the approaching devastation, but we were not allowed to interfere in that way. Ever.

Mrs. Thompson stood no more than four and a half feet tall. Her face was usually half-hidden by an oversized pair of tinted blue glasses, yet she always managed to be looking at me over the tops of her spectacles. After touching the tight curls of her white hair, arranging them vainly in the drop-down mirror I'd attached to her visor, Tee turned and gave me a smile.

"Don't cry this time, Zed-baby," she said, handing me her glasses before she stepped out of the car.

She walked to the edge of the field, slipped through the top and middle strands of the barbed wire fence, and began to turn slowly across the field of green. The wind twisted in time to her movements. Every step of her tiny white shoes took her a little bit higher into the air, her shawl opening around her like a parachute, until Tee looked like she was stepping from the tops of one soybean plant to the next. And so Mrs. Thompson spun across the field, calling to the wind, and black clouds dipped above her, forming a cone.

In the back seat of the Monte Carlo, scratching behind Walt's ears, I sniffed and wiped my eyes. Again and again. She got me with it every damn time.

#

Missy let me drive west, while Tee slept. Since we had the time, I'd convinced Missy to let us take the long way to Southern California. Being in Iowa — despite the cushion of Missouri and Kansas between us — still felt much too close to Oklahoma for my tastes. In any case, getting closer to the coast and the air currents I knew best was an added relief. I went through a carton of unfiltered Camels along the way, stubbing out each smoke in our over-flowing ashtray and immediately lighting another with the red lighter.

Tee slept most of the way through Iowa, Nebraska, and into South Dakota. She had been taking longer and longer to recover in the past few years. We were all paying the price for not finding a replacement for Robert Frost sooner. Though Tee didn't complain like Missy, I knew the added exertions were taking a toll on her.

Tiring of the road on our way through the Badlands, I stopped the car at a scenic overlook close to Cedar Pass, watching a rain squall form against the backdrop of the setting sun. Something about the farmer and his tractor back in Iowa had been sticking in my mind the entire drive. I'd been worried about the man — did he have a family? How would his crops survive? Did he have animals, pets even?

That was when I realized it, looking out at the reddish-tinted land, broken and pockmarked on either side of Highway 240. I was going soft.

Lost in my thoughts, I jumped when I heard a rustle not two feet away. Missy stepped up next to me, having slipped quietly out of the car to avoid waking Tee. I turned to look down at her unsmiling face, then checked on Walt Whitman back in the car. If he got loose out here, we'd never catch him. But he sat obediently in the back seat, peeking through the Monte's tiny rear window and grinning mindlessly at the two of us.

Missy prodded me in the ribs and held out her hand. "Keys," she said.

"With pleasure," I said, and fished the key ring out of my jeans pocket, along with the plastic lighter. I felt for the pack of Camels in my shirt pocket and offered her a smoke. I could smell the green hint of rain all these miles away.

"What's your *problem*?" Missy said, ignoring the cigarette and grabbing the keys. The light of the setting sun softened the lines of her thin face.

I looked away, trying to make like I was studying the hills behind her. The jagged landscape of misformed cliffs and mottled green trees stretched out to the west, melting into the pine forests of Roosevelt National Park and the stone majesty of Crazy Horse Monument. The rain storm was breaking, forks of lightning cutting the air ten miles to the west.

"No problems," I said at last. "Why do you ask?"

"Bullshit. Something's bugging you." She played with one of her dreads, unraveling it, then twisting it tight again. She poked me a second time. "Zed. How long have we been working together? Fifty years?"

I inhaled on the cigarette and exhaled slowly, watching my breath take shape in cigarette smoke. I knew it was impossible, but I felt addicted to nicotine, or at least the act of smoking. And where there's smoke . . .

"I lose track, Missy. From the moment I was picked, time sort of lost its shape for me."

Missy let go of her hair and jangled the keys in her hand, the sound like tiny cymbals. "The Bosses just sent our next job. For after LA."

"When it rains it pours," I said without thinking. "Sorry. Just a little weather humor there, for ya. Har-de-har-har."

Missy wasn't smiling. "We have to go to Wyoming next. Forest fire."

I heard the storm approaching from the west. I never really learned, before I started this job, how to effectively hide my emotions. I could feel my eyes betraying me, showing my fear. "I guess then we'll find out if you and Tee made the right choice."

"Damn it, Zed," Missy began, but I was already moving back to the Monte, heading for the back seat again. The rain would be upon us soon, just an innocent, nearly windless shower, but I didn't want Tee to get wet again through her open window. And Walt Whitman was getting nervous with us gone for so long.

Plus, we needed to get moving. We had a date with an earthquake in LA. Another city, much bigger than Oklahoma City.

#

The way Robert Frost went was the way all of us will go, eventually. When too much energy converges in one place at the wrong time, it happens. When the forces of nature — beyond even the knowledge of the Bosses — converge with too much strength or too quickly for us to react, shit happens.

Shit also happens when some unforeseen human element forces its way like a spike into our carefully modulated work. I've gotten to know most of those in our line of work who are responsible for the other continents, and they all give us their sympathy. Here in North America, we've been getting too many of those unexpected calls lately.

The most recent "unforeseen human element" took place in Oklahoma City.

The reception on our radio had been particularly staticky that day of April. Calls had gone out, first for Bob's services, then for Missy's, then Bob again. All three of us agreed that the call for Missy must have been wrong; she really wasn't needed in this part of the country. We'd shared a quick, nervous laugh about that — who'd ever heard of an earthquake in Oklahoma City? — before heading downtown to the Murrah building by mid-morning. Bob had whined and scratched at the driver's seat on the way there before finally relaxing next to me with his rawhide chewtoy. I almost did something about his whining. Almost, which counts for exactly nothing now.

Instead I let him do his work, even though city work was the worst part of our jobs. I always forced myself not to think of the human cost, the deaths that resulted from what we did for the Bosses. But this particular job, on this particular day, was all bad.

Bob was a true greyhound, his fur the bluish-gray tint that gave his species their name. Slender and noble, he took off at ten minutes to nine, phasing like a natural, circling the federal building as he built the heat, the *flame*. He phased through pedestrians and cars effortlessly, just as we had trained him. Don't think about them, I told myself then. Think about the natural order of our world, and how we helped maintain that balance.

He'd begun to flicker with his flame when the first tremor hit. In sympathetic reaction, Missy convulsed in the front seat as the unforeseen explosion began, and I made my fatal error. I took my eyes off Bob to tend to Missy. The Monte Carlo automatically phased us out of the blast radius. But the rest of downtown Oklahoma City was shattered and on fire from the massive explosion deep inside the federal building. The fire wasn't Bob's fire. When Missy had pulled herself together after the man-made earthquake, I looked up. The Murrah building was torn in half, and Robert Frost was gone.

All three of us phased in and out of the wreckage, moving past those we weren't allowed to help, humans that I didn't even *look* at as I blew past, trying to find our greyhound. Tee exhausted herself searching the catacombs beneath the building, while Missy beat her hands bloody trying to shake loose the foundation and uncover his whereabouts. They had both been looking in the wrong place.

We who dispense death and destruction forget too easily that we can also be destroyed. I realized the limitations of our abilities that day, and I realized the folly of our elemental powers when I found Bob twenty feet above me, impaled on a girder, his blue-gray fur singed black with his own unspent heat. We can be caught unawares by the evil that flows in the currents and tides and tremors of just one misguided human mind. We weren't as invulnerable as we'd thought.

#

I woke from my nightmare memories of Oklahoma to the blessed silence of northern Wyoming. Tee was driving, squinting through the steering wheel at Highway 89, a thirty-six pound bag of ProPlan dog food propping her up. She was singing an old gospel number softly as she barreled north toward

Old Faithful, her forgotten pipe resting beside her. The chill waters of Shoshone Lake glistened like the distant waves I'd seen too briefly in Southern California.

Missy slept in the back seat, Walt Whitman's back legs stretched onto her lap. Missy was no joke when it came to her work. Today's *LA Times*, now rolled up on the floor under my feet, had reported a magnitude of 6.5 on the Richter scale. Luckily, the quake happened at 3:30 a.m., and the buildings at the intersection of Highways 110 and 10 in southern LA were mostly empty. The sunken facade of the Staples Center and the bashed-in convention center next to it reminded me too much of the devastation in Oklahoma. Ever since the tornado in Iowa and my realization in the Badlands, I couldn't stand the thought of more lives lost, human or otherwise. The greyhound in the back seat was a constant reminder of what we'd all lost.

I never asked to be reminded.

And now, Walt Whitman was going to start earning his keep as our new flame.

"Tee," I said as she ended her song, my hands quivering. I felt as if I'd been drinking cup after cup of coffee.

"Mm-hmm?" Mrs. Thompson said. She glanced at me over the tops of her big spectacles for a quick second, then returned her gaze to the road. She continued humming the same song she'd just finished singing.

I paused for a moment, and then plowed forward. "Have you ever had doubts about what we do?" I asked, afraid to look at her. I picked up her pipe and lit it with the red lighter, bitter tobacco and spices filling my nose.

"Doubts?" Tee laughed, taking the pipe from me. "I'm too old to have doubts about anything, Zed-baby. What's there to doubt? We make the wind blow, we make the earth shake, we make the rains come. And now our puppy is gonna make the flames." She looked at me, her mouth a narrow line around her smoking pipe. "Just like Robert Frost did. Just as good as him."

"I know," I said, hearing the uncertainty in my own voice. But, I wanted to say, he's not Bob. And times are changing. Human nature was becoming stronger than *our* nature. The natural disasters we were responsible for paled in comparison to humanity's self-inflicted disasters. The polluted waters and acid rain. The acts of uncontrolled violence and rage. The dirty air. The bombings.

"What if we made it stop?" I said, the words out of my mouth before I realized it.

The big car swerved. "What?" Mrs. Thompson said with a sudden, surprising anger. "You want to make the Bosses *really* mad? That it?"

I shrugged at her and turned to the window. One and a half minutes from now, if all went according to plan, a fire would be started somewhere up ahead in Yellowstone. Summer-dried trees would go up like oversized matches, and the fire could easily spread to the houses of people miles from where Walt Whitman would start his flame. And as soon as the land was burning, we would be off to our next job, maybe one of my hurricanes, maybe one of Tee's twisters.

Tee parked the car fifteen miles southeast of Old Faithful, next to a stand of hundred-foot pines. I woke Missy and slipped the leash over Walt's narrow head. He leaped out of the car and tried to place his paws on my chest. While the fall breeze brought the scent of pines to my nose, I stepped away from him and fumbled for the comforting presence of a cigarette. The sky was unbearably blue.

"Don't worry," Tee said on her way out of the Monte. "Walt will do just fine."

Missy followed us to a clearing in the shade of the tall trees, and the three of us gathered around the prancing dog.

"Ready, rookie?" I said. Walt was pulling at his leash with anticipation, yet his smile was still there. "I hope you guys made the right choice," I said to Missy as I let Walt off the leash. By the time he'd taken five strides he was at full speed, body curved and legs blurring. I could feel his heat already. He was a wonder to watch, I remembered thinking to myself. He may just work out, after all.

Walt was phasing through trees, just as Missy and Tee had taught him, when I saw the two vans parked on the access road to the north. A campsite lay on the other side of the access road. A pair of men stood outside the vans, pacing nervously. I saw the automatic weapons an instant too late, as Walt's flame caught and the chaos began.

#

I like to think that I would've been a brave person, if I'd been allowed to grow up and live a normal, human life. Maybe I'd have been a cop, or a firemen, like any other kid in the fifties wanted to be. Or maybe I'd be a lawyer and try to put away those people who ruined a good chunk of Yellowstone in their mad cause, whatever that cause had been.

But at nineteen, my age when I was picked for this job, I would never have attempted to stand up to anyone if I'd still been human. It wasn't in my nature, back then. Even now, after Yellowstone, I wouldn't call myself brave. Just angry enough to want to change an outcome or two, if it was within my grasp.

We learned later that the men in the vans had been trying to send a message to the government for years, and they had met at Yellowstone on their way to Cheyenne. Up until that day, their group hadn't been very good at what they were doing, and more and more of their group were getting caught and sent to penitentiaries across the country. Some of them were apprehended the week before New Year's outside Seattle, while others were grabbed in a bar outside Bozeman, Montana, with a truckful of TNT. The guys at Yellowstone had been a bit quicker than their partners; if they'd made it to Cheyenne that day, it would have been their third consecutive bombing. But on that day, they weren't quick enough to avoid the heat of Walt Whitman's flame.

And so, after all these years — has it already been fifty years since I disappeared from my dorm room, smoking what would be my last true cigarette? — I finally remembered on that afternoon in Wyoming how it felt to be afraid and to be angry, angry enough to do something against my nature.

#

Walt lit the ring of trees, just as the Bosses had ordered him. He was fast and sure-footed, I gave him that. The fire followed him, lighting up the grass and trees in his wake like the tail of a comet. But Walt wasn't quick enough to avoid the explosion when his fire spread onto the brush next to the first van. As the drivers stamped hopelessly at the flames, the first van blew like thunder, picking up Walt and sending a fireball across the access road, toward the campgrounds.

I felt the cigarette fall from my mouth. This wasn't part of the plan. LA had been hard enough, after we'd seen the security guards trapped inside the convention center when it crumbled. I couldn't sit around and watch any longer.

So I called up rain clouds, thunder rolling across the sky. I knew I could use them to cover both Walt and the burning land around us with rain. But Missy and Mrs. Thompson stopped me before I could let loose the storm clouds.

"Don't," Missy said. I could barely hear her over the explosion of the second van. "Don't throw off the balance."

Walt was still running, fire licking at his legs as he struggled to keep his feet. He ran faster, but he wouldn't be able to outrun the unnatural fire roaring from the vans. He'd been too close.

"Let me," I shouted. I could see people running wildly in the campground area until yellow fire separated us. I can douse it with the rains, I wanted to say. I can save them all, not just Walt, but everyone. The hell with the balance.

Tee shook her head and hit me with a warning gust of wind that knocked me back into the Monte Carlo. She held me there with the wind, watching Walt and the surrounding countryside burn up, her face expressionless.

I glared at Missy, needing her help. Walt Whitman streaked past us once again. The greyhound was panicked, running in wide circles now, barely a step ahead of the chemical fire.

"Look at him," I shouted to Missy as we phased in and out to protect ourselves from the heat. "Not again." I struggled to lift my arm enough to gesture at the inferno taking over the campgrounds. Not again, I repeated silently.

Missy swung from side to side, taking in everything while Tee resolutely held me back. I could hear our dog yelping in pain. With the wind and the growing heat, I couldn't even scream. All I could smell was burning flesh and fur.

Finally, when I was preparing to phase out and escape the fires, Missy made a fist and punched the ground. The tremor knocked Tee off her feet and sent me up and over the Monte Carlo. At last, in the shelter of the big car, I called down all the rain scheduled for next month for the entire Pacific seaboard onto the inferno. The raindrops fell like millions of tiny bombs that covered the southwest corner of Yellowstone Park.

As the rain tore into us and filled the world with a sizzling wetness, Tee turned to me, fear and rage covering her face. She gave me the longest look of my life, and I prepared myself for another blast of wind. But I held my ground and returned her gaze. I needed her to see that what we were doing was right. Thanks to humans, the natural order of our jobs had been destroyed, yet we could still do something about it. We had to; otherwise we were just as bad as the men in the vans.

After what seemed like hours, Tee wiped rain from her tiny forehead and gave me the slightest of nods. I smiled at her and Missy and the wet dog limping our way, and I let the thunder roll across the mountains around us. The rain was cold and cleansing, reminding me that we had it in us to regain a sort of balance, in our own way. And the Bosses were just going to have to accept that.

AFTERWORD

Gunning for the Buddha

This is the first story I've written that was solely inspired by a song — in this case, Shriekback's song of the same title, which led me to research the meaning and history behind the saying "If you see the Buddha on the road, kill him." I took that idea and ran with it, playing with time travel theories and creating a nihilistic narrator who refuses to put blind faith in any religion (hence the title). It's one of my most experimental stories, one in which I tried to throw everything but the kitchen sink into the mix to see what would emerge, and it's one of my favorites.

Goddamn Redneck Surfer Zombies

This story started out as just a fun attempt at humorous horror, more of a voice story than anything else, and it's turned out to be one of my better stories. I liked the imagery of the zombies on their coffin lids, surfing one last big wave before returning to their graves, but I also loved the resilience of the narrator and how he and the other salty natives of this beach town were able to make the best of a bad situation instead of simply running away in fear. It's a great one to read out loud, too. And it has one of my favorite final lines of any story I've written (definitely in my Top Five All-Time Best Closing Lines I've Written list).

Visions of Suburban Bliss

This story comes out of a sense of despair I feel sometimes, working a nine-to-five day job and commuting from the 'burbs, witnessing urban sprawl and postage-stamp lawns, all that homogeneity and banality. The place I'm sort of poking fun of in the story is a small city right next to Raleigh, NC, called Cary. I wanted to poke fun at the almost surreal quality of the gated communities you can find in cities like Cary across the country. I've always wondered what the people who live in these places must feel like, if they really feel safe or just scared. Plus I've always wanted to put a sweat lodge in a story.

A Feast at the Manor

This story was inspired by a trip out west combined with my own desire to one day lose those extra pounds I seemed to have picked up, somewhere. I wanted to create an overweight character who's okay with being big ("big, not fat"), and I also wanted to use the setting of an old, creepy hotel in LA my wife Elizabeth and I stayed at for a week a few years ago. I really love the way Rob was still very attracted to his wife despite her own insecurity about her weight, and how he'd do whatever she wanted to make her happy.

Unplugged

Okay, I admit I came late to the cyberpunk party, but this story was my way of turning out the lights once all the revelers had left. I wrote this story in July of '96 during my last week of the Clarion Science Fiction and Fantasy Workshop. It began life as a collision of two styles: Raymond Carver's minimalism (the original story title was "Where I'm Jacking In From," which I still sort of like) and William Gibson's information-drenched land-scapes. I revamped and reworked the story over the next few years, until it finally was accepted for publication. It was during all those revisions that I started to really find my voice, so this story has a nice warm spot in my heart, even if it may sound a bit dated these days. Thanks go to my buddy Chris Babson for suggesting I write about hacker cowboys going to rehab.

Working the Game

I wanted to try something set on far-future Earth that dealt with the have-nots of society. Coming from a working-class background myself, I often feel like I've been misled about my future (for example, I'm a proud member of Generation X, and I know when I retire that I won't see any of the money I've been paying into social security since I started working). So many people of my generation have seen our parents lose their jobs and watch the American Dream crumbling around them growing up to know that the whole "dedication to the company" is a load of crap. We're all working our butts off for what? The chance to maybe retire in 40 or 50 years and then continue to eke out an existence before death comes a-knockin'? Surely there's more to life than just working the "game" that people call the real world. I for one want more out of life than collecting my points and dreaming about one day going over the wall and entering my cocoon.

Explosions

Chronologically, this story comes first out of the four Wannoshay stories, though it was the third story I'd written about the aliens who come to Earth in the near future and how the average person deals with their arrival. This story features Shontera, a hard-working, somewhat spacy single mother and blue-collar worker who dreams of escaping her dead-end job but instead becomes a part of history. I'd once given up on this story, but after dusting it off and revising the ending (so it made sense — what a concept!), I'm quite fond of it. This story and the three that follow it are part of my SF novel, *The Wannoshay Cycle*.

Wantaviewer

While the previous story was about a woman who became a part of history, this story is about a young woman with a checkered past and a very uncertain future who only wants to *record* history. Ally Trang was a fun character to get to know — a junkie who also loves making movies. The fine folks at *Strange Horizons* made this my third Wannoshay story to be published at their excellent Web site (along with "Explosions" and "Crossing the Camp"). Editors Jed Hartman, Susan Groppi, and Chris Heinemann helped me make these three stories much better than I could have on my own.

Mud and Salt

This is a guy story; it has hunting, guns, swearing, fighting, and talking about women. But I like to think it does a bit more than that, under its gruff surface. The story started as an experiment, fashioned after Tobias Wolff's "Hunters in the Snow" and quickly departed from that, showing how friendships are tested in the worst situations, and how hidden strength can emerge in the weakest of us. This was the first of my Wannoshay stories to see print. This sale really jump-started my writing career, because it allowed me to go to the Writers of the Future workshop. While I was enjoying the expenses-paid week in LA as part of the workshop, I got to meet the other writers whose stories were in the anthology, and I learned a ton of valuable information from Tim Powers, Algis Budrys, Kevin J. Anderson, and especially Dean Wesley Smith, who shared with me the secret to a successful writing career (work your ass off, basically, advice I'm still following).

Crossing the Camp

A lot of different elements went into the creation of this story, the writing of which marked a sort of watershed moment for me as an author. I felt like I'd made a major breakthrough with this story, digging deeper into the emotional wells and writing about what really mattered to me. The story was inspired in part by Sting's song "All This Time" and a story by Jason Brown called "Driving the Heart," combined with a trick I'd learned for generating ideas, which consists of putting two very unsimilar things together to see what would happen. I came up with a priest in a concentration camp, and the pieces of the story fell into place from there. This was the first story about the aliens called the Wannoshay that I wrote, and it will always be my favorite.

Black Angels

This story started with the memory of a statue in an Iowa City graveyard, and the rest came to me as I was daydreaming on my commute home from work one day. The Black Angel statue really does exist, and it's in the Iowa City cemetery described in the story. It's spooky, especially at night. This poor story has been all over the place, and it was even accepted to be published in an anthology about — of all things — vampire *cockroaches*, but the anthology died before ever seeing print. Luckily, before the anthology went down for the count, I received excellent revision advice from the editor, David Niall Wilson, who gave me a couple wonderful suggestions that made everything in the story fit together in a much more logical manner. Plus it's got angels and demons fighting in a graveyard — what's not to love?

The Disillusionist

I had a lot of fun writing this one. I was aiming for a Neil Gaiman kind of story, featuring weird magic (or *un-magic*, really) and a bizarre villain. This foray into historical fantasy and horror was the second story I wrote that was inspired by a song, this time by The Church. It was fun to fictionalize some of the wacky imagery of the song. I was stuck on this story for a while, until I realized I could make the narrator someone all Americans will recognize (those of us who have access to five dollar bills and pennies, that is). Then I had elements of alternate history mixed in with the horrific and fantastic bits, and it all clicked. I love it when that happens.

Coal Ash and Sparrows

This story began life as an outtake from my as-yet-unpublished young-adult urban fantasy novel, *The Last of the Hand*. The orphan train information was taken from research I'd been doing for an upcoming novel, and as I compared the different timelines of both novels, I saw a story taking shape as dates began to intersect. That's one of the fascinating aspects about writing fiction — when everything starts to take shape after I've done all the legwork and "heavy lifting" about the characters, plot, and setting. As Freddy Mercury sings, "It's a kind of magic . . . " (Sorry, I couldn't resist.)

An Outrider's Tale

I'd had the idea for this fairy-tale retelling for almost five years before actually figuring out how to tell it. I wanted to include it in this collection because I love the original fairy tale, and I liked the way I attempted to borrow aspects of this. Thanks to Dr. John Kessel for (among *many* other things he's done to help me as a writer) first planting the seeds for this story in his SF writing workshop class at NC State. The most interesting authorial note about this story is that two separate editors, in rejecting the tale, suggested I take the settings, characters, and situation and make a novel out of them. And so, the ideas have been percolating . . .

Natural Order

I like to think of this as the best story I've ever written in ten hours. I was reading Tim Powers' excellent novel *Last Call* at the time, and whenever I read fiction written at the level of Mr. Powers, I get inspired and want to write. And in the crazy way that events play out in the writing world, Tim Powers had a hand in this story's conception. At our Writers of the Future writing workshop, Tim was one of our teachers, and he assigned us each a unique item to write a story about it. My item was a cheap red lighter. After a couple false starts, I came up with the storm-tossed opening of this story and inserted our pet greyhound as the hero of the story. Once it was done, I barely had to change a word. I'm still not sure where that one came from, to be honest.

ACKNOWLEDGEMENTS

And that's my story collection. I thank you for reading my stories, and I hope you had as much fun reading them as I did writing them. Writing is a strange obsession, and it's usually a solitary one, but I've been very fortunate in having a strong support system of family and friends to offer their input and keep me smiling on those days when I wonder why I even bother putting two words together. I thank all of you for all you do for me.

Specifically, I want to thank fellow writers and friends Tim Pratt, Greg van Eekhout, Jay Lake, Samantha Ling, Chris Babson, Lee Capps, Scott Reilly, Jason Lundberg, Jim C. Hines, Nick Mamatas, Nick Kaufmann (how's that chest, man?), Scott Nicholson, the class of Clarion '96, the "WotF" gang (we miss ya, Mark), James Hartley, and Sarah Hoyt. Thanks to teachers John Kessel, Maureen McHugh, James Patrick Kelly, Judy Tarr, Greg Frost, Liz Hand, Gardner Dozois, Kris Rusch, Dean Smith, Tim Powers, AJ Budrys, and all the other writers and editors I've known throughout the years who have taught me so much and helped me improve. Thanks too go to Sean Wallace at Prime Books for putting all of this together.

Huge thanks to my parents and the rest of my family for putting up with me all these years.

And most of all, I wouldn't have been able to write the stories in this collection without my wonderful wife Elizabeth, and I dedicate this book to her.

Printed in the United States
200242BV00004B/327/A

9 781930 997721